THE LIFE AND
ADVENTURES OF
ROBINSON
CRUSOE

BY DANIEL DEFOE

ILLUSTRATED BY ROGER DUVOISIN

INTRODUCTION BY MAY LAMBERTON BECKER

THE WORLD PUBLISHING COMPANY

CLEVELAND AND NEW YORK

Rainbow Classics

are published by THE WORLD PUBLISHING COMPANY

2231 WEST 110TH STREET, CLEVELAND 2, OHIO

FIRST PRINTING APRIL 1946
SECOND PRINTING SEPTEMBER 1946

CONTENTS

CONTENTS

INTRODUCTION

How this story came to be written

BY MAY LAMBERTON BECKER

IN THE YEAR 1704 Alexander Selkirk, son of John Selcraig a shoemaker, who had run away to sea and joined a privateering expedition, quarreled with his captain, Thomas Stradling, and was at his own request put ashore on the uninhabited island of Juan Fernandez off the coast of Chile. There he lived, all alone, until 1709, when he was rescued by another set of privateers. It was a nine-day wonder in the days of Queen Anne.

Daniel Defoe—his father's name was Foe but he had improved it—must have thought what a good story it would make, but he was then too busy to do anything about it. He had travelled a good deal, taken part in Monmouth's Rebellion, and written political satires so biting that he had been sent to prison for them. For one he had been set in the pillory for people to throw vegetables at him—only the people were so much on his side that they threw flowers instead. He had made and lost much money; as he put it, thirteen times he had been rich and poor. But by the year 1719 he was certainly not rich, nearly sixty years old, and beginning to feel discouraged. The story of Selkirk came back to mind; Defoe had a gift for vivid reporting, especially if he did not have to stick too closely to facts. In this case he "embellished" them into the most famous adventure story of all the world's literature: "The life and strange adventures of Robinson Crusoe of York, mariner, who lived eight-and-twenty years all alone on the coast of America, near the mouth of the great river of Oroonoque; having been cast on shore by shipwreck, where-in all the men perished but himself. With an account of how he was at last as strangely delivered by pyrates. Written by himself."

It was not written for boys, and it was full of moral reflections meant for men, but every boy who could get a chance to read it promptly did so, as well as everyone else. People took all Robinson said as coming from the lips of a real man: Defoe could describe something he had never seen and make you sure you had seen it yourself. He did this in *The Apparition of Mrs. Veal* (1706) and the *Journal of the Plague Year* (1722). But of all he wrote—counting political pamphlets, more than 250 works—nothing has lasted so long or gone so far as this story of the solitary castaway, the parrot, faithful Friday, the boat that couldn't be launched, and the footprints on the sand. Most people, when you ask what they recall in the story, tell you first how their hearts missed a beat when Crusoe came upon that footprint!

The story was published, republished, condensed, edited, cut down, in language after language, for generation after generation. Boys always come upon it with the same thrill. I have seen little French boys setting off for summer holidays with pail-and-shovel under one arm and a battered copy of *Crusoe* under the other. I have seen a tiny flower-seller in Avignon stop business till he had read through the French children's paper named "Robinson." I know an American fourth-grader whose teacher read the book aloud on Friday afternoons; when the term ended before the tale was finished, he saved up and bought a second-hand copy to see how it came out. He wrote me that another boy offered to buy this copy from him, but he decided there was nothing he could get with the money that he would like so much.

The first copy of *Robinson Crusoe* marked the founding of a great publishing house, for the first Longmans brought out the book, April 25, 1719, as the first publication of what was to be the firm of Longmans, Green. So many imitations of Crusoe, conscious or unconscious, have been published that a special name has been made for them—Robinsonades—and just their titles would fill a book. Those that lasted longest were *The Adventures of Philip Quarll*, that Thackeray loved, and *The Swiss Family Robinson* that I used to act out in our big garden along with the boys from next door.

In these new drawings by Roger Duvoisin you see Robinson Crusoe's island as I am sure Defoe himself saw it. The subject has fired this sensitive and original artist and he has drawn what he seems to have seen with his own eyes, and shows actions in which you would think he had taken part. The character of the book is in these pictures, as well as its contents.

When he was a little chap Roger Duvoisin loved to draw—especially galloping horses. Their hoofs were too much for him, though; he made them look like oversized shoes, and when his uncle came for a visit Roger would always make him draw horses dashing over large sheets of paper on their elegant hoofs. His trees weren't so good, either, and his godmother, who was a well-known painter, offered to show him how to draw them. "After that," he says, "my trees were really bad." When he graduated from art school—in Switzerland, where he was born —he painted murals and stage scenery and posters, worked with ceramics and even became manager of an old French pottery plant. Then he began to design textiles, and an American firm offered to bring him to America if he would promise to stay at least four years. He is here still, an American citizen. The de-

THE LIFE AND
ADVENTURES OF
ROBINSON
CRUSOE

Chapter 1: *In which I do not heed my father's advice*

I was born in the year 1632, in the city of York, of a good family, though not of that country, my father being a foreigner, of Bremen, who settled first at Hull: he got a good estate by merchandise, and leaving off his trade, lived afterward at York; from whence he had married my mother, whose relations were named Robinson, a very good family in that country, and from whom I was called Robinson Kreutznaer; but, by the usual corruption of words in England, we are now called, nay, we call ourselves, and write our name, Crusoe; and so my companions always called me.

I had two elder brothers, one of whom was lieutenant-colonel to an English regiment of foot in Flanders, formerly commanded by the famous Colonel Lockhart, and was killed at the battle near Dunkirk against the Spaniards. What became of my second brother I never knew, any more than my father or mother knew what became of me.

Being the third son of the family, and not bred to any trade,

13

my head began to be filled very early with rambling thoughts. My father, who was very ancient, had given me a competent share of learning, as far as house education and a country free school generally goes, and designed me for the law; but I would be satisfied with nothing but going to sea; and my inclination to this led me so strongly against the will, nay, the commands of my father, and against all the entreaties and persuasions of my mother and other friends, that there seemed to be something fatal in that propension of nature tending directly to the life of misery which was to befall me.

My father, a wise and grave man, gave me serious and excellent counsel against what he foresaw was my design. He called me one morning into his chamber, where he was confined by the gout, and expostulated very warmly with me upon this subject; he asked me what reasons, more than a mere wandering inclination, I had for leaving my father's house and my native country, where I might be well introduced, and had a prospect of raising my fortune by application and industry, with a life of ease and pleasure. He told me it was for men of desperate fortunes on one hand, or for aspiring superior fortunes on the other, who went abroad upon adventures, to rise by enterprise, and make themselves famous in undertakings of a nature out of the common road; that these things were all either too far above me, or too far below me; that mine was the middle state, or what might be called the upper station of low life, which he had found by long experience was the best state in the world, the most suited to human happiness, not exposed to the miseries and hardships, the labor and sufferings of the mechanic part of mankind, and not embarrassed with the pride, luxury, ambition, and envy of the upper part of mankind. He told me, I might judge of the happiness of this state, by this one thing, namely, that this was the state of life

which all other people envied; that kings have frequently
lamented the miserable consequences of being born to great
things, and wish they had been placed in the middle of the two
extremes, between the mean and the great; that the wise man
gave his testimony to this, as the just standard of true felicity,
when he prayed to have neither poverty nor riches.

He bade me observe it, and I should always find, that the
calamities of life were shared among the upper and lower part
of mankind; but that the middle station had the fewest disasters, and was not exposed to so many vicissitudes as the higher
or lower part of mankind; nay, they were not subjected to so
many distempers and uneasinesses either of body or mind, as
those were who, by vicious living, luxury, and extravagances
on one hand, or by hard labor, want of necessaries, and mean
or insufficient diet on the other hand, bring distempers upon
themselves by the natural consequences of their way of living;
that the middle station of life was calculated for all kind of
virtues and all kind of enjoyments; that peace and plenty were
the handmaids of a middle fortune; that temperance, modera-
tion, quietness, health, society, all agreeable diversions, and all
desirable pleasures, were the blessings attending the middle
station of life; that this way men went silently and smoothly
through the world, and comfortably out of it, not embarrassed
with the labors of the hands or of the head, not sold to the life
of slavery for daily bread, or harassed with perplexed circumstances, which rob the soul of peace, and the body of rest; not
enraged with the passion of envy, or secret burning lust of ambition for great things; but in easy circumstances sliding gently
through the world, and sensibly tasting the sweets of living
without the bitter, feeling that they are happy, and learning by
every day's experience to know it more sensibly.

After this, he pressed me earnestly, and in the most affectionate manner, not to play the young man, not to precipitate myself into miseries which nature and the station of life I was born in, seemed to have provided against; that I was under no necessity of seeking my bread; that he would do well for me, and endeavor to enter me fairly into the station of life which he had been just recommending to me; and that if I was not very easy and happy in the world, it must be my mere fate or fault that must hinder it, and that he should have nothing to answer for, having thus discharged his duty in warning me against measures which he knew would be to my hurt; in a word, that as he would do very kind things for me if I would stay and settle at home as he directed, so he would not have so much hand in my misfortunes, as to give me any encouragement to go away; and to close all, he told me I had my elder brother for an example, to whom he had used the same earnest persuasions to keep him from going into the Low Country wars, but could not prevail, his young desires prompting him to run into the army, where he was killed; and though he said he would not cease to pray for me, yet he would venture to say to me, that if I did take this foolish step, God would not bless me, and I would have leisure hereafter to reflect upon having neglected his counsel when there might be none to assist in my recovery.

I observed in this last part of his discourse,—which was truly prophetic, though I suppose my father did not know it to be so himself,—I say, I observed the tears run down his face very plentifully, and especially when he spoke of my brother who was killed; and that when he spoke of my having leisure to repent, and none to assist me, he was so moved, that he broke off the discourse, and told me his heart was so full, he could say no more to me.

I was sincerely affected with this discourse, as indeed, who could be otherwise, and I resolved not to think of going abroad any more, but to settle at home according to my father's desire. But, alas! a few days wore it all off; and, in short, to prevent any of my father's further importunities, in a few weeks after I resolved to run quite away from him. However, I did not act so hastily neither, as my first heat of resolution prompted, but I took my mother, at a time when I thought her a little pleasanter than ordinary, and told her that my thoughts were so entirely bent upon seeing the world, that I should never settle to anything with resolution enough to go through with it, and my father had better give me his consent than force me to go without it; that I was now eighteen years old, which was too late to go apprentice to a trade, or clerk to an attorney; that I was sure, if I did, I should never serve out my time, and I should certainly run away from my master before my time was out, and go to sea; and if she would speak to my father to let me go but one voyage abroad, if I came home again and did not like it, I would go no more, and I would promise by a double diligence to recover that time I had lost.

This put my mother into a great passion: she told me, she knew it would be to no purpose to speak to my father upon any such subject; that he knew too well what was my interest to give his consent to anything so much for my hurt, and that she wondered how I could think of any such thing after such a discourse as I had had from my father, and such kind and tender expressions as she knew my father had used to me, and that, in short, if I would ruin myself, there was no help for me; but I might depend I should never have their consent to it; that for her part she would not have so much hand in my destruction; and I should never have it to say, that my mother was willing when my father was not.

Though my mother refused to move it to my father, yet, as I heard afterwards, she reported all the discourse to him, and that my father, after showing a great concern at it, said to her, with a sigh, "That boy might be happy if he would stay at home, but if he goes abroad, he will be the most miserable wretch that was ever born; I can give no consent to it."

It was not till almost a year after this that I broke loose, though in the mean time I continued obstinately deaf to all proposals of settling to business, and frequently expostulating with my father and mother about their being so positively determined against what they knew my inclinations prompted me to. But being one day at Hull, where I went casually, and without any purpose of making an elopement that time—but I say, being there, and one of my companions being about to sail to London, in his father's ship, and prompting me to go with them, with the common allurement of seafaring men, namely, that it should cost me nothing for my passage, I consulted neither father nor mother any more, nor so much as sent them word of it; but leaving them to hear of it as they might, without asking God's blessing, or my father's, without any consideration of circumstances or consequences, and in an ill hour —God knows—on the first of September, 1651, I went on board a ship bound for London. Never any young adventurer's misfortunes, I believe, began sooner, or continued longer than mine. The ship was no sooner gotten out of the Humber, but the wind began to blow, and the waves to rise in a most frightful manner; and as I had never been at sea before, I was most inexpressibly sick in body, and terrified in mind. I began now seriously to reflect upon what I had done, and how justly I was overtaken by the judgment of Heaven for my wicked leaving my father's house, and abandoning my duty; all the good counsel of my parents, my father's tears and my mother's entreaties, came now fresh into my mind, and my conscience, which was not yet come to the pitch of hardness to which it has been since, reproached me with the contempt of advice, and the breach of my duty to God and my father.

All this while the storm increased, and the sea, which I had never been upon before, went very high, though nothing like what I have seen many times since; no, nor like what I saw a few days after: but it was enough to affect me then, who was but a young sailor, and had never known anything of the matter. I expected every wave would have swallowed us up, and that every time the ship fell down, as I thought, in the trough or hollow of the sea, we should never rise more; and in this agony of mind I made many vows and resolutions, that if it would please God here to spare my life this one voyage, if ever I got once my foot upon dry land again I would go directly home to my father, and never set it into a ship again while I lived; that I would take his advice, and never run myself into such miseries as these any more. Now I saw plainly the goodness of his observations about the middle station of life, how easy, how comfortably he had lived all his days, and never had been exposed to tempests at sea, or troubles on shore; and I resolved that I would, like a true repenting prodigal, go home to my father.

These wise and sober thoughts continued all the while the storm continued, and indeed some time after; but the next day the wind was abated and the sea calmer, and I began to be a little inured to it: however, I was very grave for all that day, being also a little sea-sick still; but towards night the weather cleared up, the wind was quite over, and a charming fine evening followed; the sun went down perfectly clear, and rose so the next morning; and having little or no wind, and a smooth sea, the sun shining upon it, the sight was, as I thought, the most delightful that ever I saw.

I had slept well in the night, and was now no more sea-sick,

but very cheerful, looking with wonder upon the sea that was
so rough and terrible the day before, and could be so calm and
so pleasant in so little time after. And now, lest my good resolutions should continue, my companion, who had indeed enticed
me away, comes to me. "Well, Bob," says he (clapping me
upon the shoulder), "how do you do after it? I warrant you
were frighted, wan't you, last night, when it blew but a cap
full of wind?" "A cap full do you call it?" said I. "It was a terrible storm." "A storm, you fool you," replies he; "do you call
that a storm? why it was nothing at all; give us but a good ship
and sea-room, and we think nothing of such a squall of wind as
that; but you're but a fresh-water sailor, Bob: come, let us make
a bowl of punch, and we'll forget all that. Do you see what
charming weather it is now?" To make short this sad part of
my story, we went the old way of all sailors; the punch was
made, and I was made drunk with it, and in that one night's
wickedness I drowned all my repentance, all my reflections
upon my past conduct, and all resolutions for my future. In a
word, as the sea was returned to its smoothness of surface and
settled calmness by the abatement of that storm, so the hurry
of my thoughts being over, my fears and apprehensions of being
swallowed up by the sea being forgotten, and the current of my
former desires returned, I entirely forgot the vows and promises
that I made in my distress. I found indeed some intervals of reflection, and the serious thoughts did, as it were, endeavor to
return again sometimes; but I shook them off, and roused myself from them as it were from a distemper, and applying myself
to drink and company, soon mastered the return of those fits,
for so I called them, and I had in five or six days got as complete a victory over conscience as any young fellow that resolved
not to be troubled with it could desire. But I was to have another trial for it still; and Providence, as in such cases generally

it does, resolved to leave me entirely without excuse. For if I would not take this for a deliverance, the next was to be such a one as the worst and most hardened wretch among us would confess both the danger and the mercy.

CHAPTER 2: *The storm in Yarmouth Roads*

THE SIXTH day of our being at sea we came into Yarmouth Roads; the wind having been contrary, and the weather calm, we had made but little way since the storm. Here we were obliged to come to an anchor, and here we lay, the wind continuing contrary, namely, at southwest, for seven or eight days, during which time a great many ships from Newcastle came into the same roads, as the common harbor where the ships might wait for a wind from the river.

We had not, however, rid here so long, but should have tided it up the river, but that the wind blew too fresh, and after we had lain four or five days blew very hard. However, the roads being reckoned as good as a harbor, the anchorage good, and our ground-tackle very strong, our men were unconcerned, and not in the least apprehensive of danger, but spent the time in rest and mirth, after the manner of the sea; but the eighth day in the morning, the wind increased, and we had all hands at work to strike our topmasts, and make everything snug and close, that the ship might ride as easy as possible. By noon the sea went very high indeed, and our ship rid forecastle in, shipped several seas, and we thought once or twice our anchor had come home; upon which our master ordered out the sheet-anchor, so that we rode with two anchors ahead, and the cables veered out to the better end.

By this time it blew a terrible storm indeed; and now I began to see terror and amazement in the faces even of the seamen

themselves. The master, though vigilant in the business of preserving the ship, yet as he went in and out of his cabin by me,
I could hear him softly to himself say several times, "Lord, be
merciful to us; we shall be all lost, we shall be all undone," and
the like. During these first hurries, I was stupid, lying still in my
cabin, which was in the steerage, and cannot describe my
temper. I could ill reassume the first penitence which I had
so apparently trampled upon, and hardened myself against: I
thought the bitterness of death had been past, and that this
would be nothing like the first. But when the master himself
came by me, as I said just now, and said we should be all lost, I
was dreadfully frighted; I got up out of my cabin, and looked
out; but such a dismal sight I never saw: the sea went mountains high, and broke upon us every three or four minutes: when
I could look about, I could see nothing but distress round us:
two ships that rid near us, we found, had cut their masts by the
board, being deep loaden; and our men cried out, that a ship
which rid about a mile ahead of us was foundered. Two more
ships being driven from their anchors, were run out of the roads
to sea at all adventures, and that with not a mast standing.
The light ships fared the best, as not so much laboring in the
sea; but two or three of them drove, and came close by us,
running away with only their spritsail out before the wind.

Towards evening the mate and boatswain begged the master
of our ship to let them cut away the foremast, which he was
very unwilling to do; but the boatswain protesting to him, that
if he did not, the ship would founder, he consented; and when
they had cut away the foremast, the mainmast stood so loose,
and shook the ship so much, they were obliged to cut her away
also, and make a clear deck.

Any one may judge what a condition I must be in at all this,
who was but a young sailor, and who had been in such a fright

before at but a little. But if I can express at this distance the thoughts I had about me at that time, I was in ten-fold more horror of mind upon account of my former convictions, and the having returned from them to the resolutions I had wickedly taken at first, than I was at death itself; and these, added to the terror of the storm, put me into such a condition, that I can by no words describe it. But the worst was not come yet: the storm continued with such fury, that the seamen themselves acknowledged they had never known a worse. We had a good ship, but she was deep loaden, and wallowed in the sea, that the seaman every now and then cried out she would founder. It was my advantage in one respect, that I did not know what they meant by founder, till I inquired. However, the storm was so violent, that I saw what is not often seen, the master, the boatswain, and some others more sensible than the rest, at their prayers, and expecting every moment when the ship would go to the bottom. In the middle of the night, and under all the rest of our distresses, one of the men that had been down on purpose to see, cried out, we had sprung a leak; another said there was four foot water in the hold. Then all hands were called to the pump. At that very word my heart, as I thought, died within me, and I fell backwards upon the side of my bed where I sat, into the cabin. However, the men roused me, and told me, that I who was able to do nothing before, was as well able to pump as another; at which I stirred up, and went to the pump and worked very heartily. While this was doing, the master seeing some light colliers, who, not able to ride out the storm, were obliged to slip and run away to sea, and would not come near us, ordered to fire a gun as a signal of distress. I, who knew nothing what that meant, was so surprised, that I thought the ship had broke, or some dreadful thing happened. In a word I was so surprised, that I fell down in a swoon. As this was a time when everybody had his own life to think of, nobody minded me, or what was become of me; but another man stepped up to the pump, and thrusting me aside with his foot, let me lie, thinking I had been dead, and it was a great while before I came to myself.

We worked on, but the water increasing in the hold, it was apparent that the ship would founder; and though the storm began to abate a little, yet as it was not possible she could swim till we might run into a port, so the master continued firing guns for help; and a light ship who had rid it out just ahead of us, ventured a boat out to help us. It was with the utmost hazard the boat came near us, but it was impossible for us to get on board, or for the boat to lie near the ship's side; till at last, the men rowing very heartily, and venturing their lives to save ours, our men cast them a rope over the stern with the buoy to it, and then veered it out a great length, which they, after great labor and hazard, took hold of, and we hauled them close under our stern and got all into their boat. It was to no purpose for them or us after we were in the boat to think of reaching to their own ship, so all agreed to let her drive, and only to pull her in towards shore as much as we could, and our master promised them, that if the boat was staved upon shore he would make it good to their master; so partly rowing and partly driving, our boat went away to the northward, sloping towards the shore almost as far as Winterton-Ness.

We were not much more than a quarter of an hour out of our ship before we saw her sink, and then I understood for the first time what was meant by a ship foundering in the sea. I must acknowledge I had hardly eyes to look up when the seamen told me she was sinking; for from that moment they rather put me into the boat than that I might be said to go in: my heart was as it were dead within me, partly with fright, partly with horror of mind, and the thoughts of what was yet before me.

While we were in this condition, the men yet laboring at the oars to bring the boat near the shore, we could see (when, our boat mounting the waves, we were able to see the shore) a great many people running along the shore to assist us when we should come near; but we made but slow way towards the shore, nor were we able to reach the shore, till, being past the light-house at Winterton, the shore falls off to the westward toward Cromer, and so the land broke off a little the violence of the wind: here we got in, and, though not without much difficulty, got all safe on shore, and walked afterwards on foot to Yarmouth, where, as unfortunate men, we were used with great humanity, as well by the magistrates of the town, who assigned us good quarters, as by particular merchants and owners of ships, and had money given us sufficient to take us either to London or back to Hull, as we thought fit.

Had I now had the sense to have gone back to Hull, and have gone home, I had been happy, and my father, an emblem of our blessed Saviour's parable, had even killed the fatted calf for me; for hearing the ship I went away in was cast away in Yarmouth Roads, it was a great while before he had any assurance that I was not drowned.

But my ill fate pushed me on now with an obstinacy that nothing could resist; and though I had several times loud calls from my reason and my more composed judgment to go home, yet I had no power to do it. I know not what to call this, nor will I urge that it is a secret overruling decree that hurries us on to be the instruments of our own destruction, even though it be before us, and that we rush upon it with our eyes open. Certainly nothing but some such decreed unavoidable misery attending, and which it was impossible for me to escape, could have pushed me forward against the calm reasonings and persuasions of my most retired thoughts, and against two such visible instructions as I had met with in my first attempt.

My comrade who had helped to harden me before, and who was the master's son, was now less forward than I. The first time he spoke to me after we were at Yarmouth, which was not till two or three days, for we were separated in the town to several quarters,—I say, the first time he saw me, it appeared his tone was altered; and looking very melancholy, and shaking his head, asked me how I did, and telling his father who I was, and how I had come this voyage only for a trial, in order to go farther abroad; his father, turning to me with a very grave and concerned tone, "Young man," says he, "you ought never to go to sea any more; you ought to take this for a plain and visible token that you are not to be a sea-faring man." "Why, sir," said I, "will you go to sea no more?" "That is another case," said he; "it is my calling, and therefore my duty; but as you made this voyage for a trial, you see what a taste Heaven has given you of what you are to expect if you persist; perhaps this is all befallen us on your account, like Jonah, in the ship of Tarshish. Pray," continues he, "what are you? and on what account did you go to sea?" Upon that I told him some of my story; at the end of which he burst out with a strange kind of passion: "What had I done," says he, "that such an unhappy wretch should come into my ship? I would not set my foot in the same ship with thee again for a thousand pounds." However, he afterwards talked very gravely to me, and exhorted me to go back to my father and not tempt Providence to my ruin; told me I might see a visible hand of Heaven against me. "And, young man," said he, "depend upon it if you do not go back, wherever you go, you will meet with nothing but disasters and disappointments, till your father's words are fulfilled upon you."

We parted soon after; for I made him little answer, and I saw him no more; which way he went, I knew not. As for me, having some money in my pocket, I travelled to London by land; and there, as well as on the road, had many struggles with myself, what course of life I should take, and whether I should go home, or go to sea.

As to going home, shame opposed the best motions that offered to my thoughts; and it immediately occurred to me how I should be laughed at among the neighbors, and should be ashamed to see, not my father and mother only, but even everybody else; from whence I have since often observed, how incongruous and irrational the common temper of mankind is, especially of youth, to that reason which ought to guide them in such cases, namely, that they are not ashamed to sin, and yet are ashamed to repent; not ashamed of the action for which they ought justly to be esteemed fools, but are ashamed of the returning, which only can make them be esteemed wise men.

In this state of life, however, I remained some time, uncertain what measure to take, and what course of life to lead. An irresistible reluctance continued to going home; and as I stayed a while, the remembrance of the distress I had been in wore off, and as that abated, the little motion I had in my desires to a return wore off with it, till at last I quite laid aside the thoughts of it, and looked out for a voyage.

That evil influence which carried me first away from my father's house, that hurried me into the wild notion of raising my fortune, and that imprest those conceits so forcibly upon me, as to make me deaf to all good advice, and to the entreaties and even the command of my father,—I say, the same influence, whatever it was, presented the most unfortunate of all enterprises to my view; and I went on board a vessel bound to the coast of Africa, or, as our sailors vulgarly call it, a voyage to Guinea.

CHAPTER 3: *In which I make two voyages, and fall into terrible misfortunes*

IT WAS my great misfortune that in all these adventures I did not ship myself as a sailor; whereby, though I might indeed have worked a little harder than ordinary, yet at the same time I had learned the duty and office of a foremast man, and in time might have qualified myself for a mate or lieutenant, if not for a master. But as it was always my fate to choose for the worse, so I did here; for having money in my pocket, and good clothes upon my back, I would always go on board in the habit of a gentleman, and so I neither had any business in the ship, nor learned to do any.

It was my lot first of all to fall into pretty good company in London, which does not always happen to such loose and un-guided young fellows as I then was; the devil generally not omitting to lay some snare for them very early; but it was not so with me. I first fell acquainted with the master of a ship who had been on the coast of Guinea, and who, having had very good success there, was resolved to go again; and who, taking a fancy to my conversation, which was not at all disagreeable at that time, hearing me say I had a mind to see the world, told me if I would go the voyage with him I should be at no expense; I should be his messmate and his companion, and if I could carry anything with me, I should have all the advantage of it that the trade would admit, and perhaps I might meet with some encouragement.

I embraced the offer, and entering into a strict friendship

with this captain, who was an honest and plain-dealing man, I went the voyage with him, and carried a small adventure with me, which, by the disinterested honesty of my friend the captain, I increased very considerably; for I carried about 40*l.* in such toys and trifles as the captain directed me to buy. This 40*l.* I had mustered together by the assistance of some of my relations whom I corresponded with, and who, I believe, got my father, or at least my mother, to contribute so much as that to my first adventure.

This was the only voyage which I may say was successful in all my adventures, and which I owe to the integrity and honesty of my friend the captain, under whom also I got a competent knowledge of the mathematics, and the rules of navigation, learned how to keep an account of the ship's course, take an observation, and, in short, to understand some things that were needful to be understood by a sailor; for, as he took delight to instruct me, I took delight to learn, and, in a word, this voyage made me both a sailor and a merchant; for I brought home five pounds nine ounces of gold dust for my adventure, which yielded me in London at my return, almost 300*l.*, and this filled me with those aspiring thoughts which have since so completed my ruin.

Yet even in this voyage I had my misfortunes too; particularly, that I was continually sick, being thrown into a violent fever by the excessive heat of the climate; our principal trading being upon the coast, from the latitude of fifteen degrees north even to the line itself.

I was now set up for a Guinea trader; and my friend, to my great misfortune, dying soon after his arrival, I resolved to go the same voyage again, and I embarked in the same vessel with one who was his mate in the former voyage, and had now got the command of the ship. This was the unhappiest voyage that

ever man made; for though I did not carry quite 100*l.* of my
new gained wealth, so that I had 200*l.* left, and which I lodged
with my friend's widow, who was very just to me, yet I fell
into terrible misfortunes in this voyage; and the first was this,
namely: Our ship, making her course towards the Canary Islands, or rather between those islands and the African shore,
was surprised in the gray of the morning by a Turkish rover of
Sallee, who gave chase to us with all the sail she could make.
We crowded also as much canvas as our yards would spread, or
our masts carry, to have got clear; but finding the pirate gained
upon us, and would certainly come up with us in a few hours,
we prepared to fight; our ship having twelve guns, and the rogue
eighteen. About three in the afternoon he came up with us, and
bringing to, by mistake, just athwart our quarter, instead of
athwart our stern, as he intended, we brought eight of our guns
to bear on that side, and poured in a broadside upon him, which
made him sheer off again, after returning our fire, and pouring
in also his small shot from near 200 men which he had on
board. However, we had not a man touched, all our men keeping close. He prepared to attack us again, and we to defend
ourselves; but laying us on board the next time upon our other
quarter, he entered sixty men upon our decks, who immediately
fell to cutting and hacking the decks and rigging. We plied
them with small shot, half-pikes, powder-chests, and such like,
and cleared our deck of them twice. However, to cut short this
melancholy part of our story, our ship being disabled, and three
of our men killed, and eight wounded, we were obliged to yield,
and were carried all prisoners into Sallee, a port belonging to
the Moors.

The usage I had there was not so dreadful as at first I apprehended, nor was I carried up the country to the emperor's
court, as the rest of our men were, but was kept by the captain

of the rover as his proper prize, and made his slave, being young
and nimble, and fit for his business. At this surprising change
of my circumstances, from a merchant to a miserable slave, I
was perfectly overwhelmed; and now I looked back upon my
father's prophetic discourse to me, that I should be miserable,
and have none to relieve me, which, I thought, was now so
effectually brought to pass, that I could not be worse; that now
the hand of Heaven had overtaken me, and I was undone without redemption. But, alas! this was but a taste of the misery I
was to go through, as will appear in the sequel of the story.

As my new patron or master had taken me home to his house,
so I was in hopes that he would take me with him when he went
to sea again, believing that it would some time or other be his
fate to be taken by a Spanish or Portuguese man-of-war, and
that then I should be set at liberty. But this hope of mine was
soon taken away; for when he went to sea, he left me on shore
to look after his little garden, and do the common drudgery of
slaves about his house; and when he came home again from
his cruise, he ordered me to lie in the cabin to look after the
ship.

Here I meditated nothing but my escape, and what method
I might take to effect it, but found no way that had the least
probability in it: nothing presented to make the supposition of
it rational; for I had nobody to communicate it to, that would
embark with me; no fellow-slave, no Englishman, Irishman, or
Scotchman, there but myself; so that for two years, though I
often pleased myself with the imagination, yet I never had the
least encouraging prospect of putting it in practice.

After about two years an odd circumstance presented itself,
which put the old thought of making some attempt for my
liberty again in my head: my patron lying at home longer than
usual, without fitting out his ship, which, as I heard, was for

want of money, he used constantly, once or twice a week, sometimes oftener, if the weather was fair, to take the ship's pinnace,
and go out into the road a fishing; and as he always took me and
a young Maresco with him to row the boat, we made him very
merry, and I proved very dexterous in catching fish: insomuch,
that sometimes he would send me with a Moor, one of his
kinsmen, and the youth, the Maresco as they called him, to
catch a dish of fish for him.

It happened one time, that going a fishing in a stark calm
morning, a fog rose so thick, that though we were not half a
league from the shore, we lost sight of it; and rowing we knew
not whither or which way, we labored all day, and all the next
night, and when the morning came we found we had pulled
off to sea instead of pulling in for the shore, and that we were
at least two leagues from the shore; however, we got well in
again, though with a great deal of labor, and some danger; for
the wind began to blow pretty fresh in the morning, but particularly we were all very hungry.

But our patron, warned by this disaster, resolved to take
more care of himself for the future; and having lying by him
the long boat of our English ship he had taken, he resolved
he would not go a fishing any more without a compass and
some provision; so he ordered the carpenter of his ship, who
also was an English slave, to build a small state-room or cabin
in the middle of the long boat, like that of a barge, with a place
to stand behind it to steer and hale home the mainsheet, and
room before for a hand or two to stand and work the sails. She
sailed with what we call a shoulder-of-mutton sail; and the boom
gibed over the top of the cabin, which lay very snug and low,
and had in it room for him to lie, with a slave or two, and a table
to eat on, with some small lockers to put in some bottles of such
liquor as he thought fit to drink, particularly his bread, rice
and coffee.

We went frequently out with this boat a fishing, and as I was most dexterous to catch fish for him, he never went without me. It happened that he had appointed to go out in this boat, either for pleasure or for fish, with two or three Moors of some distinction in that place, and for whom he had provided extraordinarily; and had therefore sent on board the boat over night a larger store of provisions than ordinary, and had ordered me to get ready three fusees with powder and shot, which were on board his ship, for that they designed some sport of fowling as well as fishing.

I got all things ready as he directed, and waited the next morning with the boat washed clean, her flag and pendants out, and everything to accommodate his guests; when by and by my patron came on board alone, and told me his guests had put off going, upon some business that fell out, and ordered me with the man and boy, as usual to go out with the boat and catch them some fish, for that his friends were to sup at his house; and commanded that as soon as I got some fish I should bring it home to his house; all which I prepared to do.

This moment my former notions of deliverance darted into my thoughts, for now I found I was like to have a little ship at my command; and my master being gone, I prepared to furnish myself, not for a fishing business, but for a voyage; though I knew not, neither did I so much as consider, whither I should steer; for anywhere to get out of that place was my way.

My first contrivance was to make a pretense to speak to this Moor, to get something for our subsistence on board; for I told him we must not presume to eat of our patron's bread; he said, that was true; so he brought a large basket of rusk or biscuit of their kind, and three jars with fresh water, into the boat. I knew where my patron's case of bottles stood, which it was evident by the make were taken out of some English prize; and

I conveyed them into the boat while the Moor was on shore, as if they had been there before for our master. I conveyed also a great lump of bees-wax into the boat, which weighed above half a hundredweight, with a parcel of twine or thread, a hatchet, a saw, and a hammer, all which were of great use to us afterwards; especially the wax to make candles. Another trick I tried upon him, which he innocently came into also; his name was Ismael, who they call Muly, or Moley; so I called to him,—"Moley," said I, "our patron's guns are on board the boat; can you not get a little powder and shot, it may be we may kill some alcamies (a fowl like our curlews) for ourselves, for I know he keeps the gunner's stores in the ship?" "Yes," says he, "I'll bring some;" and accordingly he brought a great leather pouch which held about a pound and a half of powder, or rather more; and another with shot, that had five or six pounds, with some bullets, and put all into the boat; at the same time I had found some powder of my master's in the great cabin, with which I filled one of the large bottles in the case, which was almost empty; pouring what was in it into another: and thus furnished with everything needful, we sailed out of the port to fish. The castle which is at the entrance of the port knew who we were, and took no notice of us; and we were not above a mile out of the port before we hauled in our sail, and set us down to fish. The wind blew from the N. N. E. which was contrary to my desire; for had it blown southerly I had been sure to have made the coast of Spain, and at least reached the bay of Cadiz; but my resolutions were, blow which way it would, I would be gone from that horrid place where I was, and leave the rest to fate.

After we had fished some time and catched nothing, for when I had fish on my hook I would not pull them up, that he might not see them, I said to the Moor, "This will not do; our master will not be thus served; we must stand farther off:" he thinking no harm agreed, and being in the head of the boat set the sails; and as I had the helm I run the boat out near a league farther, and then brought her to as if I would fish, when giving the boy the helm, I stept forward to where the Moor was, and making as if I stooped for something behind him, I took him by surprise with my arm under his legs, and tossed him clear overboard into the sea. He rose immediately, for he swam like a cork, and calling to me, begged to be taken in: told me he would go all over the world with me; he swam so strong after the boat that he would have reached me very quickly, there being but little wind; upon which I stepped into the cabin, and fetching one of the fowling-pieces, I presented it at him, and told him I had done him no hurt, and if he would be quiet I would do him none: "but," said I, "you swim well enough to reach the shore, and the sea is calm; make the best of your way to shore, and I will do you no harm, but if you come near the boat I'll shoot you through the head; for I am resolved to have my liberty:" so he turned himself about and swam for the shore, and I make no doubt but that he reached it with ease, for he was an excellent swimmer.

I could have been content to have taken this Moor with me, and have drowned the boy, but there was no venturing to trust him. When he was gone I turned to the boy, who they called Xury, and said to him, "Xury, if you will be faithful to me I'll make you a great man; but if you will not stroke your face to be true to me," that is, swear by Mahomet and his father's beard, "I must throw you into the sea too;" the boy smiled in my face, and spoke so innocently that I could not mistrust him; and swore to be faithful to me, and go all over the world with me.

While I was in view of the Moor that was swimming, I stood directly to sea with the boat, rather stretching to windward, that they might think me gone towards the Straits' mouth (as indeed any one that had been in their wits must have been supposed to do), for who would have supposed we were sailed on to the southward to the truly Barbarian coast, where whole nations of Negroes were sure to surround us with their canoes, and destroy us; where we could never once go on shore but we should be devoured by savage beasts, or more merciless savages of human kind?

CHAPTER 4: *Escape and rescue*

As soon as it grew dusk in the evening, I changed my course, and steered directly south and by east, bending my course a little toward the east, that I might keep in with the shore; and having a fair fresh gale of wind, and a smooth quiet sea, I made such sail that I believe by the next day at three o'clock in the afternoon, when I first made the land, I could not be less that 150 miles south of Sallee; quite beyond the emperor of Morocco's dominions, or indeed of any other king thereabouts, for we saw no people.

Yet such was the fright I had taken at the Moors, and the dreadful apprehensions I had of falling into their hands, that I would not stop, or go on shore, or come to an anchor. The wind continuing fair till I had sailed in that manner five days, and the wind shifting to the southward, I concluded also that if any of our vessels were in chase of me, they also would now give over; so I ventured to make the coast, and come to an anchor in the mouth of a little river, I knew not what, or where; neither what latitude, what country, what nation, or what river: I neither saw, or desired to see any people, the principal thing I wanted was fresh water. We came into this creek in the evening, resolving to swim on shore as soon as it was dark, and discover the country; but as soon as it was quite dark, we heard such dreadful noises of the barking, roaring, and howling of wild creatures of we knew not what kinds, that the poor boy was ready to die with fear, and begged of me not to go on shore till day. "Well, Xury," said I, "then I won't, but it may be we may see men by day, who will be as bad to us as those lions." "Then we give them the shoot gun," says Xury, laughing; "make them run way." Such English Xury spoke by conversing among us slaves. However I was glad to see the boy so cheerful, and I gave him a dram (out of our patron's case of bottles) to cheer him up; after all Xury's advice was good, and I took it; we dropped our little anchor and lay still all night; I say still, for we slept none; for in two or three hours we saw vast great creatures (we knew not what to call them) of many sorts, come down to the sea-shore and run into the water, wallowing and washing themselves for the pleasure of cooling themselves; and they made such hideous howlings and yellings that I never indeed heard the like.

Xury was dreadfully frighted, and indeed so was I too; but we were both more frighted when we heard one of these mighty

creatures come swimming towards our boat: we could not see
him, but we might hear him by his blowing to be a monstrous
huge and furious beast. Xury said it was a lion, and it might be
so for aught I know; but poor Xury cried to me to weigh the
anchor and row away. "No," says I, "Xury, we can slip our
cable with a buoy to it and go off to sea; they cannot follow us
far." I had no sooner said so, but I perceived the creature (whatever it was) within two oars' length, which something surprised
me; however I immediately stept to the cabin-door, and taking
up my gun fired at him, upon which he immediately turned
about and swam towards the shore again.

But it is impossible to describe the horrible noises, and hideous cries and howlings, that were raised, as well upon the edge
of the shore, as higher within the country, upon the noise or
report of the gun; a think I have some reason to believe those
creatures had never heard before: this convinced me that there
was no going on shore for us in the night upon that coast, and
how to venture on shore in the day was another question too;
for to have fallen into the hands of any of the savages, had been
as bad as to have fallen into the hands of lions and tigers; at
least we were equally apprehensive of the danger of it.

Be that as it would, we were obliged to go on shore some-
where or other for water, for we had not a pint left in the boat;
when or where to get it was the point. Xury said, if I would let
him go on shore with one of the jars, he would find if there was
any water, and bring some to me. I asked him why he would
go? why I should not go, and he stay in the boat? The boy answered with so much affection that made me love him ever
after. Says he, "If wild mans come, they eat me, you go way."
"Well, Xury," said I, "we will both go, and if the wild mans
come, we will kill them: they shall eat neither of us;" so I gave
Xury a piece of rusk-bread to eat, and a dram out of our patron's

case of bottles which I mentioned before; and we hauled the boat in as near the shore as we thought was proper, and waded on shore; carrying nothing but our guns, and two jars for water.

I did not care to go out of sight of the boat, fearing the coming of canoes with savages down the river: but the boy, seeing a low place about a mile up the country, rambled to it; and by and by I saw him come running towards me. I thought he was pursued by some savage, or frighted with some wild beast, and I ran forward towards him to help him; but when I came nearer to him, I saw something hanging over his shoulders, which was a creature that he had shot, like a hare, but different in color, and longer legs; however we were very glad of it, and it was very good meat; but the great joy that poor Xury came with, was to tell me he had found good water, and seen no wild mans.

But we found afterwards that we need not take such pains for water; for a little higher up the creek where we were, we found the water fresh when the tide was out, which flowed but a little way up; so we filled our jars and feasted on the hare we had killed, and prepared to go on our way, having seen no footsteps of any human creature in that part of the country.

As I had been one voyage to this coast before, I knew very well that the islands of the Canaries, and the Cape de Verde Islands also, lay not far off from the coast. But as I had no instruments to take an observation to know what latitude we were in, and did not exactly know, or at least remember, what latitude they were in, I knew not where to look for them, or when to stand off to sea towards them; otherwise I might now easily have found some of these islands. But my hope was, that if I stood along this coast till I came to that part where the English trade, I should find some of their vessels upon their usual design of trade, that would relieve and take us in.

By the best of my calculation, that place where I now was,

must be that country, which, lying between the emperor of
Morocco's dominions and the Negroes, lies waste, and uninhabited, except by wild beasts, the Negroes having abandoned
it, and gone farther south for fear of the Moors; and the Moors
not thinking it worth inhabiting, by reason of its barrenness;
and indeed both forsaking it because of the prodigious number
of tigers, lions, leopards, and other furious creatures which
harbor there; so that the Moors use it for their hunting only,
where they go like an army, two or three thousand men at a
time; and indeed for near an hundred miles together upon this
coast, we saw nothing but a waste uninhabited country by day;
and heard nothing but howlings and roaring of wild beasts by
night.

Once or twice in the day-time I thought I saw the Peak of
Teneriffe, being the high top of the mountain Teneriffe in the
Canaries; and had a great mind to venture out in hopes of
reaching thither; but having tried twice, I was forced in again
by contrary winds, the sea also going too high for my little
vessel, so I resolved to pursue my first design and keep along
the shore.

Several times I was obliged to land for fresh water after we
had left this place; and once in particular, being early in the
morning, we came to an anchor under a little point of land
which was pretty high, and the tide beginning to flow, we lay
still to go farther in. Xury, whose eyes were more about him
than it seems mine were, calls softly to me, and tells me that
we had best go farther off the shore; "for," says he, "look,
yonder lies a dreadful monster on the side of that hillock fast
asleep." I looked where he pointed, and saw a dreadful monster
indeed, for it was a terrible great lion that lay on the side of
the shore, under the shade of a piece of the hill that hung
as it were a little over him. "Xury," says I, "you shall go on

shore and kill him:" Xury looked frighted, and said, "Me kill! he eat me at one mouth;" one mouthful he meant. However, I said no more to the boy, but bade him lie still; and took our biggest gun, which was almost musquet-bore, and loaded it with a good charge of powder, and with two slugs, and laid it down; then I loaded another gun with two bullets; and the third, for we had three pieces, I loaded with five smaller bullets. I took the best aim I could with the first piece, to have shot him into the head, but he lay so with his leg raised a little above his nose, that the slugs hit his leg about the knee, and broke the bone. He started up growling at first, but finding his leg broke, fell down again, and then got up upon three legs, and gave the most hideous roar that ever I heard. I was a little surprised that I had not hit him on the head; however, I took up the second piece immediately, and though he began to move off, fired again, and shot him into the head, and had the pleasure to see him drop, and make but little noise, but lay struggling for life. Then Xury took heart, and would have me let him go on shore. "Well, go," said I. So the boy jumped into the water, and taking a little gun in one hand, swam to the shore with the other hand, and coming close to the creature, put the muzzle of the piece to his ear, and shot him into the head, which dispatched him quite.

This was game indeed to us, but this was no food: and I was very sorry to lose three charges of powder and shot upon a creature that was good for nothing to us. However, Xury said he would have some of him; so he comes on board, and asked me to give him the hatchet. "For what, Xury?" said I. "Me cut off his head," said he. However, Xury could not cut off his head, but he cut off a foot, and brought it with him, and it was a monstrous great one.

I bethought myself, however, that perhaps the skin of him

might one way or other be of some value to us; and I resolved
to take off his skin, if I could. So Xury and I went to work with
him; but Xury was much the better workman at it, for I knew
very ill how to do it. Indeed it took us up both the whole
day; but at last we got the hide off him, and spreading it on the
top of our cabin, the sun effectually dried it in two days' time,
and it afterwards served me to lie upon.

After this stop, we made on to the southward continually for
ten or twelve days, living very sparing on our provisions, which
began to abate very much, and going no oftener into the shore
than we were obliged to for fresh water: my design in this was,
to make the river Gambia or Senegal, that is to say anywhere
about the Cape de Verde, where I was in hopes to meet with
some European ship; and if I did not, I knew not what course
I had to take, but to seek for the Islands, or perish there among
the Negroes. I knew that all the ships from Europe, which
sailed either to the coast of Guinea or to Brazil, or to the East
Indies, made this Cape, or those Islands; and, in a word, I put
the whole of my fortune upon this single point, either that I
must meet with some ship or must perish.

When I had pursued this resolution about ten days longer,
as I have said, I began to see that the land was inhabited; and
in two or three places, as we sailed by, we saw people stand
upon the shore to look at us; we could also perceive they were
quite black, and stark naked. I was once inclined to have gone
on shore to them; but Xury was my better counsellor, and said
to me, "No go, no go:" however I hauled in nearer the shore
that I might talk to them, and I found they ran along the shore
by me a good way. I observed they had no weapons in their
hands except one, who had a long slender stick, which Xury
said was a lance, and that they would throw them a great way
with good aim. So I kept at a distance, but talked with them by

signs as well as I could; and particularly made signs for something to eat: they beckoned to me to stop my boat, and they would fetch me some meat; upon this I lowered the top of my sail, and lay by, and two of them ran up into the country, and in less than half an hour came back, and brought with them two pieces of dry flesh and some corn, as is the produce of their country; but we neither knew what the one nor the other was: however, we were willing to accept it, but how to come at it was our next dispute, for I was not for venturing on shore to them, and they were as much afraid of us; but they took a safe way for us all, for they brought it to the shore and laid it down, and went and stood a great way off till we fetched it on board, and then came close to us again.

We made signs of thanks to them, for we had nothing to make them amends; but an opportunity offered that very instant to oblige them wonderfully; for while we were lying by the shore, came two mighty creatures, one pursuing the other (as we took it) with great fury, from the mountains towards the sea: whether it was the male pursuing the female, or whether they were in sport or in rage, we could not tell, any more than we could tell whether it was usual or strange, but I believe it was the latter; because, in the first place, those ravenous creatures seldom appear but in the night; and in the second place, we found the people terribly frighted, especially the women. The man that had the lance or dart did not fly from them, but the rest did; however, as the two creatures ran directly into the water, they did not seem to offer to fall upon any of the Negroes, but plunged themselves into the sea, and swam about as if they had come for their diversion. At last one of them began to come nearer our boat than at first I expected, but I lay ready for him, for I had loaded my gun with all possible expedition, and bade Xury load both the others. As soon as he came fairly within my reach, I fired, and shot him directly into the head. Immediately he sunk down into the water, but rose instantly, and plunged up and down as if he was struggling for life; and so indeed he was: he immediately made to the shore, but between the wound, which was his mortal hurt, and the strangling of the water, he died just before he reached the shore.

It is impossible to express the astonishment of these poor creatures at the noise and the fire of my gun; some of them were even ready to die for fear, and fell down as dead with the very terror. But when they saw the creature dead, and sunk in the water, and that I made signs to them to come to the shore, they took heart and came to the shore, and began to search for the creature. I found him by his blood staining the water; and by the help of a rope, which I slung round him, and gave the Negroes to haul, they dragged him on shore, and found that it was a most curious leopard, spotted and fine to an admirable degree, and the Negroes held up their hands with admiration to think what it was I had killed him with.

The other creature, frighted with the flash of fire and the noise of the gun, swam on shore, and ran up directly to the mountains from whence they came, nor could I at that distance know what it was. I found quickly the Negroes were for eating the flesh of this creature, so I was willing to have them take it as a favor from me, which when I made signs to them that they might take him, they were very thankful for. Immediately they fell to work with him, and though they had no knife, yet with a sharpened piece of wood they took off his skin as readily, and much more readily, then we could have done with a knife: they offered me some of the flesh, which I declined, making as if I would give it them, but made signs for the skin, which they gave me very freely, and brought me a great deal more of their provision, which, though I did not understand, yet I accepted; then I made signs to them for some water, and held out one of my jars to them, turning it bottom upward, to show that it was empty, and that I wanted to have it filled. They called immediately to some of their friends, and there came two women, and brought a great vessel made of earth, and burnt, as I suppose, in the sun; this they set down for me, as before, and I sent Xury on shore with my jars, and filled them all three.

I was now furnished with roots and corn, such as it was, and water; and, leaving my friendly Negroes, I made forward for about eleven days more, without offering to go near the shore, till I saw the land run out a great length into the sea, at about the distance of four or five leagues before me; and, the sea being very calm, I kept a large offing to make this point: at length, doubling the point at about two leagues from the land, I saw plainly land on the other side to seaward; then I concluded, as it was most certain indeed, that this was the Cape de Verde, and those the islands, called from thence Cape de Verde Islands. However, they were at a great distance, and I could not tell what I had best do, for if I should be taken with a fresh of wind I might neither reach one nor the other.

In this dilemma, as I was very pensive, I stept into the cabin and set me down, Xury having the helm, when on a sudden the boy cried out, "Master, master, a ship with a sail;" and the foolish boy was frighted out of his wits, thinking it must needs be some of his master's ships sent to pursue us, when I knew we were gotten far enough out of their reach. I jumped out of the cabin, and immediately saw not only the ship, but that it was a Portuguese ship, and, as I thought, was bound to the coast of Guinea for Negroes. But when I observed the course she steered, I was soon convinced they were bound some other way,

and did not design to come any nearer to the shore; upon which
I stretched out to sea as much as I could, resolving to speak
with them if possible.

With all the sail I could make, I found I should not be able
to come in their way, but they would be gone by before I
could make any signal to them. But after I had crowded to
the utmost, and began to despair, they, it seems, saw me by the
help of their perspective-glasses, and that it was some European
boat, which, as they supposed, must belong to some ship that
was lost; so they shortened sail to let me come up. I was encouraged with this, and as I had my patron's flag on board, I
made a waft of it to them for a signal of distress, and fired a gun,
both which they saw; for they told me they saw the smoke,
though they did not hear the gun. Upon these signals they very
kindly brought-to, and lay-by for me, and in about three hours'
time I came up with them.

They asked me what I was, in Portuguese, and in Spanish,
and in French; but I understood none of them; but at last a
Scottish sailor, who was on board, called to me, and I answered
him, and told him I was an Englishman, that I had made my
escape out of slavery from the Moors at Sallee. Then they bade
me come on board, and very kindly took me in, and all my
goods.

Chapter 5: *My plantation in the Brazils*

It was inexpressible joy to me, that any one would believe,
that I was thus delivered, as I esteemed it, from such a miserable and almost hopeless condition as I was in, and immediately offered all I had to the captain of the ship, as a return for
my deliverance; but he generously told me he would take nothing from me, but that all I had should be delivered safe to me

when I came to the Brazils; "for," says he, "I have saved your life on no other terms than I would be glad to be saved myself; and it may one time or other be my lot to be taken up in the same condition: besides," says he, "when I carry you to the Brazils, so great a way from your own country, if I should take away from you what you have, you will be starved there, and then I only take away that life I have given. No, no, Seignor, Mr. Englishman, I will carry you thither in charity, and those things will help you to buy your subsistence there, and your passage home again."

As he was charitable in his proposal, so he was just in the performance to a tittle, for he ordered the seamen that none should offer to touch anything I had; then he took everything into his own possession, and gave me back an exact inventory of them, that I might have them; even so much as my earthen jars.

As to my boat, it was a very good one, and that he saw, and told me he would buy it of me for the ship's use, and asked me what I would have for it? I told him he had been so generous to me in everything that I could not offer to make any price of the boat, but left it entirely to him; upon which he told me he would give me a note of his hand to pay me 80 pieces of eight for it at Brazil; and when it came there, if any one offered to give more, he would make it up; he offered me also 60 pieces of eight more for my boy Xury, which I was loth to take; not that I was not willing to let the captain have him, but I was very loth to sell the poor boy's liberty, who had assisted me so faithfully in procuring my own. However, when I let him know my reason, he owned it to be just, and offered me this medium, that he would give the boy an obligation to set him free in ten years, if he turned Christian. Upon this, and Xury saying he was willing to go to him, I let the captain have him.

We had a very good voyage to the Brazils, and arrived in All-Saints-Bay, in about twenty-two days after. And now I was once more delivered from the most miserable of all conditions of life, and what to do next with myself I was now to consider.

The generous treatment the captain gave me, I can never enough remember; he would take nothing of me for my passage, gave me twenty ducats for the leopard's skin, and forty for the lion's skin, which I had in my boat, and caused everything I had in the ship to be punctually delivered me; and what I was willing to sell he bought, such as the case of bottles, two of my guns, and a piece of the lump of bees-wax, for I had made candles of the rest; in a word, I made about 220 pieces of eight of all my cargo, and with this stock I went on shore in the Brazils.

I had not been long here, but being recommended to the house of a good honest man like himself, who had an Ingenio, as they call it, that is, a plantation and a sugar house; I lived with him some time, and acquainted myself by that means with the manner of their planting and making of sugar; and seeing how well the planters lived, and how they grew rich suddenly, I resolved, if I could get license to settle there, I would turn planter among them, resolving in the mean time to find out some way to get my money, which I had left in London, remitted to me. To this purpose, getting a kind of a letter of naturalization, I purchased as much land that was uncured as my money would reach, and formed a plan for my plantation and settlement, and such a one as might be suitable to the stock which I proposed to myself to receive from England.

I had a neighbor, a Portuguese of Lisbon, but born of English parents, whose name was Wells, and in much such circumstances as I was. I call him neighbor, because his plantation lay next to mine, and we went on very sociably together. My stock was but low, as well as his; and we rather planted for food, than anything else, for about two years. However, we began to increase, and our land began to come into order; so that the third year we planted some tobacco, and made each of us a large piece of ground ready for planting canes in the year to come; but we both wanted help; and now I found more than before, I had done wrong in parting with my boy Xury.

But alas! for me to do wrong that never did right, was no great wonder: I had no remedy but to go on; I was gotten into an employment quite remote to my genius, and directly contrary to the life I delighted in, and for which I forsook my father's house, and broke through all his good advice; nay, I was coming into the very middle station, or upper degree of low life, which my father advised me to before; and which if I resolved to go on with, I might as well have staid at home, and never have fatigued myself in the world as I had done, and I used often to say to myself, I could have done this as well in England among my friends, as have gone five thousand miles off to do it among strangers and savages in a wilderness, and at such distance as never to hear from any part of the world that had the least knowledge of me.

In this manner I used to look up my condition with the utmost regret. I had nobody to converse with, but now and then this neighbor: no work to be done, but by the labor of my hands; and I used to say, I lived just like a man cast away upon some desolate island, that had nobody there but himself. But how just has it been, and how should all men reflect, that, when they compare their present conditions with others that are worse, Heaven may oblige them to make the exchange, and be convinced of their former felicity, by their experience; I say how just has it been, that the truly solitary life I reflected on in an island of mere desolation should be my lot, who had so often unjustly compared it with the life which I then led, in which, had I continued, I had in all probability been exceeding prosperous and rich.

I was in some degree settled in my measures for carrying on the plantation, before my kind friend, the captain of the ship that took me up at sea, went back; for the ship remained there, providing his loading and preparing for his voyage, near three months; when, telling him what little stock I had left behind me in London, he gave me this friendly and sincere advice: "Seignor Inglese," says he (for so he always called me), "if you will give me letters, and a procuration here in form to me, with orders to the person who has your money in London, to send your effects to Lisbon, to such persons as I shall direct, and in such goods as are proper for this country, I will bring you the produce of them, God willing, at my return; but since human affairs are all subject to changes and disasters, I would have you give orders but for one hundred pounds sterling, which you say is half your stock, and let the hazard be run for the first; so that if it come safe, you may order the rest the same way; and if it miscarry, you may have the other half to have recourse to it for your supply."

This was so wholesome advice, and looked so friendly, that I could not but be convinced it was the best course I could take; so I accordingly prepared letters to the gentle-woman with whom I had left my money, and a procuration to the Portuguese captain, as he desired.

I wrote the English captain's widow a full account of all my adventures, my slavery, escape, and how I had met with the Portugal captain at sea, the humanity of his behavior, and what condition I was now in, with all other necessary directions for my supply; and when this honest captain came to Lisbon, he found means, by some of the English merchants there, to send over, not the order only, but a full account of my story, to a merchant at London, who represented it effectually to her; whereupon, she not only delivered the money, but out of her own pocket sent the Portugal captain a very handsome present for his humanity and charity to me.

The merchant in London vesting this hundred pounds in English goods, such as the captain had written for, sent them directly to him at Lisbon, and he brought them all safe to me to the Brazils; among which, without my directions (for I was too young in my business to think of them), he had taken care to have all sorts of tools, iron-work, and utensils necessary for my plantation, and which were of great use to me.

When this cargo arrived I thought my fortune made, for I was surprised with joy of it; and my good steward the captain had laid out the five pounds which my friend had sent him for a present for himself, to purchase, and bring me over a servant under bond for six years' service, and would not accept of any consideration, except a little tobacco, which I would have him accept, being of my own produce.

Neither was this all; but my goods being all England manufactures, such as cloth, stuffs, baize, and things particularly valuable and desirable in the country, I found means to sell them to a very great advantage, so that I may say I had more than four times the value of my first cargo, and was now infinitely beyond my poor neighbor, I mean in the advancement of my plantation: for the first thing I did, I bought me a Negro slave, and an European servant also; I mean another besides that which the captain brought me from Lisbon.

But as abused prosperity is oftentimes made the very means of our greatest adversity, so it was with me. I went on the next

year with great success in my plantation; I raised fifty great rolls
of tobacco on my own ground, more than I had disposed of for
necessaries among my neighbors; and these fifty rolls, being
each of above an hundred-weight, were well cured and laid by
against the return of the fleet from Lisbon. And now, increasing in business and in wealth, my head began to be full of proj-
ects and undertakings beyond my reach; such as are indeed
often the ruin of the best heads in business.

Had I continued in the station I was now in, I had room for
all the happy things to have yet befallen me, for which my
father so earnestly recommended a quiet retired life, and of
which he had so sensibly described the middle station of life to
be full; but other things attended me, and I was still to be the
willful agent of all my own miseries; and particularly to increase
my fault, and double the reflections upon myself, which in my
future sorrows I should have leisure to make. All these miscarriages were procured by my apparent obstinate adhering to my
foolish inclination of wandering abroad, and pursuing that inclination in contradiction to the clearest views of doing myself
good in a fair and plain pursuit of those prospects and those
measures of life, which nature and Providence concurred to
present me with, and to make my duty.

As I had done thus in breaking away from my parents, so I
could not be content now, but I must go and leave the happy
view I had of being a rich and thriving man in my new plantation, only to pursue a rash and immoderate desire of rising
faster than the nature of the thing admitted; and thus I cast
myself down again into the deepest gulf of human misery that
ever man fell into, or perhaps could be consistent with life and
a state of health in the world.

To come then by the just degrees to the particulars of this
part of my story; you may suppose, that having now lived almost

four years in the Brazils, and beginning to thrive and prosper very well upon my plantation, I had not only learned the language, but had contracted acquaintance and friendship among my fellow planters, as well as among the merchants at St. Salvadore, which was our port; and that in my discourses among them I had frequently given them an account of my two voyages to the coast of Guinea, the manner of trading with the Negroes there, and how easy it was to purchase upon the coast, for trifles, such as beads, toys, knives, scissors, hatchets, bits of glass, and the like, not only gold dust, Guinea grains, elephants' teeth, &c., but Negroes for the service of the Brazils, in great numbers.

They listened always very attentively to my discourses on these heads, but especially to that part which related to the buying Negroes, which was a trade at that time not only not far entered into, but as far as it was, had been carried on by the Assientos, or permission of the kings of Spain and Portugal, and engrossed in the public, so that few Negroes were bought, and those excessively dear.

It happened, being in company with some merchants and planters of my acquaintance, and talking of those things very earnestly, three of them came to me the next morning, and told me they had been musing very much upon what I had discoursed with them of the last night, and they came to make a secret proposal to me; and after enjoining me in secrecy, they told me that they had a mind to fit out a ship to go to Guinea; that they had all plantations as well as I, and were straitened for nothing so much as servants; that as this was a trade that could not be carried on, because they could not publicly sell the Negroes when they came home: so they desired to make but one voyage, to bring the Negroes on shore privately, and divide them among their own plantations; and in a word, the question was, whether I would go as their supercargo in the ship, to manage the trading part upon the coast of Guinea; and they offered me that I should have my equal share of the Negroes, without providing any part of the stock.

This was a fair proposal, it must be confessed, had it been made to any one that had not had a settlement and plantation of his own to look after, which was in a fair way of becoming very considerable, and with a good stock upon it. But for me, that was thus entered and established, and had nothing to do but go on as I had begun, for three or four years more, and to have sent for the other hundred pounds from England, and who in that time, and with that little addition, could scarce have failed of being worth three or four thousand pounds sterling, and that increasing too; for me to think of such a voyage was the most preposterous thing that ever man in such circumstances could be guilty of.

But I, that was born to be my own destroyer, could no more resist the offer, than I could restrain my first rambling designs, when my father's good counsel was lost upon me. In a word, I told them I would go with all my heart, if they would undertake to look after my plantation in my absence, and would dispose of it to such as I should direct if I miscarried. This they all engaged to do, and entered into writings or covenants to do so; and I made a formal will, disposing of my plantation and effects, in case of my death, making the captain of the ship that saved my life, as before, my universal heir, but obliging him to dispose of my effects as I had directed in my will, one half of the produce being to himself, and the other to be shipped to England.

In short, I took all possible caution to preserve my effects, and keep up my plantation. Had I used half as much prudence

to have looked into my own interest, and have made a judgment of what I ought to have done and not to have done, I had
certainly never gone away from so prosperous an undertaking,
leaving all the probable views of a thriving circumstance, and
gone upon a voyage to sea, attended with all its common hazards; to say nothing of the reasons I had to expect particular
misfortunes to myself.

But I was hurried on, and obeyed blindly the dictates of my
fancy rather than my reason; and, accordingly, the ship being
fitted out, and the cargo furnished, and all things done as by
agreement by my partners in the voyage, I went on board in an
evil hour, the 1st of September, 1659—being the same day eight
years that I went from my father and mother at Hull, in order
to act the rebel to their authority, and the fool to my own
interest.

CHAPTER 6: *A violent storm and a shipwreck*

OUR SHIP was about 120 tons burden, carried 6 guns, and 14
men, besides the master, his boy, and myself. We had on board
no large cargo of goods, except of such toys as were fit for our
trade with the Negroes, such as beads, bits of glass, shells, and
odd trifles, especially little looking-glasses, knives, scissors,
hatchets, and the like.

The same day I went on board we set sail, standing away to
the northward upon our own coast, with design to stretch over
for the African coast when they came about ten or twelve degrees of northern latitude, which it seems was the manner of
their course in those days. We had very good weather, only
excessive hot, all the way upon our own coast till we came to
the height of Cape St. Augustino; from whence, keeping farther

off at sea, we lost sight of land, and steered as if we were bound for the isle Fernand de Noronha, holding our course N. E. by N. and leaving those isles on the east. In this course we passed the line in about twelve days' time, and were by our last observation in seven degrees twenty-two minutes northern latitude, when a violent tornado or hurricane took us quite out of our knowledge. It began from the south-east, came about to the north-west, and then settled into the north-east, from whence it blew in such a terrible manner, that for twelve days together we could do nothing but drive, and scudding away before it, let it carry us whither ever fate and the fury of the winds directed; and during these twelve days I need not say that I expected every day to be swallowed up, nor indeed did any in the ship expect to save their lives.

In this distress, we had, besides the terror of the storm, one of our men died of fever, and one man and the boy washed overboard. About the twelfth day, the weather abating a little, the master made an observation as well as he could, and found he was in about eleven degrees north latitude, but that he was twenty-two degrees of longitude difference west from Cape St. Augustino: so that he found he was gotten upon the coast of Guinea, or the north part of Brazil, beyond the river Amazones, toward that of the river Oronoque, commonly called the Great River, and began to consult with me what course he should take, for the ship was leaky and very much disabled, and he was going directly back to the coast of Brazil.

I was positively against that; and looking over the charts of the sea-coast of America with him, we concluded there was no inhabited country for us to have recourse to, till we came within the circle of the Caribbee Islands, and therefore resolved to stand away for Barbadoes, which, by keeping off at sea, to avoid the indraught of the bay or gulf of Mexico, we might easily perform, as we hoped, in about fifteen days' sail; whereas, we could not possibly make our voyage to the coast of Africa without some assistance, both to our ship and to ourselves.

With this design we changed our course, and steered away N. W. by W. in order to reach some of our English islands, where I hoped for relief; but our voyage was otherwise determined; for being in the latitude of twelve degrees eighteen minutes, a second storm came upon us, which carried us away with the same impetuosity westward, and drove us so out of the very way of all human commerce, that had all our lives been saved, as to the sea, we were rather in danger of being devoured by savages than ever returning to our own country.

In this distress, the wind still blowing very hard, one of our men early in the morning cried out, "Land!" and we had no sooner run out of the cabin to look out, in hopes of seeing whereabouts in the world we were, but the ship struck upon a sand, and in a moment, her motion being so stopped, the sea broke over her in such a manner, that we expected we should all have perished immediately; and we were immediately driven into our close quarters, to shelter us from the very foam and spray of the sea.

It is not easy for any one, who has not been in the like condition, to describe or conceive the consternation of men in such circumstances. We knew nothing where we were, or upon what land it was we were driven, whether an island or the main, whether inhabited or not inhabited; and as the rage of the wind was still great, though rather less than at first, we could not so much as hope to have the ship hold many minutes without breaking in pieces, unless the winds, by a kind of miracle, should turn immediately about. In a word, we sat looking one upon another, and expecting death every moment, and every man acting accordingly as preparing for another world, for there was little or nothing more for us to do in this. That which was our present comfort, and all the comfort we had, was, that contrary to our expectation the ship did not break yet, and that the master said the wind began to abate.

Now, though we found that the wind did a little abate, yet the ship having thus struck upon the sand, and sticking too fast for us to expect her getting off, we were in a dreadful condition indeed, and had nothing to do but to think of saving our lives as well as we could. We had a boat at our stern just before the storm, but she was first staved by dashing against the ship's rudder, and in the next place she broke away, and either sunk or was driven off to sea, so there was no hope from her. We had another boat on board but how to get her off into the sea was a doubtful thing; however there was no room to debate, for we fancied the ship would break in pieces every minute, and some told us she was actually broken already.

In this distress, the mate of our vessel lays hold of the boat, and with the help of the rest of the men, they got her slung over the ship's side, and getting all into her, let go, and committed ourselves, being eleven in number, to God's mercy and the wild sea; for though the storm was abated considerably, yet the sea went dreadful high upon the shore, and might well be called *den wild zee*, as the Dutch call the sea in a storm.

And now our case was very dismal indeed; for we all saw plainly that the sea went so high, that the boat could not live, and that we should be inevitably drowned. As to making sail, we had none, nor, if we had, could we have done anything with it, so we worked at the oar towards the land, though with heavy hearts, like men going to execution; for we all knew that when the boat came nearer the shore she would be dashed in a thousand pieces by the breach of the sea. However, we committed our souls to God in the most earnest manner, and the wind

driving us toward the shore, we hastened our destruction with our own hands, pulling as well as we could towards land.

What the shore was, whether rock or sand, whether steep or shoal, we knew not; the only hope that could rationally give us the least shadow of expectation was, if we might happen into some bay or gulf, or the mouth of some river, where by great chance we might have run our boat in, or got under the lee of the land, and perhaps made smooth water. But there was nothing of this appeared; but as we made nearer and nearer the shore, the land looked more frightful than the sea.

After we had rowed, or rather driven, about a league and a half, as we reckoned it, a raging wave, mountain-like, came rolling a-stern of us, and plainly bade us expect the *coup-de-grace*. In a word, it took us with such a fury that it overset the boat at once; and separating us, as well from the boat as from one another, gave us not time hardly to say, O God! for we were all swallowed up in a moment.

Nothing can describe the confusion of thought which I felt when I sunk into the water; for though I swam very well, yet I could not deliver myself from the waves so as to draw breath, till that wave having driven me, or rather carried me, a vast way on towards the shore, and having spent itself went back, and left me upon the land almost dry, but half dead with the water I took in. I had so much presence of mind, as well as breath left, that seeing myself nearer the main land than I expected, I got upon my feet, and endeavored to make on towards the land as fast as I could, before another wave should return and take me up again. But I soon found it was impossible to avoid it; for I saw the sea come after me as high as a great hill, and as furious as an enemy which I had no means or strength to contend with. My business was to hold my breath, and raise myself upon the water, if I could; and so by swimming to preserve my breathing, and pilot myself towards the shore, if possible. My greatest concern now being that the sea, as it would carry me a great way towards the shore when it came on, might not carry me back again with it when it gave back towards the sea.

The wave that came upon me again buried me at once 20 or 30 feet deep in its own body, and I could feel myself carried with a mighty force and swiftness towards the shore a very great way; but I held my breath, and assisted myself to swim still forward with all my might. I was ready to burst with holding my breath, when, as I felt myself rising up, so, to my immediate relief, I found my head and hands shoot out above the surface of the water; and thought it was not two seconds of time that I could keep myself so, yet it relieved me greatly, gave me breath and new courage. I was covered again with water a good while, but not so long but I held it out; and finding the water had spent itself, and began to return, I struck forward against the return of the waves, and felt ground again with my feet. I stood still a few moments to recover breath, and till the water went from me, and then took to my heels and ran with what strength I had farther towards the shore. But neither would this deliver me from the fury of the sea, which came pouring in after me again, and twice more I was lifted up by the waves and carried forwards as before, the shore being very flat.

The last time of these two had well near been fatal to me; for the sea having hurried me along as before, landed me, or rather dashed me, against a piece of a rock, and that with such force, as it left me senseless, and indeed helpless, as to my own deliverance; for the blow taking my side and breast, beat the breath as it were quite out of my body; and had it not returned again immediately, I must have been strangled in the water; but I recovered a little before the return of the waves, and seeing I should be covered again with the water, I resolved to hold fast by a piece of the rock, and so hold my breath, if possible, till the wave went back. Now as the waves were not so high as at first, being near land, I held my hold till the wave abated, and then fetched another run, which brought me so near the shore that the next wave, though it went over me, yet did not swallow me up as to carry me away; and the next run I took I got to the main-land, where, to my great comfort, I clambered up the clefts of the shore, and sat me down upon the grass, free from danger, and quite out of the reach of the water.

I was now landed and safe on shore, and began to look up and thank God that my life was saved in a case wherein there was some minutes before scarce any room to hope. I believe it is impossible to express to the life what the ecstasies and transports of the soul are, when it is so saved, as I may say, out of the very grave. I walked about on the shore, lifting up my hands, and my whole being, as I may say, wrapt up in the contemplation of my deliverance, making a thousand gestures and motions which I cannot describe, reflecting upon all my comrades that were drowned, and that there should not be one soul saved but myself; for, as for them, I never saw them afterwards, or any sign of them, except three of their hats, one cap, and two shoes that were not fellows.

I cast my eyes to the stranded vessel, when the breach and froth of the sea being so big, I could hardly see it, it lay so far off, and considered, Lord! how was it possible I could get on shore!

After I had solaced my mind with the comfortable part of my condition, I began to look around me, to see what kind of place I was in, and what was next to be done; and I soon found my comforts abate, and that, in a word, I had a dreadful deliverance. For I was wet, had no clothes to shift me, nor any thing either to eat or drink to comfort me; neither did I see any prospect before me, but that of perishing with hunger, or being devoured by wild beasts; and that which was particularly afflicting to me, was, that I had no weapon either to hunt and kill any creature for my sustenance, or to defend myself against any other creature that might desire to kill me for theirs. In a word, I had nothing about me but a knife, a tobacco-pipe, and a little tobacco in a box; this was all my provision, and this threw me into terrible agonies of mind, that for a while I ran about like a madman. Night coming upon me, I began with a heavy heart to consider what would be my lot if there were any ravenous beasts in that country, seeing at night they always come aboard for their prey.

All the remedy that offered to my thoughts at that time was, to get up into a thick bushy tree like a fir, but thorny, which grew near me, and where I resolved to sit all night, and consider the next day what death I should die, for as yet I saw no prospect of life. I walked about a furlong from the shore, to see if I could find any fresh water to drink, which I did, to my great joy; and having drank, and put a little tobacco in my mouth to prevent hunger, I went to the tree, and getting up into it endeavored to place myself so as that if I should sleep I might not fall; and having cut me a short stick, like a truncheon, for my defence, I took up my lodging, and having been excessively fatigued I fell fast asleep, and slept as comfortably as, I believe, few could have done in my condition, and found myself the most refreshed with it that I think I ever was on such an occasion.

When I waked it was broad day, the weather clear, and the storm abated, so that the sea did not rage and swell as before; but that which surprised me most was, that the ship was lifted off in the night from the sand where she lay by the swelling of the tide, and was driven up almost as far as the rock which I first mentioned, where I had been so bruised by the dashing me against it. This being within about a mile from the shore where I was, and the ship seeming to stand upright still, I wished myself on board, that, at least, I might save some necessary things for my use.

When I came down from my apartment in the tree, I looked about me again, and the first thing I found was the boat, which lay as the wind and the sea had tossed her, up upon the land, about two miles on my right hand. I walked as far as I could upon the shore to have got to her, but found a neck or inlet of water between me and the boat, which was about half a mile broad; so I came back for the present, being more intent upon getting at the ship, where I hoped to find something for my present subsistence.

A little after noon I found the sea very calm, and the tide ebbed so far out that I could come within a quarter of a mile of the ship, and here I found a fresh renewing of my grief; for I saw evidently, that if we had kept on board, we had been all safe, that is to say, we had all got safe on shore, and I had not been so miserable as to be left entirely destitute of all comfort and company, as I now was. This forced tears from my eyes again, but as there was little relief in that, I resolved, if possible, to get to the ship, so I pulled off my clothes, for the weather was hot to extremity, and took the water; but when I came to the ship, my difficulty was still greater to know how to get on board, for as she lay aground, and high out of the water, there was nothing within my reach to lay hold of. I swam round her twice, and the second time I spied a small piece of rope, which I wondered I did not see at first, hang down by the fore-chains so low as that with great difficulty I got hold of it, and by the help of that rope got up into the forecastle of the ship. Here I found that the ship was bulged, and had a great deal of water

I thought myself pretty well freighted

in her hold, but that she lay so on the side of a bank of hard sand, or rather earth, that her stern lay lifted up upon the bank, and her head low almost to the water. By this means all her quarter was free, and all that was in that part was dry; for you may be sure my first work was to search and to see what was spoiled and what was free; and first I found that all the ship's provisions were dry and untouched by the water; and being very well disposed to eat, I went to the bread-room and filled my pockets with biscuit, and eat it as I went about other things, for I had no time to lose. I also found some rum in the great cabin, of which I took a large dram, and which I had indeed need enough of to spirit me for what was before me. Now I wanted nothing but a boat to furnish myself with many things which I foresaw would be very necessary to me.

It was in vain to sit still and wish for what was not to be had, and this extremity roused my application. We had several spare yards, and two or three large spars of wood, and a spare topmast or two in the ship. I resolved to fall to work with these, and flung as many of them overboard as I could manage for their weight, tying every one with a rope that they might not drive away; when this was done I went down the ship's side, and pulling them to me, I tied four of them fast together at both ends, as well as I could, in the form of a raft, and laying two or three short pieces of plank upon them cross-ways, I found I could walk upon it very well, but that it was not able to bear any great weight, the pieces being too light; so I went to work, and with the carpenter's saw I cut a spare topmast into three lengths, and added them to my raft, with a great deal of labor and pains: but hope of furnishing myself with necessaries encouraged me to go beyond what I should have been able to have done upon another occasion.

My raft was now strong enough to bear any reasonable

weight; my next care was what to load it with, and how to preserve what I laid upon it from the surf of the sea; but I was not long considering this. I first laid all the planks or boards upon it that I could get, and having considered well what I most wanted, I first got three of the seamen's chests, which I had broken open and emptied, and lowered them down upon my raft. The first of these I filled with provisions, namely, bread, rice, three Dutch cheeses, five pieces of dried goat's flesh, which we lived much upon, and a little remainder of European corn which had been laid by for some fowls which we brought to sea with us, but the fowls were killed. There had been some barley and wheat together; but, to my great disappointment, I found afterwards that the rats had eaten or spoiled it all. As for liquors, I found several cases of bottles belonging to our skipper, in which were some cordial waters, and in all about five or six gallons of rack; these I stowed by themselves, there being no need to put them into the chest, nor no room for them. While I was doing this, I found the tide began to flow, though very calm; and I had the mortification to see my coat, shirt, and waist-coat which I had left on shore, upon the sand, swim away; as for my breeches, which were only linen and open-kneed, I swam on board in them and my stockings. However, this put me upon rummaging for clothes, of which I found enough, but took no more than I wanted for present use; for I had other things which my eye was more upon—as, first, tools to work with on shore; and it was after long searching that I found out the carpenter's chest, which was indeed a very useful prize to me, and much more valuable than a ship-loading of gold would have been at that time. I got it down to my raft, even whole as it was, without losing time to look into it, for I knew in general what it contained.

My next care was for some ammunition and arms. There

were two very good fowling-pieces in the great cabin, and two pistols; these I secured first, with some powder-horns, and a small bag of shot, and two old rusty swords. I knew there were three barrels of powder in the ship, but knew not where our gunner had stowed them; but with much search I found them, two of them dry and good, the third had taken water. Those two I got to my raft, with the arms; and now I thought myself pretty well freighted, and began to think how I should get to shore with them, having neither sail, oar, nor rudder, and the least capful of wind would have overset all my navigation.

I had three encouragements: a smooth, calm sea, the tide

rising and setting into the shore, and what little wind there was blew me towards the land; and thus, having found two or three broken oars belonging to the boat, and besides the tools which were in the chest, I found two saws, an axe and a hammer, and with this cargo I put to sea. For a mile, or thereabouts, my raft went very well, only that I found it drive a little distant from the place where I had landed before, by which I perceived that there was some indraft of the water, and consequently I earnestly hoped to find some creek or river there, which I might make use of as a port to get to land with my cargo.

As I imagined, so it was. There appeared before me a little opening of the land, and I found a strong current of the tide set into it, so I guided my raft as well as I could to keep in the middle of the stream; but here I had like to have suffered a second shipwreck, which, if I had, I think verily would have broke my heart; for knowing nothing of the coast, my raft run aground at one end of it upon a shoal, and not being aground at the other end, it wanted but a little that all my cargo had slipped off towards that end that was afloat, and so fallen into the water. I did my utmost, by setting my back against the chests, to keep them in their places, but could not thrust off the raft with all my strength, neither durst I stir from the posture I was in; but holding up the chests with all my might, stood in that manner near half an hour, in which time the rising of the water brought me a little more upon a level; and a little after, the water still rising, my raft floated again, and I thrust her off with the oar I had into the channel; and then driving up higher, I at length found myself in the mouth of a little river, with land on both sides, and a strong current or tide running up. I looked on both sides for a proper place to get to shore, for I was not willing to be driven too high up the river, hoping in time to see some ship at sea, and therefore resolved to place myself as near the coast as I could.

At length I spied a little cove on the right shore of the creek, to which, with great pain and difficulty, I guided my raft, and at last got so near, as that, reaching ground with my oar, I could thrust her directly in. But here I had liked to have dipped all my cargo into the sea again: for that shore lying pretty steep, that is to say sloping, there was no place to land, but where one end of the float, if it run on shore, would lie so high, and the other sink lower as before, that it would endanger my cargo again. All that I could do, was to wait till the tide was at the highest, keeping the raft with my oar like an anchor to hold the side of it fast to the shore, near a flat piece of ground, which I expected the water would flow over; and so it did. As soon as I found water enough (for my raft drew about a foot of water), I thrust her on upon that flat piece of ground, and there fastened or moored her by sticking my two broken oars into the ground; one on one side near one end, and one on the other side near the other end; and thus I lay till the water ebbed away, and left my raft and all my cargo safe on shore.

CHAPTER 7: *My fortress*

My NEXT work was to view the country, and seek a proper place for my habitation, and where to stow my goods to secure them from whatever might happen. Where I was I yet knew not; whether on the continent or on an island, whether inhabited or not inhabited, whether in danger of wild beasts or not. There was a hill not above a mile from me, which rose up very steep and high, and which seemed to overtop some other hills which lay as in a ridge from it northward. I took out one of the fowling-pieces, and one of the pistols, and an horn of powder, and thus armed, I travelled for discovery up to the top of that hill; where, after I had with great labor and difficulty got to the top,

I saw my fate to my great affliction, namely, that I was in an island environed every way with the sea, no land to be seen, except some rocks which lay a great way off, and two small islands less than this, which lay about three leagues to the west.

I found also that the island I was in was barren, and, as I saw good reason to believe, uninhabited, except by wild beasts, of whom however I saw none; yet I saw abundance of fowls, but knew not their kinds, neither when I killed them could I tell what was fit for food, and what not. At my coming back, I shot at a great bird, which I saw sitting upon a tree on the side of a great wood—I believe it was the first gun that had been fired there since the creation of the world. I had no sooner fired, but from all parts of the wood there arose an innumerable number of fowls of many sorts, making a confused screaming, and crying every one according to his usual note; but not one of them of any kind that I knew. As for the creature I killed, I took it to be a kind of hawk, its color and beak resembling it, but had no talons or claws more than common; its flesh was carrion and fit for nothing.

Contented with this discovery, I came back to my raft, and fell to work to bring my cargo on shore, which took me up the rest of that day; and what to do with myself at night, I knew not, nor indeed where to rest; for I was afraid to lie down on the ground, not knowing but some wild beast might devour me, though, as I afterwards found, there was really no need for those fears.

However, as well as I could, I barricaded myself round with the chests and boards that I had brought on shore, and made a kind of a hut for that night's lodging. As for food, I yet saw not which way to supply myself, except that I had seen two or three creatures, like hares, run out of the wood where I shot the bird.

I now began to consider that I might yet get a great many

things out of the ship which would be useful to me, and particularly some of the rigging and sails, and such other things as might come to land, and I resolved to make another voyage on board the vessel, if possible; and I knew that the first storm that blew must necessarily break her all in pieces, I resolved to set all other things apart till I got everything out of the ship that I could get. Then I called a council, that is to say, in my thoughts, whether I should take back the raft; but this appeared impracticable, so I resolved to go as before, when the tide was down, and I did so, only that I stripped before I went from my hut, having nothing on but a checkered shirt, and a pair of linen trousers, and a pair of pumps on my feet.

I got on board the ship, as before, and prepared a second raft, and having had experience of the first, I neither made this so unwieldy, nor loaded it so hard; but yet I brought away several things very useful to me; as first, in the carpenter's stores, I found two or three bags full of nails and spikes, a great screw jack, a dozen or two of hatchets, and above all, that most useful thing called a grindstone. All these I secured, together with several things belonging to the gunner, particularly two or three iron crows, and two barrels of musket-bullets, seven muskets, and another fowling-piece, with some small quantity of powder, a large bag full of small shot, and a great roll of sheet lead; but this last was so heavy, I could not hoist it up to get it over the ship's side.

Besides these things, I took all the men's clothes that I could find, and a spare foretop-sail, hammock, and some bedding; and with this I loaded my second raft, and brought them all safe on shore, to my very great comfort.

I was under some apprehensions during my absence from the land, that at least my provisions might be devoured on shore; but when I came back, I found no sign of any visitor, only there sat a creature like a wild cat upon one of the chests, which, when I came towards it, ran away a little distance, and then stood still. She sat very composed and unconcerned, and looked full in my face, as if she had a mind to be acquainted with me. I presented my gun at her, but as she did not understand it, she was perfectly unconcerned at it, nor did she offer to stir away; upon which I tossed her a bit of biscuit, though by the way I was not very free of it, for my store was not great. However, I spared her a bit, I say, and she went to it, smelled it, ate it, and looked as pleased, for more; but I thanked her, and could spare no more, so she marched off.

Having got my second cargo on shore, though I was fain to open the barrels of powder, and bring them by parcels (for they were too heavy, being large casks), I went to work to make me a little tent with the sail and some poles which I cut for that purpose; and into this tent I brought everything that I knew would spoil, either with rain or sun, and I piled all the empty chests and casks up in a circle round the tent, to fortify it from any sudden attempt, either from man or beast.

When I had done this, I blocked up the door of the tent with some boards within, and an empty chest set up on end without; and spreading one of the beds on the ground, laying my two pistols just at my head, and my gun at length by me, I went to bed for the first time, and slept very quietly all night, for I was very weary and heavy; for the night before I had slept little, and had labored very hard all day, as well to fetch all those things from the ship as to get them on shore.

I had the biggest magazine of all kinds now that ever were laid up, I believe, for one man, but I was not satisfied still; for while the ship sat upright in that posture, I thought I ought to get everything out of her that I could: so every day at low water I went on board, and brought away something or other; but particularly the third time I went, I brought away as much of the rigging as I could, as also all the small ropes and rope twine I could get, with a piece of spare canvas, which was to mend the sails upon occasion, and the barrel of wet gunpowder. In a word, I brought away all the sails first and last, only that I was fain to cut them in pieces, and bring as much at a time as I could; for they were no more useful to be sails, but as mere canvas only.

But that which comforted me more still, was that, last of all, after I had made five or six such voyages as these, and thought I had nothing more to expect from the ship that was worth my meddling with; I say, after all this, I found a great hogshead of bread, and three large runlets of rum or spirits, and a box of sugar, and a barrel of fine flour. This was surprising to me, because I had given over expecting any more provisions, except what was spoiled by the water. I soon emptied the hogshead of that bread, and wrapped it up, parcel by parcel, in pieces of the sails, which I cut out; and, in a word, I got all this safe on shore also.

The next day I made another voyage; and now, having plundered the ship of what was portable and fit to hand out, I began with the cables; and cutting the great cable into pieces, such as I could move, I got two cables and a hawser on shore, with all the iron-work I could get; and having cut down the spritsail-yard, and the mizzen-yard, and everything I could to make a large raft, I loaded it with all those heavy goods and came away. But my good luck began now to leave me; for this raft was so unwieldy and so overladen, that after I had entered the little cove, where I had landed the rest of my goods, not being able to guide it so handily as I did the other, it overset, and threw me and all my cargo into the water. As for myself it was no great harm, for I was near the shore; but as to my cargo, it was a great part of it lost, especially the iron, which I expected would have been of great use to me. However, when the tide was out, I got most of the pieces of cable ashore, and some of the iron, though with infinite labor; for I was fain to dip for it into the water—a work which fatigued me very much. After this, I went every day on board and brought away what I could get.

I had been now thirteen days on shore, and had been eleven times on board the ship, in which time I had brought away all that one pair of hands could be well supposed capable to bring; though I believe verily, had the calm weather held, I should have brought away the whole ship, piece by piece. But preparing the twelfth time to go on board, I found the wind begin to rise; however, at low water I went on board, and though I thought I had rummaged the cabin so effectually, as that nothing more could be found, yet I discovered a locker with drawers in it, in one of which I found two or three razors, and one pair of large scissors, with some ten or a dozen of good knives and forks; in another I found about thirty-six pounds value in money, some European coin, some Brazil, some pieces of eight, some gold, some silver.

I smiled to myself at the sight of this money. "O Drug!" said I, aloud, "what art thou good for? thou art not worth to me, no not the taking off the ground. One of these knives is worth all this heap. I have no manner of use for thee, even remain where thou art and go to the bottom, as a creature whose life is not worth saving." However, upon second thoughts, I took it away, and wrapping all this in a piece of canvas, I began to think of making another raft; but while I was preparing this, I found the sky overcast, and the wind began to rise, and in a quarter of an hour it blew a fresh gale from the shore. It presently occurred to me, that it was in vain to pretend to make a raft with the wind off shore, and that it was my business to be gone before the tide of flood began, otherwise I might not be able to reach the shore at all: accordingly I let myself down into the water, and swam across the channel, which lay between the ship and the sands, and even that with difficulty enough, partly with the weight of things I had about me, and partly the roughness of the water; for the wind rose very hastily, and before it was quite high water it blew a storm.

But I was gotten home to my little tent, where I lay with all my wealth about me very secure. It blew very hard all that night; and in the morning when I looked out, behold no more ship was to be seen. I was a little surprised, but recovered myself with this satisfactory reflection; namely, that I had lost no time, nor abated any diligence, to get everything out of her that could be useful to me; and that indeed there was little left in her that I was able to bring away, if I had had more time.

I now gave over any more thoughts of the ship, or of anything out of her, except what might drive on shore from her wreck, as indeed divers pieces of her afterwards did; but those things were of small use to me.

My thoughts were now wholly employed about securing myself against either savages (if any should appear) or wild beasts, if any were in the island; and I had many thoughts of the method how to do this, and what kind of dwelling to make; whether I should make me a cave in the earth, or a tent upon the earth; and, in short, I resolved upon both, of the manner, and description of which it may not be improper to give an account.

I soon found the place I was in was not for my settlement, particularly because it was upon a low moorish ground near the sea, and I believed would not be wholesome, and more particularly because there was no fresh water near it, so I resolved to find a more healthy and more convenient spot of ground.

I consulted several things in my situation which I found would be proper for me. Health, and fresh water, I just now mentioned; shelter from the heat of the sun; security from ravenous creatures, whether man or beast; a view to the sea, that if God sent any ship in sight, I might not lose any advantage for my deliverance, of which I was not willing to banish all my expectation yet.

In search of a place proper for this, I found a little plain on the side of a raising hill, whose front towards this little plain was steep as a house-side, so that nothing could come down upon me from the top; on the side of this rock there was a hollow place, worn a little way in, like the entrance or door of a cave; but there was not really any cave or way into the rock at all.

On the flat of the green, just before this hollow place, I resolved to pitch my tent. This plain was not above an hundred yards broad, and about twice as long, and lay like a green before my door, and at the end it descended irregularly every way down into the low grounds by the sea-side. It was on the N. N. W. side of the hill, so that I was sheltered from the heat every day, till it came to a W. and by S. sun, or thereabouts, which in those countries is near the setting.

Before I set up my tent, I drew a half circle before the hollow place, which took in about ten yards in its semi-diameter, from the rock, and twenty yards in its diameter, from its beginning and ending.

In this half circle I pitched two rows of strong stakes, driving them into the ground till they stood very firm, like piles, the biggest end being out of the ground about five foot and a half, and sharpened on the top; the two rows did not stand above six inches from one another.

Then I took the pieces of cable which I had cut in the ship, and laid them in rows one upon another, within the circle between these two rows of stakes, up to the top, placing other stakes in the inside, leaning against them, about two foot and a half high, like a spur to a post; and this fence was so strong, that neither man nor beast could get into it or over it. This cost me a great deal of time and labor, especially to cut the piles in the woods, bring them to the place, and drive them into the earth.

The entrance into this place I made to be not by a door, but by a short ladder to go over the top; which ladder, when I was in, I lifted over after me: and so I was completely fenced in and fortified, as I thought, from all the world, and consequently slept secure in the night, which otherwise I could not have done; though, as it appeared afterward, there was no need of all this caution from the enemies that I apprehended danger from.

Into this fence or fortress, with infinite labor, I carried all my riches, all my provisions, ammunition, and stores, of which you have the account above; and I made me a large tent, which, to preserve me from the rains, that in one part of the year are very violent there, I made double, namely, one smaller tent within, and one larger tent above it, and covered the uppermost with a a large tarpaulin which I had saved among the sails.

And now I lay no more for a while in the bed which I had brought on shore, but in a hammock, which was indeed a very good one, and belonged to the mate of the ship.

Into this tent I brought all my provisions, and everything that would spoil by the wet; and having thus inclosed all my goods I made up the entrance, which till now I had left open, and so passed and repassed, as I said, by a short ladder.

When I had done this, I began to work my way into the rock; and bringing all the earth and stones that I dug down out through my tent, I laid them up within my fence in the nature of a terrace, that so it raised the ground within about a foot and a half; and thus I made me a cave just behind my tent, which served me like a cellar to my house.

It cost me much labor, and many days, before all these things were brought to perfection, and therefore I must go back to some other things which took up some of my thoughts. At the same time it happened, after I had laid my scheme for the setting up my tent and making the cave, that a storm of rain falling from a thick, dark cloud, a sudden flash of lightning happened, and after that a great clap of thunder, as is naturally the effect of it. I was not so much surprised with the lightning, as I was with a thought which darted into my mind as swift as the lightning itself. O my powder! my very heart sunk within me, when I thought that at one blast all my powder might be destroyed; on which, not my defense only, but the providing me food, as I thought, entirely depended. I was nothing near so anxious about my own danger, though, had the powder took fire, I had never known who had hurt me.

Such impression did this make upon me, that after the storm was over I laid aside all my works, my building, and fortifying, and applied myself to make bags and boxes to separate the powder, and to keep it only a little in a parcel, in hope, that whatever might come, it might not all take fire at once; and to keep it so apart, that it should not be possible to make one part fire another. I finished this work in about a fortnight; and I think my powder, which in all was about 240 pounds weight, was divided in not less than a hundred parcels. As to the barrel that had been wet, I did not apprehend any danger from that, so I placed it in my new cave, which in my fancy I called my kitchen; and the rest I hid up and down in holes among the rocks, so that no wet might come to it, marking very carefully where I laid it.

In the interval of time while this I was doing, I went out once at least every day with my gun, as well to divert myself as to see if I could kill anything fit for food, and, as near as I could, to acquaint myself with what the island produced. The first time I went out I presently discovered that there were goats in the island, which was a great satisfaction to me; but then it was attended with this misfortune to me, namely, that they were so shy, so subtle, and so swift of foot, that it was the most difficult thing in the world to come at them. But I was not discouraged at this, not doubting but I might now and then shoot one, as it soon happened; for after I had found their haunts a little, I laid wait in this manner for them: I observed, if they saw me in the valleys, though they were upon the rocks, they would run away as in a terrible fright; but if they were feeding in the valleys, and I was upon the rocks, they took no notice of me: from whence I concluded, that by the position of their optics, their sight was so directed downward, that they did not readily see objects that were above them; so afterwards I took this method: I always climbed the rocks first, to get above them, and then I had frequently a fair mark. The first shot I made among these creatures I killed a she-goat, which had a little kid by her, which she gave suck to, which grieved me heartily; but when the old one fell, the kid stood stock still by her till I came and took her up; and not only so, but when I carried the old one with me upon my shoulders, the kid followed me quite to my inclosure, upon which I laid down the dam, and took the kid in my arms and carried it over my pale, in hopes to have bred it up tame, but it would not eat, so I was forced to kill it and eat it myself. These two supplied me with flesh a great while, for I ate sparingly, and saved my provisions (my bread especially) as much as possibly I could.

Having now fixed my habitation, I found it absolutely necessary to provide a place to make a fire in, and fuel to burn; and what I did for that, as also how I enlarged my cave, and what conveniences I made, I shall give a full account of in its place; but I must first give some little account of myself, and of my thoughts about living, which it may well be supposed were not a few.

I had a dismal prospect of my condition; for as I was not cast away upon that island without being driven, as is said, by a violent storm quite out of the course of our intended voyage, and a great way, some hundreds of leagues, out of the ordinary course of the trade of mankind, I had great reason to consider it as a determination of Heaven that in this desolate place and in this desolate manner, I should end my life. The tears would run plentifully down my face when I made these reflections, and sometimes I would expostulate with myself, why Providence should thus completely ruin his creatures, and render them so absolutely miserable, so without help abandoned, so entirely depressed, that it could hardly be rational to be thankful for such a life.

But something always returned swift upon me to check these thoughts and reprove me; and particularly one day, walking with my gun in my hand by the sea-side, I was very pensive upon the subject of my present condition, when reason as it were expostulated with me the other way, thus: Well, you are in a desolate condition, it is true; but pray remember, where are the rest of you? Did not you come eleven of you into the boat? Where are the ten? Why were they not saved and you lost? Why were you singled out? Is it better to be here or there? and then I pointed to the sea. All evils are to be considered with the good that is in them, and with what worse attends them.

Then it occurred to me again, how well I was furnished for my subsistence, and what would have been my case if it had not happened, which was a hundred thousand to one, that the ship floated from the place where she first struck, and was driven so near the shore that I had time to get all these things out of her? What would have been my case if I had been left to have lived in the condition in which I at first came on shore, without necessaries of life or necessaries to supply and procure them? Particularly, said I aloud (though to myself), what should I have done without a gun, without ammunition, without any tools to make anything, or to work with; without clothes, bedding, a tent, or any manner of covering? And that now I had all these to a sufficient quantity, and was in a fair way to provide myself in such a manner, as to live without my gun when my ammunition was spent, so that I had a tolerable view of subsisting, without any want, as long as I lived; for I considered from the beginning how I should provide for the accidents that might happen and for the time that was to come, even not only after my ammunition should be spent, but even after my health or strength should decay.

I confess I had not entertained any notion of my ammunition being destroyed at one blast, I mean, my powder being blown up by lightning; and this made the thoughts of it so surprising to me when it lightened and thundered, as I observed just now.

And now being about to enter into a melancholy relation of a scene of silent life, such, perhaps, as was never heard of in the world before, I shall take it from its beginning, and continue it in its order. It was, by my account, the 30th of September, when, in the manner as above said, I first set foot upon this horrid island, when the sun being, to us, in its autumnal equinox, was almost just over my head; for I reckoned myself, by observation, to be in the latitude of 9 degrees and 22 minutes north of the line.

After I had been there about ten or twelve days, it came into my thoughts that I should lose my reckoning of time for want of books, and pen and ink, and should even forget the Sabbath days from the working days; but to prevent this, I cut it with my knife upon a large post in capital letters, and making it into a great cross, I set it up on the shore where I first landed, namely, I CAME ON SHORE HERE ON THE 30TH OF SEPT. 1659. Upon the sides of this square post I cut every day a notch with my knife, and every seventh notch was as long again as the rest, and every first day of the month as long again as that long one; and thus I kept my calendar, or weekly, monthly, and yearly reckoning of time.

In the next place we are to observe, that among the many things which I brought out of the ship in the several voyages, which, as above mentioned, I made to it, I got several things of less value, but not all less useful to me, which I omitted setting down before; as in particular, pens, ink, and paper; several parcels in the captain's, mate's, gunner's, and carpenter's keeping; three or four compasses, some mathematical instruments, dials, perspective glasses, charts, and books of navigation; all which I huddled together, whether I might want them or no;

also, I found three very good Bibles which came to me in my cargo from England, and which I had packed up among my things; some Portuguese books also, and among them two or three Popish prayer-books, and several other books, all which I carefully secured. And I must not forget, that we had in the ship a dog and two cats, of whose eminent history I may have occasion to say something in its place; for I carried both the cats with me; and as for the dog, he jumped out of the ship of himself, and swam on shore to me the day after I went on shore with my first cargo, and was a trusty servant to me many years. I wanted nothing that he could fetch me, or any company that he could make up to me; I only wanted to have him talk to me, but that he could not do. As I observed before, I found pen, ink, and paper, and I husbanded them to the utmost; and I shall show, that while my ink lasted, I kept things very exact; but after that was gone I could not, for I could not make any ink, by any means that I could devise.

And this put me in mind that I wanted many things, not-withstanding all that I had amassed together; and of these this of ink was one, as also spade, pickaxe, and shovel, to dig or remove the earth; needles, pins, and thread; as for linen, I soon learned to want that without much difficulty.

This want of tools made every work I did go on heavily, and it was near a whole year before I had entirely finished my little pale or surrounded habitation. The piles or stakes, which were as heavy as I could well lift, were a long time in cutting and preparing in the woods, and more by far in bringing home; so that I spent sometimes two days in cutting and bringing home one of those posts, and a third day in driving it into the ground; for which purpose I got a heavy piece of wood at first, but at last bethought myself of one of the iron crows, which, however, though I found it, yet it made driving those posts or piles very laborious and tedious work.

But what need I have been concerned at the tediousness of anything I had to do, seeing I had time enough to do it in, nor had I any other employment if that had been over, at least, that I could foresee, except the ranging the island to seek for food, which I did more or less every day.

I have already described my habitation, which was a tent under the side of a rock, surrounded with a strong pale of posts and cables, but I might now rather call it a wall, for I raised a kind of wall up against it of turfs, about two feet thick on the outside, and after some time, I think it was a year and a half, I raised rafters from it, leaning to the rock, and thatched or covered it with boughs of trees, and such things as I could get to keep out the rain, which I found at some times of the year very violent.

I have already observed how I brought all my goods into this pale, and into the cave which I had made behind me; but I must observe too, that at first this was a confused heap of goods, which, as they lay in no order, so they took up all my place, I had no room to turn myself; so I set to work to enlarge my cave and work farther into the earth; for it was a loose, sandy rock, which yielded easily to the labor I bestowed on it. And so when I found I was pretty safe as to beasts of prey, I worked sideways to the right hand into the rock; and then turning to the right again, worked quite out, and made me a door to come out, on the outside of my pale or fortification.

This gave me not only egress and regress, as it were a back way to my tent and to my store-house, but gave me room to stow my goods. And now I began to apply myself to such necessary things as I found I most wanted, as particularly a chair and a table; for without these I was not able to enjoy the few comforts I had in the world. I could not write or eat, or do several things with so much pleasure without a table.

So I went to work; and here I must needs observe, that as reason is the substance and original of the mathematics, so by stating and squaring everything by reason, and by making the most rational judgment of things, every man may be in time master of every mechanic art. I had never handled a tool in my life, and yet in time by labor, application, and contrivance, I found at last that I wanted nothing but I could have made it, especially if I had had tools; however, I made abundance of things, even without tools, and some with no more tools than an adze and a hatchet, which, perhaps, were never made that way before, and that with infinite labor; for example, if I wanted a board, I had no other way but to cut down a tree, set it on a hedge before me, and hew it flat on either side with my axe, till I had brought it to be as thin as a plank, and then dub it smooth with my adze. It is true, by this method I could make but one board out of a whole tree, but this I had no remedy for but patience, any more than I had for the prodigious deal of time and labor which it took me up to make a plank or board; but my time or labor was little worth, and so it was as well employed one way as another.

However, I made me a table and a chair, as I observed above, in the first place, and this I did out of the short pieces of boards which I brought on my raft from the ship; but when I had wrought out some boards, as above, I made large shelves, of the breadth of a foot and a half, one over another, all along one side of my cave, to lay all my tools, nails, and iron-work, and in a word, to separate everything at large in their places, that I might come easily at them. I knocked pieces into the wall of the rock to hang my guns and all things that would hang up.

So that had my cave been to be seen, it looked like a general magazine of all necessary things; and I had everything so ready at my hand, that it was a great pleasure to me to see all my goods in such order, and especially to find my stock of all necessaries so great.

CHAPTER 8: *In which is given a copy of my journal*

AND NOW it was that I began to keep a journal of every day's employment; for indeed at first I was in too much hurry, and not only hurry as to labor, but in too much discomposure of mind, and my journal would have been full of many dull things.

I shall here give you the copy (though in it will be told many particulars over again) as long as it lasted; for having no more ink, I was forced to leave it off.

THE JOURNAL

September 30, 1659. I, poor, miserable Robinson Crusoe, being shipwrecked, during a dreadful storm, in the offing, came on shore on this dismal, unfortunate island, which I called the Island of Despair, all the rest of the ship's company being drowned, and myself almost dead.

All the rest of that day I spent in afflicting myself, at the dismal circumstances I was brought to, namely, I had neither food, house, clothes, weapon, nor place to fly to, and in despair of any relief, saw nothing but death before me, either that I should be devoured by wild beasts, murdered by savages, or starved to death for want of food. At the approach of night I slept in a tree, for fear of wild creatures, but slept soundly though it rained all night.

October 1. In the morning I saw, to my great surprise, the ship had floated with the high tide, and was driven on shore again much nearer the island, which as it was some comfort on one hand, for seeing her sit upright, and not broken to pieces, I hoped, if the wind abated, I might get on board, and get some food or necessaries out of her for my relief; so, on the other hand, it renewed my grief at the loss of my comrades, who I imagined if we had all stayed on board might have saved the ship, or at least that they would not have been all drowned, as they were; and that, had the men been saved, we might perhaps have built us a boat out of the ruins of the ship, to have carried us to some other part of the world. I spent great part of this day in perplexing myself on these things; but at length, seeing the ship almost dry, I went upon the sand as near as I could, and then swam on board: this day also it continued raining, though with no wind at all.

From the 1st of *October* to the 24th. All these days entirely spent in making several voyages to get all I could out of the ship, which I brought on shore, every tide of flood, upon rafts. Much rain also in these days, though with some intervals of fair weather; but, it seems, this was the rainy season.

Oct. 20. I overset my raft, and all the goods I had got upon it; but being in shoal water, and the things being chiefly heavy, I recovered many of them when the tide was out.

Oct. 25. It rained all night and all day, with some gusts of wind, during which time the ship broke in pieces, the wind blowing a little harder than before, and was no more to be seen, except the wreck of her, and that only at low water. I spent this day in covering and securing the goods which I had saved, that the rain might not spoil them.

Oct. 26. I walked about the shore almost all day, to find out a place to fix my habitation, greatly concerned to secure myself from any attack in the night, either from wild beasts or men. Toward night I fixed upon a proper place under a rock, and marked out a semicircle for my encampment, which I resolved to strengthen with a work, wall, or fortification made of double piles, lined within with cables, and without with turf.

From the 26th to the 30th, I worked very hard in carrying all my goods to my new habitation, though some part of the time it rained exceeding hard.

The 31st, in the morning, I went out into the island with my gun, to seek for some food, and discover the country, when I killed a she-goat, and her kid followed me home; which I afterwards killed also, because it would not feed.

November 1. I set up my tent under a rock, and lay there for the first night, making it as large as I could with stakes driven in to swing my hammock upon.

Nov. 2. I set up all my chests and boards, and the pieces of timber which made my rafts, and with them formed a fence round me, a little within the place I had marked out for my fortification.

Nov. 3. I went out with my gun, and killed two fowls like

ducks, which were very good food. In the afternoon went to
work to make me a table.

Nov. 4. This morning I began to order my times of work, of
going out with my gun, time of sleep, and time of diversion.
Every morning I walked out with my gun for two or three
hours, if it did not rain, then employed myself to work till
about eleven o'clock, then eat what I had to live on, and from
twelve to two I lay down to sleep, the weather being excessive
hot, and then in the evening to work again. The working part
of this day, and of the next, were wholly employed in making
my table, for I was yet but a very sorry workman, though time
and necessity made me a complete natural mechanic soon after,
as I believe it would do any one else.

Nov. 5. This day went I abroad with my gun and my dog,
and killed a wild cat; her skin pretty soft, but her flesh good
for nothing; every creature I killed I took off the skins and preserved them. Coming back to the seashore I saw many sorts of
sea-fowls, which I did not understand; but was surprised and
almost frighted with two or three seals, which, while I was
gazing, not well knowing what they were, got into the sea,
and escaped me for that time.

Nov. 6. After my morning walk I went to work with my table
again, and finished it, though not to my liking; nor was it long
before I learned to mend it.

Nov. 7. Now it began to be settled fair weather. The 7th,
8th, 9th, 10th, and a part of the 12th (for the 11th was Sun-
day), I took wholly up to make me a chair, and with much ado
brought it to a tolerable shape, but never to please me; and
even in the making I pulled it in pieces several times. *Note.*—I
soon neglected my keeping Sundays, for omitting my mark for
them on my post, I forgot which was which.

Nov. 13. This day it rained, which refreshed me exceedingly, and cooled the earth; but it was accompanied with terrible thunder and lightning, which frighted me dreadfully for fear of my powder. As soon as it was over I resolved to separate my stock of powder into as many little parcels as possible, that it might not be in danger.

Nov. 14, 15, 16. These three days I spent in making little square chests or boxes, which might hold about a pound, or two pounds at most, of powder; and so putting the powder in, I stowed it in places as secure and remote from one another as possible. On one of these three days I killed a large bird that was good to eat, but I know not what to call it.

Nov. 17. This day I began to dig behind my tent into the rock, to make room for my farther conveniency. *Note.*—Three things I wanted exceeding for this work, namely, a pickaxe, a shovel, and a wheelbarrow or basket, so I desisted from my work, and began to consider how to supply that want, and make me some tools. As for a pickaxe, I made use of the iron crows, which were proper enough, though heavy; but the next thing was a shovel or spade. This was so absolutely necessary, that indeed I could do nothing effectually without it; but what kind of one to make I knew not.

Nov. 18. The next day, in searching the woods, I found a tree of that wood, or like it, which in the Brazils they call the Iron Tree, for its exceeding hardness; of this, with great labor and almost spoiling my axe, I cut a piece and brought it home too with difficulty enough, for it was exceeding heavy.

The excessive hardness of the wood, and having no other way, made me a long while upon this machine; for I worked it effectually by little and little into the form of a shovel or spade, the handle exactly shaped like ours in England, only that the broad part having no iron shod upon it at bottom, it would

not last me so long; however, it served well enough for the uses which I had occasion to put it to; but never was a shovel, I believe, made after that fashion, or so long a making.

I was still deficient, for I wanted a basket or a wheelbarrow. A basket I could not make by any means, having no such things as twigs that would bend to make wicker ware, at least none yet found out; and as to a wheelbarrow, I fancied I could make all but the wheel, but that I had no notion of, neither did I know how to go about it; besides, I had no possible way to make the iron gudgeons for the spindle or axis of the wheel to run in, so I gave it over; and so for carrying away the earth which I dug out of the cave, I made me a thing like a hod which the laborers carry mortar in, when they serve the brick-layers.

This was not so difficult to me as the making the shovel; and yet this, and the shovel, and the attempt which I made in vain to make a wheelbarrow, took me up no less than four days, I mean always excepting my morning walk with my gun, which I seldom failed; and very seldom failed also bringing home something to eat.

Nov. 23. My other work having now stood still, because of my making these tools, when they were finished I went on, and working every day, as my strength and time allowed, I spent eighteen days entirely in widening and deepening my cave, that it might hold my goods commodiously.

Note.—During all this time, I worked to make this room or cave spacious enough to accommodate me as a warehouse or magazine, a kitchen, a dining-room, and a cellar; as for my lodg-ing, I kept to the tent, except that sometimes in the wet season of the year, it rained so hard that I could not keep myself dry, which caused me afterwards to cover all my place within my pale with long poles in the form of rafters, leaning against the rock, and load them with flags and large leaves of trees like a thatch.

December 10. I began now to think my cave or vault finished, when on a sudden (it seems I had made it too large) a great quantity of earth fell down from the top and one side, so much, that in short it frighted me, and not without reason too; for if I had been under it, I had never wanted a grave-digger. Upon this disaster I had a great deal of work to do over again; for I had the loose earth to carry out, and, which was of more importance, I had the ceiling to prop up, so that I might be sure no more would come down.

Dec. 11. This day I went to work with it accordingly, and got two shores or posts pitched upright to the top, with two pieces of boards across over each post; this I finished the next day, and setting more posts up with boards, in about a week more I had the roof secured; and the posts, standing in rows, served me for partitions to part off my house.

Dec. 17. From this day to the twentieth I placed shelves, and knocked up nails on the posts to hang everything up that could be hung up; and now I began to be in some order within doors.

Dec. 20. Now I carried everything into the cave, and began to furnish my house, and set up some pieces of boards, like a dresser, to order my victuals upon; but boards began to be very scarce with me; also, I made me another table.

Dec. 24. Much rain all night and all day; no stirring out.

Dec. 25. Rain all day.

Dec. 26. No rain; and the earth much cooler than before, and pleasanter.

Dec. 27. Killed a young goat, and lamed another, so that I caught it, and led it home by a string; when I had it home, I bound and splintered up its leg, which was broke. *N. B.* I took such care of it, that it lived, and the leg grew well and as strong

as ever; but by nursing it so long it grew tame, and fed upo
the little green at my door, and would not go away. This wa
the first time that I entertained a thought of breeding up som
tame creatures, that I might have food when my powder an
shot was all spent.

Dec. 28, 29, 30. Great heats and no breeze, so that there wa
no stirring abroad, except in the evening for food; this time
spent in putting all my things in order within doors.

January 1. Very hot still, but I went abroad early and lat
with my gun, and lay still in the middle of the day. This eve
ning, going farther into the valleys, which lay towards the centr
of the island, I found there was plenty of goats, though exceed
ing shy and hard to come at; however, I resolved to try if I coul
not bring my dog to hunt them down.

Jan. 2. Accordingly, the next day, I went out with my dog
and set him upon the goats; but I was mistaken, for they al
faced about upon the dog; and he knew his danger too well
for he would not come near them.

Jan. 3. I began my fence or wall; which, being still jealou
of my being attacked by somebody, I resolved to make ver
thick and strong.

N. B. This wall being described before, I purposely omi
what was said in the Journal. It is sufficient to observe, that
was no less time than from the 3d of *January* to the 14th o
April, working, finishing, and perfecting this wall, though i
was no more than about twenty-four yards in length, being a
half circle from one place in the rock to another place abou
eight yards from it; the door of the cave being in the centr
behind it.

All this time I worked very hard, the rains hindering me man
days, nay, sometimes weeks together; but I thought I shoul
never be perfectly secure until this wall was finished; and it i

scarce credible what inexpressible labor everything was done with, especially the bringing piles out of the woods, and driving them into the ground, for I made them much bigger than I need to have done.

When this wall was finished, and the outside double fence with a turf-wall raised up close to it, I persuaded myself that if any people were to come on shore there, they would not perceive anything like a habitation; and it was very well I did so, as may be observed hereafter upon a very remarkable occasion.

During this time I made my rounds in the woods for game every day, when the rain permitted me, and made frequent discoveries in these walks of something or other to my advantage; particularly I found a kind of wild pigeon, who built not as wood pigeons, in a tree, but rather as house pigeons, in the holes of the rocks; and taking some young ones, I endeavored to breed them up tame; and did so; but when they grew older they flew away, which perhaps was at first for want of feeding them, for I had nothing to give them; however, I frequently found their nests, and got their young ones, which were very good meat.

And now, in the managing of my household affairs, I found myself wanting in many things, which I thought at first it was impossible for me to make, as indeed, as to some of them, it was; for instance, I could never make a cask to be hooped. I had a small runlet or two, as I observed before, but I could never arrive to the capacity of making one by them, though I spent many weeks about it; I could neither put in the heads, or joint the staves so true to one another as to make them hold water, so I gave that also over.

In the next place, I was at a great loss for candles; so that as soon as ever it was dark, which was generally by seven o'clock, I was obliged to go to bed. I remembered the lump of bees-wax with which I made candles in my African adventure, but I had none of that now; the only remedy I had was, that when I had killed a goat I saved the tallow, and with a little dish made of clay, which I baked in the sun, to which I added a wick of some oakum, I made me a lamp; and this gave me light, though not a clear, steady light like a candle. In the middle of all my labors it happened, that rummaging my things, I found a little bag, which, as I hinted before, had been filled with corn for the feeding of poultry, not for this voyage, but before, as I suppose, when the ship came from Lisbon; what little remainder of corn had been in the bag, was all devoured with the rats, and I saw nothing in the bag but husks and dust; and being willing to have the bag for some other use, I think it was to put powder in, when I divided it for fear of the lightning, or some such use, I shook the husks of corn out of it on one side of my fortification under the rock.

It was a little before the great rains, just now mentioned, that I threw this stuff away, taking no notice of anything, and not so much as remembering that I had thrown anything there; when about a month after, or thereabouts, I saw some few stalks of something green shooting out of the ground, which I fancied might be some plant I had not seen; but I was surprised and perfectly astonished, when after a little longer time I saw about ten or twelve ears come out, which were perfect green barley of the same kind as our European, nay, as our English barley.

It is impossible to express the astonishment and confusion of my thoughts on this occasion. I had hitherto acted upon no religious foundation at all; indeed, I had very few notions of religion in my head, or had entertained any sense of anything that had befallen me, otherwise than as a chance, or, as we lightly say, what pleases God; without so much as inquiring into the end of Providence in these things, or his order in governing events in the world; but after I saw barley grow there, in a climate which I knew was not proper for corn, and especially that I knew not how it came there, it startled me strangely; and I began to suggest, that God had miraculously caused this grain to grow without any help of seed sown, and that it was so directed purely for my sustenance on that wild, miserable place.

This touched my heart a little, and brought tears out of my eyes, and I began to bless myself, that such a prodigy of nature should happen upon my account; and this was the more strange to me, because I saw near it still, all along by the side of the rock, some other straggling stalks, which proved to be stalks of rice, and which I knew, because I had seen it grow in Africa, when I was ashore there.

I not only thought these the pure productions of Providence for my support, but not doubting but that there was more in the place, I went all over that part of the island, where I had been before, peeping in every corner and under every rock to see for more of it, but I could not find any; at last it occurred to my thought, that I had shook a bag of chicken's meat out in that place, and then the wonder began to cease. And I must confess, my religious thankfulness to God's providence began to abate too, upon discovering that all this was nothing but what was common; though I ought to have been as thankful for so strange and unforeseen a providence as if it had been miraculous; for it was really the work of Providence as to me that should order or appoint ten or twelve grains of corn to remain unspoiled, when the rats had destroyed all the rest, as if it had been dropped from heaven; as also, that I should throw it out in that particular place, where, it being in the shade of a high rock, it sprang up immediately; whereas, if I had thrown it anywhere else at that time, it had been burnt up and destroyed.

I carefully saved the ears of this corn, you may be sure, in their season, which was about the end of June, and laying up every corn, I resolved to sow them all again, hoping in time to have some quantity sufficient to supply me with bread; but it was not till the fourth year that I could allow myself the least grain of this corn to eat, and even then but sparingly, as I shall say afterwards in its order; for I lost all that I sowed the first season, by not observing the proper time; for I sowed it just before the dry season, so that it never came up at all, at least not as it would have done; of which in its place.

Besides this barley, there were, as above, twenty or thirty stalks of rice, which I preserved with the same care, and whose use was of the same kind or to the same purpose, namely, to make me bread, or rather food; for I found ways to cook it up without baking, though I did that also after some time. But to return to my Journal.

I worked excessive hard these three or four months to get my wall done; and the 14th of April I closed it up, contriving to go into it not by a door, but over the wall by a ladder, that there might be no sign in the outside of my habitation.

April 16. I finished the ladder, so I went up with the ladder to the top, and then pulled it up after me, and let it down on the inside. This was a complete inclosure to me; for within I had room enough, and nothing could come at me from without, unless it could first mount my wall.

The very next day after this wall was finished, I had almost had all my labor overthrown at once, and myself killed. The case was thus. As I was busy in the inside of it, behind my tent, just in the entrance into my cave, I was terribly frighted with a most dreadful surprising thing indeed; for on a sudden I found the earth come crumbling down from the roof of my cave, and from the edge of the hill, over my head, and two of the posts I had set up in the cave cracked in a frightful manner. I was heartily scared, but thought nothing of what was really the cause, only thinking that the top of my cave was falling in, as some of it had done before; and, for fear I should be buried in it, I ran forward to my ladder; and not thinking myself safe there neither, I got over my wall for fear of the pieces of the hill which I expected might roll down upon me. I was no sooner stepped down upon the firm ground, but I plainly saw it was a terrible earthquake, for the ground I stood on shook three times at about eight minutes' distance, with three such shocks as would have overturned the strongest building that could be supposed to have stood on the earth; and a great piece of the top of a rock, which stood about half a mile from me next the sea, fell down with such a terrible noise as I never heard in all my life. I perceived also the very sea was put into violent motion by it; and I believe the shocks were stronger under the water than on the island.

I was so amazed with the thing itself, having never felt the like, or discoursed with any one that had, that I was like one dead or stupefied; and the motion of the earth made my stomach sick, like one that was tossed at sea. But the noise of the falling of the rock awaked me, as it were, and rousing me from the stupefied condition I was in, filled me with horror, and I thought of nothing then but the hill falling upon my tent, and all my household goods, and burying all at once; and this sunk my very soul within me a second time.

After the third shock was over, and I felt no more for some time, I began to take courage, and yet I had not heart enough to get over my wall again, for fear of being buried alive, but sat still upon the ground, greatly cast down and disconsolate, not knowing what to do. All this while I had not the least serious religious thought, nothing but the common, "Lord, have mercy upon me;" and when it was over, that went away too.

While I sat thus, I found the air overcast, and grow cloudy, as if it would rain; soon after that the wind rose by little and little, so that in less than half an hour it blew a most dreadful hurricane. The sea was all on a sudden covered over with foam and froth, the shore was covered with the breach of the water, the trees were torn up by the roots, and a terrible storm it was; and this held about three hours, and then began to abate, and in two hours more it was stark calm, and began to rain very hard.

All this while I sat upon the ground, very much terrified and dejected, when on a sudden it came into my thoughts, that these winds and rain being the consequences of the earthquake, the earthquake itself was spent and over, and that I might venture into my cave again. With this thought my spirits began to revive, and the rain also helping to persuade me, I went in and sat down in my tent, but the rain was so violent, that my tent was ready to be beaten down with it; and I was forced to go into my cave, though very much afraid and uneasy, for fear it should fall on my head.

This violent rain forced me to a new work, namely, to cut a hole through my new fortification like a sink to let water go out, which would else have drowned my cave. After I had been in my cave some time, and found still no more shocks of the earthquake followed, I began to be more composed. And now, to support my spirits, which indeed wanted it very much, I went to my little store, and took a small sup of rum, which however I did then, and always, very sparingly, knowing I could have no more when that was gone.

It continued raining all that night, and a great part of the next day, so that I could not stir abroad; but my mind being more composed, I began to think of what I had best do, concluding, that if the island was subject to these earthquakes, there would be no living for me in a cave, but I must consider of building me some little hut in an open place, which I might surround with a wall as I had done here, and so make myself secure from wild beasts or men: but concluded if I stayed where I was, I should certainly, one time or other, be buried alive.

With these thoughts I resolved to remove my tent from the place where it stood, which was just under the hanging precipice of the hill, and which, if it should be shaken again, would certainly fall upon my tent. And I spent the next two days, being the 19th and 20th of April, in contriving where and how to remove my habitation.

The fear of being swallowed up alive, made me that I never slept in quiet: and yet the apprehension of lying abroad, without any fence, was almost equal to it; but still, when I looked about and saw how everything was put in order, how pleasantly concealed I was, and how safe from danger, it made me very loth to remove.

In the mean time, it occurred to me that it would require a vast deal of time for me to do this, and that I must be contented to run the venture where I was, till I had formed a camp for myself, and had secured it so as to remove to it; so with this resolution I composed myself for a time, and resolved that I would go to work with all speed to build me a wall with piles and cables, in a circle as before; and set my tent up in it when it was finished, but that I would venture to stay where I was till it was finished and fit to remove to. This was the 21st.

April 22. The next morning I began to consider of means to put this resolve in execution, but I was at a great loss about my tools; I had three large axes and abundance of hatchets (for we carried the hatchets for traffic with the Indians), but with much chopping and cutting knotty hard wood, they were all full of notches and dull, and though I had a grindstone, I could not turn it and grind my tools too: this cost me as much thought as a statesman would have bestowed upon a grand point of politics, or a judge upon the life and death of a man. At length I contrived a wheel with a string, to turn it with my foot, that I might have both my hands at liberty. I had never seen any such thing in England, or at least not to take notice how it was done, though since I have observed it is very common there; besides that, my grindstone was very large and heavy. This machine cost me a full week's work to bring it to perfection.

April 28, 29. These two whole days I took up in grinding my tools, my machine for turning my grindstone performing very well.

April 30. Having perceived my bread had been low a great while, now I took a survey of it, and reduced myself to one biscuit cake a day, which made my heart very heavy.

May 1. In the morning, looking towards the sea-side, the tide being low, I saw something lie on the shore bigger than ordinary; and it looked like a cask. When I came to it, I found a small barrel, and two or three pieces of the wreck of the ship, which were driven on shore by the late hurricane; and looking towards the wreck itself, I thought it seemed to lie higher out of the water than it used to do. I examined the barrel which was driven on shore, and soon found it was a barrel of gunpowder, but it had taken water, and the powder was caked as hard as a stone; however, I rolled it farther on shore for the present, and went on upon the sands as near as I could to the wreck of the ship, to look for more.

When I came down to the ship, I found it strangely removed: the forecastle, which lay before buried in sand, was heaved up at least six feet; and the stern, which was broken to pieces and parted from the rest by the force of the sea, soon after I had left rummaging her, was tossed, as it were, up, and cast on one side, and the sand was thrown so high on that side next her stern, that whereas there was a great place of water before, so that I could not come within a quarter of a mile of the wreck without swimming, I could now walk quite up to her when the tide was out. I was surprised with this at first, but soon concluded that it must be done by the earthquake. And as by this violence the ship was more broken open than formerly, so many things came daily on shore, which the sea had loosened, and which the winds and water rolled by degrees to the land. This wholly diverted my thoughts from the

design of removing my habitation; and I busied myself mightily
that day especially, in searching whether I could make any way
into the ship; but I found nothing was to be expected of that
kind, for that all the inside of the ship was choked up with sand.
However, as I had learnt not to despair of anything, I resolved
to pull everything to pieces that I could of the ship, concluding,
that everything I could get from her would be of some use or
other to me.

May 3. I began with my saw, and cut a piece of a beam
through, which I thought held some of the upper part or
quarter-deck together; and when I had cut it through, I cleared
away the sand as well as I could from the side which lay highest; but the tide coming in, I was obliged to give over for
that time.

May 4. I went a fishing, but caught not one fish that I durst
eat of, till I was weary of my sport; when just going to leave off,
I caught a young dolphin. I had made me a long line of some
rope yarn, but I had no hooks, yet I frequently caught fish
enough, as much as I cared to eat; all which I dried in the sun,
and eat them dry.

May 5. Worked on the wreck, cut another beam asunder,
and brought three great fir planks off from the decks, which
I tied together, and made swim on shore when the tide of
flood came on.

May 6. Worked on the wreck, got several iron bolts out of
her, and other pieces of iron-work; worked very hard, and came
home very much tired, and had thoughts of giving it over.

May 7. Went to the wreck again, but with an intent not to
work, but found the weight of the wreck had broke itself down,
the beams being cut, that several pieces of the ship seemed to
lie loose: and the inside of the hold lay so open, that I could
see into it, but almost full of water and sand.

May 8. Went to the wreck, and carried an iron crow to

wrench up the deck, which lay now quite clear of the water or sand; I wrenched open two planks, and brought them on shore also with the tide. I left the iron crow in the wreck for next day.

May 9. Went to the wreck, and with the crow made way into the body of the wreck, and felt several casks, and loosened them with the crow, but could not break them up; I felt also the roll of English lead, and could stir it, but it was too heavy to remove.

May 10, 11, 12, 13, 14. Went every day to the wreck, and got a great many pieces of timber, and boards, or plank, and two or three hundred weight of iron.

May 15. I carried two hatchets, to try if I could not cut a piece off the roll of lead, by placing the edge of one hatchet, and driving it with the other; but as it lay about a foot and a half in the water, I could not make any blow to drive the hatchet.

May 16. It had blowed hard in the night, and the wreck appeared more broken by the force of the water; but I staid so long in the woods to get pigeons for food, that the tide prevented me going to the wreck that day.

May 17. I saw some pieces of the wreck blown on shore, at a great distance, near two miles off me, but resolved to see what they were, and found it was a piece of the head, but too heavy for me to bring away.

May 24. Every day to this day I worked on the wreck, and with hard labor I loosened some things so much with the crow, that the first blowing tide several casks floated out, and two of the seamen's chests; but the wind blowing from the shore, nothing came to land that day but pieces of timber, and a hogshead, which had some Brazil pork in it, but the salt water and sand had spoiled it. I continued this work every day to the 15th of June, except the time necessary to get food, which I always appointed, during this part of my employment, to be when the tide was up, that I might be ready when it was ebbed out; and by this time I had gotten timber, and plank, and iron-work enough to have built a good boat, if I had known how; and also, I got at several times, and in several pieces, near a hundred weight of the sheet-lead.

June 16. Going down to the sea-side, I found a large tortoise or turtle; this was the first I had seen, which it seems was only my misfortune, not any defect of the place, or scarcity; for had I happened to be on the other side of the island, I might have had hundreds of them every day; as I found afterwards; but perhaps had paid dear enough for them.

June 17. I spent in cooking the turtle. I found in her three-score eggs; and her flesh was to me at that time the most savory and pleasant that ever I tasted in my life, having had no flesh, but of goats and fowls, since I landed in this horrid place.

June 18. Rained all day, and I stayed within. I thought at this time the rain felt cold, and I was something chilly, which I knew was not usual in that latitude.

June 19. Very ill, and shivering, as if the weather had been cold.

June 20. No rest all night, violent pains in my head, and feverish.

June 21. Very ill, frighted almost to death with the apprehensions of my sad condition, to be sick and no help. Prayed to God for the first time since the storm off Hull, but scarce knew what I said, or why; my thoughts being all confused.

June 22. A little better, but under dreadful apprehensions of sickness.

June 23. Very bad again, cold and shivering, and then a violent headache.

June 24. Much better.

June 25. An ague very violent; the fit held me seven hours, cold fit and hot, with faint sweats after it.

June 26. Better; and having no victuals to eat, took my gun, but found myself very weak; however, I killed a she-goat, and with much difficulty got it home, and broiled some of it, and ate; I would fain have stewed it and made some broth, but had no pot.

June 27. The ague again so violent, that I lay abed all day, and neither eat nor drank. I was ready to perish for thirst, but so weak I had not strength to stand up, or to get myself any water to drink. Prayed to God again, but was light-headed; and when I was not, I was so ignorant that I knew not what to say; only I lay and cried, Lord, look upon me; Lord, pity me; Lord, have mercy upon me. I suppose I did nothing else for two or three hours, till the fit wearing off, I fell asleep, and did not wake till far in the night; when I waked I found myself much refreshed, but weak and exceeding thirsty: however, as I had no water in my whole habitation, I was forced to lie till morning, and went to sleep again. In this second sleep I had this terrible dream.

I thought that I was sitting on the ground on the outside

of my wall, where I sat when the storm blew after the earth-quake, and that I saw a man descend from a great black cloud, in a bright flame of fire, and alight upon the ground. He was all over as bright as a flame, so that I could but just bear to look towards him; his countenance was most inexpressibly dreadful, impossible for words to describe; when he stepped upon the ground with his feet I thought the earth trembled just as it had done before in the earthquake, and all the air looked to my apprehension as if it had been filled with flashes of fire.

He was no sooner landed upon the earth, but he moved forward toward me, with a long spear or weapon in his hand to kill me; and when he came to a rising ground, at some distance, he spoke to me, or I heard a voice so terrible, that it is impossible to express the terror of it; all that I can say I understood was this, "Seeing all these things have not brought thee to repentance, now thou shalt die;" at which words I thought he lifted up the spear that was in his hand to kill me.

No one, that shall ever read this account, will expect that I should be able to describe the horrors of my soul at this terrible vision; I mean, that even while it was a dream, I even dreamed of those horrors; nor is it any more possible to describe the impression that remained upon my mind, when I awaked, and found it was but a dream.

June 28. Having been somewhat refreshed with the sleep I had had, and the fit being entirely off, I got up; and though the fright and terror of my dream was very great, yet I considered, that the fit of the ague would return again next day, and now was my time to get something to refresh and support myself when I should be ill. And the first thing I did, I filled a large square case-bottle with water, and set it upon my table, in reach of my bed; and to take off the chill or aguish disposition of the water, I put about a quarter of a pint of rum into it, and mixed them together. Then I got me a piece of goat's flesh, and broiled it on the coals, but could eat very little. I walked about, but was very weak, and withal, very sad and heavy-hearted under a sense of my miserable condition, dreading the return of my distemper the next day. At night I made my supper of three of the turtle's eggs, which I roasted in the ashes, and eat, as we call it, in the shell; and this was the first bit of meat I had ever asked God's blessing to, even, as I could remember, in my whole life.

After I had eaten I tried to walk; but found myself so weak that I could hardly carry the gun (for I never went out without that); so I went but a little way, and sat down upon the ground, looking out upon the sea, which was just before me, and very calm and smooth.

I rose up pensive and sad, walked back to my retreat, and went up over my wall, as if I had been going to bed; but my thoughts were sadly disturbed, and I had no inclination to sleep; so I sat down in my chair, and lighted my lamp, for it began to be dark. Now as the apprehension of the return of my distemper terrified me very much, it occurred to my thought, that the Brazilians take no physic but their tobacco for almost all distempers; and I had a piece of a roll of tobacco in one of the chests, which was quite cured, and some also that was green, and not quite cured. I went, directed by Heaven, no doubt! for in this chest I found a cure both for soul and body! I opened the chest, and found what I looked for, namely, the tobacco; and as the few books I had saved lay there too, I took out one of the Bibles which I mentioned before, and which, to this time, I had not found leisure, or so much as inclination, to look into; I say I took it out, and brought both that and the tobacco with me to the table.

What use to make of the tobacco I knew not, as to my distemper, or whether it was good for it or no; but I tried several experiments with it, as if I resolved it should hit one way or other: I first took a piece of a leaf, and chewed it in my mouth, which indeed at first almost stupefied my brain, the tobacco being green and strong, and that I had not been used to it; then I took some, and steeped it an hour or two in some rum, and resolved to take a dose of it when I lay down; and, lastly, I burnt some upon a pan of coals, and held my nose close over the smoke of it, as long as I could bear it, and I held almost to suffocation.

In the interval of this operation, I took up the Bible, and began to read; but my head was too much disturbed with the tobacco to bear reading, at least at that time. Only having opened the book casually, the first words that occurred to me were these: "Call on me in the day of trouble, and I will deliver thee, and thou shalt glorify me."

The words were very apt to my case, and made some impression upon my thoughts at the time of reading them, though not so much as they did afterwards; for, as for being delivered, the word had no sound, as I may say, to me; the thing was so remote, so impossible in my apprehension of things, that I began to say as the children of Israel did when they were promised flesh to eat, "Can God spread a table in the wilderness?" so I began to say, Can God himself deliver me from this place? And as it was not for many years that any hope appeared, this prevailed very often upon my thoughts; but, however, the words made a very great impression upon me, and I mused upon them very often. It grew now late, and the tobacco had, as I said, dozed my head so much, that I inclined to sleep; so I left my lamp burning in the cave, lest I should want anything in the night, and went to bed; but before I lay down, I did what I never had done in all my life; I kneeled down and prayed to God to fulfill the promise to me, that if I called upon him in the day of trouble, he would deliver me. After my broken and imperfect prayer was over, I drank the rum in which I had steeped the tobacco, which was so strong and rank of the tobacco, that indeed I could scarce get it down. Immediately upon this I went to bed, and I found presently it flew up into my head violently; but I fell into a sound sleep, and waked no more, till noon the next day; nay, to this hour. I am partly of the opinion that I slept all the next day and night, and till almost three the day after; for otherwise I knew not how I should lose a day out of my reckoning in the days of the week, as it appeared some years after I had done; for if I had lost it by crossing and recrossing the line, I should have lost more than one day: but certainly I lost a day in my account, and never knew which way.

Be that however one way or other, when I waked I found myself exceedingly refreshed, and my spirits lively and cheerful. When I got up, I was stronger than I was the day before, and my stomach better, for I was hungry; and, in short, I had no fit the next day, but continued much altered for the better. This was the 29th.

The 30th was my well day, of course; and I went abroad with my gun, but did not care to travel too far. I killed a seafowl or two, something like a brand goose, and brought them home, but was not very forward to eat them; so I eat some more of the turtle's eggs, which were very good. This evening I renewed the medicine which I had supposed did me good the day before, namely, the tobacco steeped in rum; only I did not take so much as before, nor did I chew any of the leaf, or hold my head over the smoke. However, I was not so well the next day, which was the first of July, as I hoped I should have been; for I had a little spice of the cold fit, but it was not much.

July 2. I renewed the medicine all the three ways, and dosed myself with it at first, and doubled the quantity which I drank.

July 3. I missed the fit for good and all, though I did not recover my full strength for some weeks after. While I was thus gathering strength, my thoughts run exceedingly upon the Scripture, "I will deliver thee;" and the impossibility of my deliverance lay much upon my mind, in bar of my ever expecting it: but as I was discouraging myself with such thoughts, it occurred to my mind that I pored so much on my deliverance from the main affliction, that I disregarded the deliverance I had received; and I was, as it were, made to ask myself such questions as these; namely, Have I not been delivered, and wonderfully, too, from sickness? from the most distressed condition that could be, and that was so frightful to me? and what notice had I taken of it? had I done my part? "God had delivered me; but I had not glorified him:" that is to say, I had not owned and been thankful for that as a deliverance; and how could I expect greater deliverance?

This touched my heart very much, and immediately I kneeled down and gave God thanks, aloud, for my recovery from my sickness.

July 4. In the morning I took the Bible; and, beginning at the New Testament, I began seriously to read it, and imposed upon myself to read awhile every morning and every night, not tying myself to the number of chapters, but as long as my thoughts should engage me. It was not long after I set seriously to this work, but I found my heart more deeply and sincerely affected with the wickedness of my past life.

Now I began to construe the words mentioned above, "Call on me, and I will deliver thee," in a different sense from what I had ever done before; for then I had no notion of anything being called deliverance, but my being delivered from the captivity I was in: for though I was indeed at large in the place, yet the island was certainly a prison to me, and that in the worst sense in the world; but now I learned to take it in another sense. Now I looked back upon my past life with such horror, and my sins appeared so dreadful, that my soul sought nothing of God but deliverance from the load of guilt that bore down all my comfort. As for my solitary life, it was nothing. I did not so much as pray to be delivered from it, or think of it; it was all of no consideration in comparison to this. And I add this part here, to hint to whoever shall read it, that whenever they come to a true sense of things, they will find deliverance from sin a much greater blessing than deliverance from affliction.

But, leaving this part, I return to my Journal:—

My condition began now to be, though not less miserable as to my way of living, yet much easier to my mind: and my thoughts being directed, by a constant reading the Scripture, and praying to God, to things of a higher nature, I had a great deal of comfort within, which till now I knew nothing of; also as my health and strength returned I bestirred myself to furnish myself with everything that I wanted, and make my way of living as regular as I could.

From the 4th of *July* to the 14th, I was chiefly employed in walking about with my gun in my hand, a little and a little at a time, as a man that was gathering up his strength after a fit of sickness; for it is hardly to be imagined how low I was, and to what weakness I was reduced. The application which I made use of was perfectly new, and perhaps what had never cured an ague before; neither can I recommend it to any one to practice by this experiment; and though it did carry off the fit, yet it rather contributed to weaken me; for I had frequent convulsions in my nerves and limbs for some time.

I learnt from it also this, in particular, that being abroad in the rainy season was the most pernicious thing to my health that could be, especially in those rains which came attended with storms and hurricanes of wind; for as the rain which came in the dry season was always most accompanied with such storms, so I found this rain was much more dangerous than the rain which fell in September and October.

I had been now in this unhappy island above ten months; all possibility of deliverance from this condition seemed to be entirely taken from me; and I firmly believed that no human shape had ever set foot upon that place. Having now secured my habitation, as I thought, fully to my mind, I had a great desire to make a more perfect discovery of the island, and to see what other productions I might find, which I yet knew nothing of.

It was on the 15th of July that I began to take a more par- ticular survey of the island itself; I went up the creek first, where, as I hinted, I brought my rafts on shore. I found, after I came about two miles up, that the tide did not flow any higher, and that it was no more than a little brook of running water, and very fresh and good; but this being the dry season, there was hardly any water in some parts of it, at least not enough to run in any stream, so as it could be perceived.

On the banks of this brook I found many pleasant savannas or meadows, plain, smooth, and covered with grass; and on the rising parts of them next to the higher grounds, where the water, as it might be supposed, never overflowed, I found a great deal of tobacco, green, and growing to a great and very strong stalk. There were divers other plants which I had no notion of, or understanding about; and might perhaps have virtues of their own, which I could not find out.

I searched for the cassava root, which the Indians in all that

climate make their bread of, but I could not find none. I saw
large plants of aloes, but did not then understand them. I saw
several sugar-canes, but wild, and, for want of cultivation, imperfect, I contented myself with these discoveries for this time,
and came back musing with myself what course I might take to
know the virtue and goodness of any of the fruits or plants
which I should discover, but could bring it to no conclusion:
for, in short, I had made so little observation while I was in the
Brazils, that I knew little of the plants of the field, at least very
little that might serve me to any purpose now in my distress.

The next day, the 16th, I went up the same way again; and,
after going something farther than I had done the day before,
I found the brook and the savannas began to cease, and the
country became more woody than before. In this part I found
different fruits, and particularly I found melons upon the
ground in great abundance, and grapes upon the trees; the vines
had spread indeed over the trees, and the clusters of grapes were
just now in their prime, very ripe and rich. This was a surprising
discovery, and I was exceedingly glad of them; but I was warned
by my experience to eat sparingly of them, remembering that,
when I was ashore in Barbary, the eating of grapes killed several
of our Englishmen who were slaves there, by throwing them
into fluxes and fevers; but I found an excellent use for these
grapes, and that was to cure or dry them in the sun and keep
them as dried grapes or raisins are kept, which I thought would
be, as indeed they were, as wholesome, and as agreeable to eat,
when no grapes might be had.

I spent all that evening there, and went not back to my habitation, which, by the way, was the first night, as I might say, I
had lain from home. In the night I took my first contrivance, and
got up into a tree, where I slept well, and the next morning pro-
ceeded upon my discovery, travelling near four miles, as I might

judge by the length of the valley, keeping still due north, with a ridge of hills on the south and north side of me.

At the end of this march I came to an opening, where the country seemed to descend to the west; and a little spring of fresh water, which issued out of the side of the hill by me, ran the other way, that is, due east; and the country appeared so fresh, so green, so flourishing, everything being in a constant verdure or flourishing of spring, that it looked like a planted garden.

I descended a little on the side of that delicious valley, surveying it with a secret kind of pleasure (though mixed with other afflicting thoughts), to think that this was all my own, that I was king and lord of all this country indefeasibly, and had a right of possession; and if I could convey it, I might have it in inheritance, as completely as any lord of a manor in England. I saw here abundance of cocoa-trees, orange and lemon, and citron-trees, but all wild, and few bearing any fruit; at least not then. However, the green limes that I gathered were not only pleasant to eat, but very wholesome; and I mixed their juice afterwards with water, which made it very wholesome, and very cool and refreshing.

I found now I had business enough to gather and carry home; and resolved to lay up a store, as well of grapes, as limes and lemons, to furnish myself for the wet season, which I knew was approaching.

In order to do this I gathered a heap of grapes in one place, and a lesser heap in another place; and a great parcel of limes and lemons in another place; and taking a few of each with me, I travelled homeward, and resolved to come again, and bring a bag or sack, or what I could make, to carry the rest home.

Accordingly, having spent three days in this journey, I came home (so I must now call my tent and my cave); but before I got thither the grapes were spoiled; the richness of the fruit and the weight of the juice having broken them and bruised them, they were good for little or nothing; as to the limes, they were good, but I could bring but a few.

The next day, being the 19th, I went back, having made me two small bags to bring home my harvest. But I was surprised when, coming to my heap of grapes, which were so rich and fine when I gathered them, I found them all spread abroad, trod to pieces, and dragged about, some here, some there, and abundance eaten and devoured. By this I concluded there were some wild creatures thereabouts which had done this; but what they were I knew not.

However, as I found there was no laying them up on heaps, and no carrying them away in a sack, but that one way they would be destroyed, and the other way they would be crushed with their own weight, I took another course; for I gathered a large quantity of the grapes and hung them upon the out branches of the trees, that they might cure and dry in the sun; and as for the limes and lemons, I carried as many back as I could well stand under.

When I came home from this journey, I contemplated with great pleasure on the fruitfulness of that valley, and the pleasantness of the situation, the security from storms on that side of the water, and the wood; and concluded that I had pitched upon a place to fix my abode, which was by far the worst part of the country. Upon the whole, I began to consider of removing my habitation, and to look out for a place equally safe as where I now was situated, if possible, in that pleasant and fruitful part of the island.

This thought ran long in my head, and I was exceeding fond of it for some time, the pleasantness of the place tempting me; but when I came to a nearer view of it, and to consider that I was now by the sea-side, where it was at least possible that something might happen to my advantage, and that the same ill fate that brought me hither, might bring some other unhappy wretches to the same place, and though it was scarce probable that any such thing should ever happen, yet to inclose myself among the hills and woods, in the centre of the island, was to anticipate my bondage, and to render such an affair not only improbable, but impossible; and that therefore I ought not by any means to remove.

However, I was so enamored of this place, that I spent much of my time there for the whole remaining part of the month of July and though, upon second thoughts, I resolved as above, not to remove, yet I built me a little kind of bower, and surrounded it at a distance with a strong fence, being a double hedge, as high as I could reach, well staked and filled between with brushwood; and here I lay very secure, sometimes two or three nights together, always going over it with a ladder, as before; so that I fancied now I had my country house, and my sea-coast house: and this work took me up to the beginning of August.

I had but newly finished my fence, and began to enjoy my labor, but the rains came on, and made me stick close to my first habitation; for though I had made me a tent like the other, with a piece of a sail, and spread it very well, yet I had not the shelter of a hill to keep me from storms, nor a cave behind me to retreat into when the rains were extraordinary.

About the beginning of August, as I said, I had finished my bower, and began to enjoy myself. The 3d of August I found the grapes I had hung up were perfectly dried, and indeed were excellent good raisins of the sun: so I began to take them down from the trees, and it was very happy that I did so; for the rains which followed would have spoiled them, and I had lost the best part of my winter food; for I had above two hundred large bunches of them. No sooner had I taken them all down, and carried most of them home to my cave, but it began to rain; and from thence, which was the 14th of August, it rained more or less every day, till the middle of October; and sometimes so violently, that I could not stir out of my cave for several days.

In this season I was much surprised with the increase of my family: I had been concerned for the loss of one of my two cats, who ran away from me, or, as I thought, had been dead; and I heard no more tidings of her, till, to my astonishment, she came home about the end of August, with three kittens. This was the more strange to me, because though I had killed a wild cat, as I called it, with my gun, yet I thought it was a quite different kind from our European cats; yet the young cats were the same kind of house breed like the old one; and both my cats being females, I thought it very strange: but from these three cats, I afterwards came to be so pestered with cats, that I was forced to kill them like vermin, or wild beasts, and to drive them from my house as much as possible.

From the 14th of August to the 26th, incessant rain, so that I could not stir, and was now very careful not to be much wet. In this confinement I began to be straitened for food: but venturing out twice, I one day killed a goat: and the last day, which was the 26th, found a very large tortoise, which was a treat to me; and my food was regulated thus:—I eat a bunch of raisins for my breakfast, a piece of the goat's flesh, or of the turtle, for my dinner, broiled (for to my great misfortune I had no vessel to boil or stew anything), and two or three of the turtle's eggs for supper.

During this confinement in my cover, by the rain, I worked daily two or three hours at enlarging my cave; and, by degrees, worked it on towards one side, till I came to the outside of the hill, and made a door or way out, which came beyond my fence or wall; and so I came in and out this way. But I was not perfectly easy at lying so open; for as I had managed myself before, I was in a perfect inclosure, whereas now I thought I lay exposed; and yet I could not perceive that there was any living thing to fear, the biggest creature that I had seen upon the island being a goat.

September 30. I was now come to the unhappy anniversary of my landing. I cast up the notches on my post, and found I had been on shore three hundred and sixty-five days. I had kept this day as a solemn fast, setting it apart to a religious exercise, prostrating myself on the ground with the most serious humiliation, confessing my sins to God, acknowledging his righteous judgments upon me, and praying to him to have mercy on me, through Jesus Christ; and having not tasted the least refreshment for twelve hours, even to the going down of the sun, I then ate a biscuit cake, and a bunch of grapes, and went to bed, finishing the day as I began it.

I had all this time observed no Sabbath-day; for as at first I had no sense of religion upon my mind, I had after some time omitted to distinguish the weeks, by making a longer notch than ordinary for the Sabbath-day, and so did not really know what any of the days were; but now, having cast up the days as above, I found I had been there a year; so I divided it into weeks, and set apart every seventh day for a Sabbath; though I found at the end of my account I had lost a day or two in my reckoning.

A little after this my ink began to fail me, and so I contented myself to use it more sparingly, and to write down only the most remarkable events of my life, without continuing a daily memorandum of other things.

CHAPTER 9: *In which I make baskets, and explore my island home*

THE RAINY season, and the dry season, began now to appear regular to me, and I learned to divide them so as to provide for them accordingly. But I bought all my experience before I had it; and this I am going to relate, was one of the most discouraging experiments that I made at all. I have mentioned, that I had saved the few ears of barley and rice which I had so surprisingly found spring up, as I thought, of themselves, and believe there were about thirty stalks of rice, and about twenty of barley; and now I thought it a proper time to sow it after the rains, the sun being in its southern position going from me.

Accordingly I dug up a piece of ground, as well as I could, with my wooden spade, and dividing it into two parts, I sowed my grain; but as I was sowing, it casually occurred to my thought, that I would not sow it all at first, because I did not know when was the proper time for it; so I sowed about two-thirds of the seeds, leaving about a handful of each. It was a great comfort to me afterwards that I did so, for not one grain of that I sowed this time came to anything; for the dry months following, the earth having had no rain after the seed was sown, it had no moisture to assist its growth, and never came up at all, till the wet season had come again, and then it grew as if it had been newly sown.

Finding my first seed did not grow, which I easily imagined was by the drought, I sought for a moister piece of ground to make another trial in; and I dug up a piece of ground near my new bower, and sowed the rest of my seed in February, a little before the vernal equinox; and this, having the rainy months of March and April to water it, sprung up very pleasantly, and

121

yielded a very good crop; but having part of the seed left only, and not daring to sow all that I had yet, I had but a small quantity at last, my whole crop not amounting to above half a peck of each kind.

But by this experience I was made master of my business, and knew exactly when the proper season was to sow; and that I might expect two seed-times, and two harvests every year.

While this corn was growing, I made a little discovery, which was of use to me afterwards. As soon as the rains were over, and the weather began to settle, which was about the month of November, I made a visit up the country to my bower, where, though I had not been some months, yet I found all things just as I left them. The circle or double hedge that I had made, was not only firm and entire, but the stakes which I had cut off of some trees that grew thereabouts, were all shot out, and grown with long branches, as much as a willow-tree usually shoots the first year after lopping its head. I could not tell what tree to call it that these stakes were cut from. I was surprised, and yet very well pleased, to see the young trees grow; and I pruned them, and led them to grow as much alike as I could, and it is scarce credible, how beautiful a figure they grew into in three years; so that though the hedge made a circle of about twenty-five yards in diameter, yet the trees, for such I might now call them, soon covered it; and it was a complete shade, sufficient to lodge under all the dry season.

This made me resolve to cut some more stakes, and make me a hedge like this in a semicircle round my wall, I mean that of my first dwelling, which I did; and placing the trees or stakes in a double row, at about eight yards' distance from my first fence, they grew presently, and were at first a fine cover to my habitation, and afterwards served for a defence also, as I shall observe in its order.

I found now, that the seasons of the year might generally be divided, not into summer and winter, as in Europe, but into the rainy seasons and the dry seasons, which were generally thus:

Half February, March, half April—Rainy, the sun being then on or near the equinox.

Half April, May, June, July, half August—Dry, the sun being then to the north of the line.

Half August, September, half October—Rainy, the sun then being come back.

Half October, November, December, January, half February—Dry, the sun being then to the south of the line.

The rainy season sometimes held longer or shorter, as the winds happened to blow; but this was the general observation I made. After I had found, by experience, the ill consequences of being abroad in the rain, I took care to furnish myself with provisions beforehand, that I might not be obliged to go out; and I sat within doors as much as possible during the wet months.

In this time I found much employment (and very suitable also to the time), for I found great occasion for many things which I had no way to furnish myself with, but by hard labor and constant application. Particularly, I tried many ways to make myself a basket; but all the twigs I could get for the purpose proved so brittle that they would do nothing. It proved of excellent advantage to me now, that when I was a boy, I used to take great delight in standing at a basket-maker's in the town where my father lived, to see them make their wicker ware; and being, as boys usually are, very officious to help, and a great observer of the manner how they worked those things, and sometimes lending a hand, I had by this means so full knowledge of the methods of it, that I wanted nothing but the materials; when it came into my mind, that the twigs of that tree from whence I cut my stakes that grew, might possibly be as tough as the sallows, and willows, and osiers in England, and I resolved to try.

Accordingly, the next day I went to my country house, as I called it, and cutting some of the smaller twigs, I found them to my purpose as much as I could desire; whereupon I came the next time prepared with a hatchet to cut down a quantity which I soon found, for there was a great plenty of them. These I set up to dry within my circle of hedges; and when they were fit for use, I carried them to my cave; and here, during the next season, I employed myself in making (as well as I could) a great many baskets, both to carry earth, or to carry or lay up anything, as I had occasion; and though I did not finish them very handsomely, yet I made them sufficiently serviceable for my purpose; and thus afterwards I took care never to be without them; and as my wicker ware decayed, I made more; especially I made strong, deep baskets to place my corn in, instead of sacks, when I should come to have any quantity of it.

Having mastered this difficulty, and employed a world of time about it, I bestirred myself to see, if possible, how to supply two wants. I had no vessels to hold anything that was liquid, except two runlets, which were almost full of rum, and some glass bottles, some of the common size, and others, which were case-bottles, square, for the holding of waters, spirits, &c. I had not so much as a pot to boil anything in, except a great kettle which I saved out of the ship, and which was too big for such uses as I desired for it, namely, to make broth, and stew a bit of meat by itself. The second thing I would fain have had, was a tobacco-pipe, but it was impossible for me to make one; however, I found a contrivance for that, too, at last.

I employed myself in planting my second rows of stakes or piles, and in this wicker work, all the summer, or dry season;

hen another business took me up more time than it could be
nagined I could spare.

I mentioned before, that I had a great mind to see the whole
land, and that I had travelled up the brook, and so on to where
built my bower, and where I had an opening quite to the sea,
n the other side of the island. I now resolved to travel quite
cross the sea-shore on that side; so taking my gun, and hatchet,
nd my dog, and a larger quantity of powder and shot than
sual, with two biscuit cakes, and a great bunch of raisins in my
ouch, for my store, I began my journey. When I had passed
ne vale where my bower stood, as above, I came within view
f the sea, to the west; and it being a very clear day, I fairly de-
ried land, whether an island or continent I could not tell; but
lay very high, extending from the west to the W. S. W. at a
ery great distance; by my guess it could not be less than fifteen
r twenty leagues off.

I could not tell what part of the world this might be, other-
ise than that I knew it must be part of America; and, as I con-
luded by all my observations, must be near the Spanish do-
inions, and perhaps was all inhabited by savages, where, if I
nould have landed, I had been in a worse condition than I was
ow; and therefore I acquiesced in the dispositions of Provi-
ence, which I began now to own, and to believe, ordered every-
ning for the best; I say I quieted my mind with this, and left
flicting myself with fruitless wishes of being there.

Besides, after some pause upon this affair, I considered, that
this land was the Spanish coast, I should certainly, one time
r other, see some vessel pass or repass one way or other; but
not, then it was the savage coast between the Spanish country
nd Brazil, which is inhabited by the worst of savages; for they
e cannibals, or man-eaters, and fail not to murder and devour
l the human bodies that fall into their hands.

With these considerations I walked very leisurely forward. I found that side of the island where I now was, much pleasanter than mine, the open or savanna fields sweet, adorned with flowers and grass, and full of very fine woods. I saw abundance of parrots, and fain would I have caught one, if possible, to have kept it to be tame, and taught it to speak to me. I did, after some pains taken, catch a young parrot, for I knocked it down with a stick, and, having recovered it, I brought it home, but it was some years before I could make him speak. However, at last I taught him to call me by my name, very familiarly; but the accident that followed, though it be a trifle, will be very diverting in its place.

I was exceedingly diverted with this journey. I found in the low grounds, hares, as I thought them to be, and foxes, but they differed greatly from all other kinds I had met with, nor could I satisfy myself to eat them, though I killed several: but I had no need to be venturous, for I had no want of food, and of that which was very good too; especially these three sorts, goats, pigeons, and turtle or tortoise; which, added to my grapes, Leadenhall Market could not have furnished a better table than I, in proportion to the company: and though my case was deplorable enough, yet I had great cause for thankfulness, that I was not driven to any extremities for food; but rather plenty, even to dainties.

I never travelled in this journey above two miles outright in a day, or thereabouts; but I took so many turns and returns, to see what discoveries I could make, that I came weary enough to the place where I resolved to sit down for all night; and then either reposed myself in a tree, or surrounded myself with a row of stakes set upright in the ground, either from one tree or another, or so as no wild creature could come at me without waking me.

As soon as I came to the sea-shore, I was surprised to see that I had taken up my lot on the worst side of the island; for here indeed the shore was covered with innumerable turtles, whereas on the other side I had found but three in a year and a half. Here was also an infinite number of fowls of many kinds, some of which I had not seen before, and many of them very good meat; but such as I knew not the names of, except those called penguins.

I could have shot as many as I pleased, but was very sparing of my powder and shot; and therefore had more mind to kill a she-goat, if I could, which I could better feed on; and though there were many more goats here than on the other side of the island, yet it was with much more difficulty that I could come near them, the country being flat and even, so that they saw me much sooner than when I was on the hills.

I confess this side of the country was much pleasanter than mine, but yet I had not the least inclination to remove; for, as I was fixed in my habitation, it became natural to me; and I seemed all the while I was here to be, as it were, upon a journey, and from home. However, I travelled along the shore of the sea toward the east, I suppose about twelve miles; and then setting up a great pole upon the shore for a mark, I concluded I would go home again; and the next journey I took should be on the other side of the island, east from my dwelling, and so round, till I came to my post again, of which in its place.

I took another way to come back than that I went, thinking I could easily keep all the island so much in my view, that I could not miss finding my first dwelling by viewing the country; but I found myself mistaken; for being come about two or three miles, I found myself descended into a very large valley, but so surrounded with hills, and those hills covered with woods, that I could not see which was my way by any direction but that

I lived mighty comfortably

of the sun; nor even then, unless I knew very well the position of the sun at that time of the day.

It happened, to my farther misfortune, that the weather proved hazy for three or four days while I was in this valley; and not being able to see the sun, I wandered about very uncomfortably, and at last was obliged to find out the sea-side, look for my post, and come back the same way I went; and then by easy journeys I turned homeward, the weather being exceeding hot, and my gun, ammunition, hatchet, and other things very heavy.

In this journey my dog surprised a young kid, and seized upon it; and I, running to take hold of it, caught it, and saved it alive from the dog. I had a great mind to bring it home, if I could; for I had often been musing whether it might not be possible to get a kid or two, and so raise a breed of tame goats, which might supply me when my powder and shot should be spent.

I made a collar for this little creature; and with a string which I made of some rope-yarn, which I always carried about me, I led him along, though with some difficulty, till I came to my bower, and there I inclosed him, and left him; for I was very impatient to be at home, from whence I had been absent above a month.

I cannot express what a satisfaction it was to me to come into my old hutch and lie down in my hammock-bed: this little wandering journey, without a settled place of abode, had been so unpleasant to me, that my own house, as I called it to myself, was a perfect settlement to me, compared to that; and it rendered everything about me so comfortable, that I resolved that I would never go a great way from it again, while it should be my lot to stay on the island.

CHAPTER 10: *The second anniversary and beginning of the third year*

I REPOSED myself here a week, to rest and regale myself after my long journey; during which, most of the time was taken up in the weighty affair of making a cage for my Poll, who began now to be a mere domestic, and to be mighty well acquainted with me. Then I began to think of the poor kid, which I had pent in within my little circle, and resolved to go and fetch it home, and give it some food: accordingly I went, and found it where I left it; for indeed it could not get out, but was almost starved for want of food. I went and cut boughs of trees and branches of such shrubs as I could find, and threw over to it; and having fed it, I tied it as I did before to lead it away; but it was so tame with being hungry, that I had no need to have tied it; for it followed me like a dog; and as I continually fed it, the creature became so loving, so gentle, and so fond, that it became from that time one of my domestics also, and would never leave me afterwards.

The rainy season of the autumnal equinox was now come, and I kept the 30th of September in the same solemn manner as before, being the anniversary of my landing on the island, having now been there two years, and no more prospect of being delivered than the first day I came there. I spent the whole day in humble and thankful acknowledgments of the many wonderful mercies which my solitary condition was attended with, and without which it might have been infinitely more miserable. I gave humble and hearty thanks, that God had been pleased to discover to me, even that it was possible I might be more happy in this solitary condition, than I should have been in society, and in all the pleasures of the world: that he could fully make up to me the deficiencies of my solitary state and the want of human society, by his presence, and the communications of his grace to my soul, supporting, comforting, and encouraging me to depend upon his providence here, and hope for his eternal presence hereafter.

Before, as I walked about, either on my hunting, or for viewing the country, the anguish of my soul at my condition would break upon me on a sudden, and my very heart would die within me, to think of the woods, the mountains, the deserts I was in; and how I was a prisoner, locked up with the eternal bolts and bars of the ocean, in an uninhabited wilderness, without redemption. In the midst of the greatest composures of my mind, this would break out upon me like a storm, and make me wring my hands, and weep like a child. Sometimes it would take me in the middle of my work, and I would immediately sit down and sigh, and look down upon the ground for an hour or two together; and this was still worse to me; for if I could burst out into tears, or vent myself by words, it would go off, and the grief, having exhausted itself, would abate.

But now I began to exercise myself with new thoughts; I daily read the word of God, and applied all the comforts of it to my present state. One morning, being very sad, I opened the Bible upon these words, "I will never, never leave thee, nor forsake thee!" Immediately it occurred, that these words were to me, why else should they be directed in such a manner, just at the moment when I was mourning over my condition, as one forsaken of God and man? Well then, said I, if God does not forsake me, of what ill consequence can it be, or what matters it, though the world should all forsake me: seeing on the other hand, if I had all the world, and should lose the favor and blessing of God, there would be no comparison in the loss.

I never opened the Bible, or shut it, but my very soul within me blessed God for directing my friend in England, without any order of mine, to pack it up among my goods; and for assisting me afterwards to save it out of the wreck of the ship.

In this disposition of mind, I began my third year; and though I have not given the reader the trouble of so particular an account of my works this year as at the first, yet in general it may be observed, that I was very seldom idle; having regularly divided my time, according to the several daily employments that were before me, such as first, my duty to God, and reading the Scriptures, which I constantly set apart some time for, thrice every day. Secondly, the going abroad with my gun for food, which generally took me up three hours every morning when it did not rain. Thirdly, the ordering, curing, preserving, and cooking what I had killed or caught for my supply. These took up a great part of the day. Also it is to be considered, that in the middle of the day, the violence of the heat was too great to stir out; so that about four hours in the evening was all the time I could be supposed to work in; with this exception, that sometimes I changed my hours of hunting and working, and went to work in the morning, and abroad with my gun in the afternoon.

To this short time allowed for labor, I desire may be added the exceedinging laboriousness of my work; the many hours which, for want of tools, want of help, and want of skill, everything that I did took up out of my time: for example, I was full two-and-forty days making me a board for a long shelf, which I wanted in my cave; whereas two sawyers, with their tools and saw-pit, would have cut six of them out of the same tree in half a day. My case was this: It was to be a large tree which was to be cut down, because my board was to be a broad one. The tree I was three days a cutting down, and two more cutting off the boughs, and reducing it to a log, or piece of timber. With inexpressible hacking and hewing, I reduced both the sides of it into

chips, till it began to be light enough to move; then I turned it,
and made one side of it smooth and flat as a board, from end to
end: then turning that side downward, cut the other side till I
brought the plank to be about three inches thick, and smooth
on both sides. Any one may judge the labor of my hands in such
a piece of work; but labor and patience carried me through that
and many other things.

I was now in the months of November and December, expecting my crop of barley and rice. The ground I had manured
or dug up for them was not great; for, as I observed, my seed of
each was not above the quantity of half a peck; for I had lost one
whole crop by sowing in the dry season; but now my crop promised very well, when on a sudden I found I was in danger of losing it all again by enemies of several sorts, which it was scarce
possible to keep from it; at first, the goats, and wild creatures
which I called hares, which, tasting the sweetness of the blade,
lay in it night and day, as soon as it came up, and eat it so close,
that it could get no time to shoot up into stalks.

This I saw no remedy for, but my making an inclosure about
it with a hedge, which I did with a great deal of toil; and the
more, because it required a great deal of speed; the creatures
daily spoiling my corn. However, as my arable land was but
small, suited to my crop, I got it totally well fenced in about
three weeks' time; and shooting some of the creatures in the
day-time, I set my dog to guard it in the night, tying him up to
a stake at the gate, where he would stand and bark all night
long: so in a little time the enemies forsook the place, and the
corn grew very strong and well, and began to ripen apace.

But as the beasts ruined me before, while my corn was in the
blade, so the birds were as like to ruin me now, when it was in
the ear; for going along by the place to see how it throve, I saw
my little crop surrounded with fowls of I know not how many

sorts, which stood as it were watching till I should be gone. I immediately let fly among them, (for I always had my gun with me). I had no sooner shot, but there arose up a little cloud of fowls, which I had not seen at all, from among the corn itself.

This touched me sensibly, for I foresaw, that in a few days they would devour all my hopes: that I should be starved, and never be able to raise a crop at all; and what to do I could not tell; however, I resolved not to lose my corn, if possible, though I should watch it night and day. In the first place, I went among it to see what damage was already done, and found they had spoiled a good deal of it; but that, as it was yet too green for them, the loss was not so great, but the remainder was like to be a good crop, if it could be saved.

I stayed by it to load my gun, and then coming away, I could easily see the thieves sitting upon all the trees about me, as if they only waited till I was gone away, and the event proved it to be so; for as I walked off, as if I was gone, I was no sooner out of their sight, but they dropped down one by one into the corn again. I was so provoked, that I could not have patience to stay till more came on, knowing that every grain that they eat now was, as it might be said, a peck loaf to me in the consequence. But coming up to the hedge, I fired again, and killed three of them. This was what I wished for; so I took them up, and served them, as we serve notorious thieves in England, that is, hanged them in chains, for a terror to others. It is almost impossible to imagine, that this should have such an effect as it had, for the fowls would not only not come at the corn, but in short they forsook all that part of the island, and I could never see a bird near the place as long as my scarecrows hung there. This I was very glad of, you may be sure, and about the latter end of December, which was our second harvest of the year, I reaped my corn.

Chapter 11: *Farming operations*

I was sadly put to it for a scythe or a sickle to cut it down, and all I could do was to make one as well as I could, out of one of the broadswords, or cutlasses, which I saved among the arms out of the ship. However, as my crop was but small, I had no great difficulty to cut it down; in short, I reaped it my way, for I cut nothing off but the ears, and carried it away in a great basket which I had made, and so rubbed it out with my hands. And at the end of all my harvesting I found, that out of my half peck of seed, I had near two bushels of rice, and above two bushels and a half of barley, that is to say, by my guess, for I had no measure at that time.

However, this was a great encouragement to me, and I foresaw that in time it would please God to supply me with bread; and yet here I was perplexed again, for I neither knew how to grind or make meal of my corn, or indeed how to clean it and part it; nor, if made into meal, how to make bread of it; and if how to make it, yet I knew not how to bake it. These things being added to my desire of having a good quantity for store, and to secure a constant supply, I resolved not to taste any of this crop, but to preserve it all for seed against the next season, and in the meantime to employ all my study and hours of working to accomplish this great work of providing myself with corn and bread.

It might be truly said, that now I worked for my bread. It is a little wonderful, and what I believe few people have thought much upon; namely, the strange multitude of little things necessary in the providing, producing, curing, dressing, making, and finishing, this one article of bread.

First, I had no plough to turn the earth, no spade or shovel

135

to dig it. Well, this I conquered by making a wooden spade, as I observed before, but this did my work in but a wooden manner; and though it cost me a great many days to make it, yet, for want of iron, it not only wore out the sooner, but made my work the harder, and made it be performed much worse.

However, this I bore with too, and was content to work it out with patience, and bear with the badness of the performance. When the corn was sowed, I had no harrow, but was forced to go over it myself, and drag a great heavy bough of a tree over it, to scratch the earth, as it may be called, rather than rake or harrow it.

When it was growing or grown, I have observed already how many things I wanted, to fence it, secure it, mow or reap it, cure or carry it home, thresh, part it from the chaff, and save it. Then I wanted a mill to grind it, sieves to dress it, yeast and salt to make it into bread, and an oven to bake it in; and all these things I did without, as shall be observed; and yet the corn was an inestimable comfort and advantage to me too. But all this, as I said, made everything laborious and tedious to me, but that there was no help for, neither was my time so much loss to me, because I had divided it. A certain part of it was every day appointed to these works, and as I resolved to use none of the corn for bread till I had a greater quantity by me, I had the next six months to apply myself, wholly by labor and invention, to furnish myself with utensils proper for the performing all the operations necessary for the making the corn, when I had it, fit for my use.

But first I was to prepare more land, for I had now seed enough to sow above an acre of ground. Before I did this, I had a week's work at least to make me a spade, which, when it was done, was a very sorry one indeed, and very heavy, and required double labor to work with it; however, I went through that, and sowed my seeds in two large flat pieces of ground, as near my house as I could find them to my mind, and fenced them in with a good hedge, the stakes of which were all cut off that wood which I had set before, which I knew would grow; so that in one year's time I knew I should have a quick or living hedge, that would want but little repair. This work was not so little as to take me up less than three months; because a great part of that time was in the wet season, when I could not go abroad.

Within-door, that is, when it rained, and I could not go out, I found employment on the following occasion, always observing, that all the while I was at work, I diverted myself with talking to my parrot, and teaching him to speak; and I quickly learnt him to know his own name; at least to speak it out pretty loud, Poll; which was the first word I ever heard spoken in the island by any mouth but my own. This therefore, was not my work, but an assistant to my work; for now, as I said, I had a great employment upon my hands, as follows: I had long studied, by some means or other, to make myself some earthen vessels, which indeed I wanted sorely, but knew not where to come at them; however, considering the heat of the climate, I did not doubt, but if I coud find out any such clay, I might botch up some such pot, as might, being dried by the sun, be hard enough, and strong enough, to bear handling, and to hold anything that was dry, and required to be kept so; and as this was necessary in preparing corn, meal, &c., which was the thing I was upon, I resolved to make some as large as I could, and fit only to stand like jars to hold what should be put into them.

It would make the reader pity me, or rather laugh at me, to tell how many awkward ways I took to raise this paste, what odd, misshapen, ugly things I made, how many of them fell in, and how many fell out, the clay not being stiff enough to bear its own weight; how many cracked by the over violent heat of the sun, being set out too hastily; and how many fell to pieces with only removing, as well before as after they were dried; and, in a word, how, after having labored hard to find the clay, to dig it, to temper it, to bring it home, and work it, I could not make above two large earthen ugly things, I cannot call them jars, in about two months' labor.

However, as the sun baked these two very dry and hard, I lifted them very gently up, and set them down again in two greater wicker baskets, which I had made on purpose for them, that they might not break, and, as between the pot and the basket there was a little room to spare, I stuffed it full of the rice and barley straw; and these two pots being to stand always dry, I thought it would hold my dry corn, and perhaps the meal when the corn was bruised.

Though I miscarried so much in my design for large pots, yet I made several smaller things with better success, such as little round pots, flat dishes, pitchers, and pipkins, and anything my hand turned to, and the heat of the sun baked them strangely hard.

But all this would not answer my end, which was to get an earthen pot to hold what was liquid, and bear the fire, which none of these could do. It happened after some time, making a pretty large fire for cooking my meat, when I went to put it out after I had done with it, I found a broken piece of one of my earthen ware vessels in the fire, burnt as hard as a stone, and red as a tile. I was agreeably surprised to see it, and said to myself, that certainly they might be made to burn whole, if they would burn broken.

This set me to study how to order my fire, so as to make it burn me some pots. I had no notion of a kiln, such as the potters burn in, or of glazing them with lead, though I had some lead to do it with; but I placed three large pipkins, and two or three pots, in a pile one upon another, and placed my firewood all round it, with a great heap of embers under them; I plied the fire with fresh fuel round the outside, and upon the top, till I saw the pots in the inside red-hot quite through, and observed that they did not crack at all; when I saw them clear red, I let them stand in that heat about five or six hours, till I found one of them, though it did not crack, did melt or run. For the sand which was mixed with the clay, melted by the violence of the heat, and would have run into glass, if I had gone on; so I slacked my fire gradually, till the pots began to abate of the red color, and watching them all night that I might not let the fire abate too fast, in the morning I had three very good, I will not say handsome pipkins, and two other earthen pots, as hard burnt as could be desired, and one of them perfectly glazed with the running of the sand.

After this experiment, I need not say that I wanted no sort of earthen ware for my use, but I must needs say as to the shapes of them, they were very indifferent, as any one may suppose, when I had no way of making them, but as the children make dirt pies, or as a woman would make pies that had never learnt to raise paste.

No joy at a thing of so mean a nature was ever equal to mine, when I found I had made an earthen pot that would bear the fire; and I had hardly patience to stay till they were cold, before I set one upon the fire again, with some water in it, to boil me some meat, which it did admirably well; and with a piece of a kid I made some very good broth, though I wanted oatmeal, and several other ingredients requisite to make it so good as I would have had it.

My next concern was to get me a stone mortar to stamp or beat some corn in; for as to the mill, there was no thought of arriving to that perfection of art with one pair of hands. To

supply this want, I was at a great loss; for of all trades in the
world I was as perfectly unqualified for a stone-cutter, as for any
whatever; neither had I any tools to go about it with. I spent
many a day to find out a great stone big enough to cut hollow,
and make fit for a mortar, and could find none at all, except
what was in the solid rock, and which I had no way to dig or
cut out; nor indeed were the rocks in the island of hardness
sufficient, but were all of a sandy crumbling stone, which would
neither bear the weight of a heavy pestle, nor would break the
corn without filling it with sand; so, after a great deal of time
lost in searching for a stone, I gave it over, and resolved to look
out for a great block of hard wood, which I found indeed much
easier; and getting one as big as I had strength to stir, I rounded
it, and formed it on the outside with my axe and hatchet; and
then, with the help of fire and infinite labor, made a hollow
place in it, as the Indians in Brazil make their canoes. After
this, I made a great heavy pestle or beater, of the wood called
the ironwood; and this I prepared and laid by against I had my
next crop of corn, when I proposed to myself to grind, or rather
pound, my corn or meal to make my bread.

My next difficulty was to make a sieve, to dress my meal and
part it from the bran and the husk, without which I did not see
it possible I could have any bread. This was a most difficult
thing, so much as but to think on; for, to be sure, I had nothing
like the necessary things to make it with; I mean fine thin canvas, or stuff, to sift the meal through. And here I was at a full
stop for many months; nor did I really know what to do: linen
I had none left but what was mere rags; I had goat's hair, but
neither knew I how to weave or spin it; and had I known how,
here were no tools to work it with. All the remedy that I found
for this, was, that at last I did remember I had among the seamen's clothes, which were saved out of the ship, some neck-

cloths of calico or muslin; and with some pieces of these I made three small sieves, but proper enough for the work: and thus I made shift for some years; how I did afterwards, I shall show in its place.

The baking part was the next thing to be considered, and how I should make bread when I came to have corn; for, first, I had no yeast. As to that part, as there was no supplying the want, so I did not concern myself much about it. But for an oven I was indeed in great pain. At length I found out an experiment for that also, which was this: I made some earthen vessels very broad, but not deep; that is to say, about two feet diameter, and not above nine inches deep; these I burnt in the fire, as I had done the other, and laid them by; and when I wanted to bake, I made a great fire upon the hearth, which I had paved with some square tiles of my own making and burning also; but I should not call them square. When the firewood was burnt pretty much into embers, or live coals, I drew them forward upon this hearth, so as to cover it all over; and there I let them lie, till the hearth was very hot: then sweeping away all the embers, I set down my loaf, or loaves; and whelming down the earthen pot upon them, drew the embers all round the outside of the pot, to keep in, and add to the heat: and thus, as well as in the best oven in the world, I baked my barley-loaves, and became in a little time a pastry-cook into the bargain, for I made myself several cakes of the rice, and puddings.

It need not be wondered at, if all these things took me up most part of the third year of my abode here; for it is to be observed, that in the intervals of these things, I had my new harvest and husbandry to manage; for I reaped my corn in its season, and carried it home as well as I could, and laid it up in the ear, in my large baskets, till I had time to rub it out; for I had no floor to thrash it on, or instrument to thrash it with.

And now indeed, my stock of corn increasing, I really wanted to build my barns bigger: I wanted a place to lay it up in; for the increase of the corn now yielded me so much, that I had of the barley about twenty bushels, and of the rice, as much, or more; insomuch that I now resolved to begin to use it freely, for my bread had been quite gone a great while: also I resolved to see what quantity would be sufficient for me a whole year, and to sow but once a year.

Upon the whole, I found that the forty bushels of barley and rice were much more than I could consume in a year; so I resolved to sow just the same quantity every year that I sowed the last, in hopes that such a quantity would fully provide me with bread.

CHAPTER 12: *Hopes of escape*

ALL THE while these things were doing, you may be sure my thoughts ran many times upon the prospect of land which I had seen from the other side of the island; and I was not without secret wishes that I was on shore there, fancying that seeing the main-land, and an inhabited country, I might find some way or other to convey myself farther, and perhaps at last find some means of escape.

But all this while I made no allowance for the dangers of such a condition, and how I might fall into the hands of savages, and perhaps such as I might have reason to think far worse than the lions and tigers of Africa. That if I once came into their power, I should run a hazard more than a thousand to one of being killed, and perhaps of being eaten; for I had heard that the people of the Caribbean coast were cannibals, or men-eaters; and I knew by the latitude that I could not be far off from that shore. All these things, I say, which I ought to have considered well of, and I did cast up in my thoughts afterwards, yet took none of my apprehensions at first; and my head ran mightily upon the thoughts of getting over to that shore.

Now I wished for my boy Xury, and the long boat with the shoulder-of-mutton sail, with which I sailed above a thousand miles on the coast of Africa; but this was in vain. Then I thought I would go and look on our ship's boat, which, as I have said, was blown up upon the shore a great way in the storm, when we were first cast away. She lay almost where she did at first, but not quite; and was turned by the force of the waves, and the winds, almost bottom upwards, against the high ridge of a beachy rough sand, but no water about her as before.

Had I had hands to have refitted her, and have launched her into the water, the boat would have done well enough, and I might have gone back into the Brazils with her easily enough; but I might have easily foreseen that I could no more turn her, and set her upright upon her bottom, than I could remove the island. However, I went to the wood, and cut levers and rollers, and brought them to the boat, resolving to try what I could do; suggesting to myself, that if I could but turn her down, I might easily repair the damage she had received, and she would be a very good boat, and I might go to sea in her very easily.

I spared no pains indeed in this piece of fruitless toil, and spent, I think, three or four weeks about it. At last, finding it impossible to heave it up with my little strength, I fell to digging away the sand to undermine it, and so to make it fall down, setting pieces of wood to thrust and guide it right in the fall.

But when I had done this, I was unable to stir it up again, or to get under it, much less to move it forwards towards the water; so I was forced to give it over: and yet, though I gave over hopes of the boat, my desire to venture over for the main increased, rather than decreased, as the means for it seemed impossible.

This at length set me upon thinking whether it was not possible to make myself a canoe or periagua, such as the natives of those climates make, even without tools, or as I might say, without hands, namely of the trunk of a great tree. This I not only thought possible, but easy; and pleased myself extremely with my thoughts of making it, and with my having much more convenience for it than any of the Negroes or Indians; but not at all considering the particular inconveniences which I lay under more than the Indians did, namely, want of hands to move it into the water, when it was made; a difficulty much harder for me to surmount than all the consequences of want of tools could be to them. But my thoughts were so intent upon my voyage over the sea in it, that I never once considered how I should get it off the land; and it was really in its own nature more easy for me to guide it over forty-five miles of sea than above forty-five fathom of land, where it lay to set it afloat in the water.

I went to work upon this boat the most like a fool that ever man did, who had any of his senses awake. I pleased myself with the design, without determining whether I was ever able to undertake it; not but that the difficulty of launching my boat came often into my head; but I put a stop to my own inquiries into it by this foolish answer which I gave myself: Let me first make it, I will warrant I will find some way or other to get it along when it is done.

This was a most preposterous method; but the eagerness of my fancy prevailed, and to work I went, and felled a cedar-tree. I question much whether Solomon ever had such a one for the building the temple of Jerusalem. It was five feet ten inches diameter at the lower part next the stump, and four feet eleven inches diameter at the end of twenty-two feet, after which it lessened for a while and then parted into branches. It was not without infinite labor that I felled this tree; I was twenty days hacking and hewing at it at the bottom; I was fourteen more getting the branches and limbs and the vast spreading head of it cut off, which I hacked and hewed through with my axe and hatchet, with inexpressible labor; after this it cost me a month to shape it and dub it to a proportion, and to something like the bottom of a boat, that it might swim upright as it ought. It cost me near three months more to clear the inside, and work it out so as to make an exact boat of it; this I did indeed without fire, by mere mallet and chisel, and by the dint of hard labor; till I had brought it to be a very handsome periagua, and big enough to have carried six and twenty men, and consequently big enough to have carried me and all my cargo.

When I had gone through this work, I was extremely delighted with it: the boat was really much bigger than I ever saw a canoe or periagua, that was made of one tree, in my life. Many a weary stroke it had cost, you may be sure, for there remained nothing but to get it into the water; and had I gotten it into the water, I made no question but I should have begun the maddest voyage, and the most unlikely to be performed, that ever was undertaken.

But all my devices to get it into the water failed me, though they cost infinite labor too; it lay about one hundred yards from the water, and not more; but the first inconvenience was, it was up hill towards the creek. Well, to take away this discouragement, I resolved to dig into the surface of the earth, and so make a declivity; this I began, and it cost me a prodigious deal of pains; but who grudge pains that have their deliverance in view? But when this was worked through, and this difficulty managed, it was still much at one; for I could no more stir the canoe than I could the other boat.

Then I measured the distance of ground, and resolved to cut
a dock, or canal, to bring the water up to the canoe, seeing I
could not bring the canoe down to the water. Well, I began
this work, and when I began to enter into it, and calculated
how deep it was to be dug, how broad, how the stuff to be
thrown out, I found that by the number of hands I had, being
none but my own, it must have been ten or twelve years before
I should have gone through with it; for the shore lay high, so
that at the upper end it must have been at least twenty feet
deep; so at length, though with great reluctancy, I gave this
attempt over also.

This grieved me heartily; and now I saw, though too late, the
folly of beginning a work before we count the cost, and before
we judge rightly of our own strength to go through with it.

In the middle of this work I finished my fourth year in this
place, and kept my anniversary with the same devotion, and
with as much comfort, as ever before; for by a constant study,
and serious application of the word of God, and by the assistance of his grace, I gained a different knowledge from what I
had before. I entertained different notions of things; I looked
now upon the world as a thing remote; which I had nothing
to do with, no expectation from, and indeed no desires about;
in a word, I had nothing indeed to do with it, nor was ever
like to have; so I thought it looked, as we may perhaps look
upon it hereafter, namely as a place I had lived in, but was
come out of it. And well might I say, as Father Abraham to
Dives, "Between me and thee there is a great gulf fixed."

In the first place, I was removed from all the wickedness of
the world here: I had neither the lust of the flesh, the lust of
the eye, or the pride of life: I had nothing to covet, for I had
all I was now capable of enjoying. I was lord of the manor; or,
if I pleased, I might call myself king or emperor over the whole

country which I had possession of; there were no rivals; I had
no competitor, none to dispute sovereignty or command with
me. I might have raised ship-loadings of corn, but I had no use
for it; so I let as little grow as I thought enough for my occasion;
I had tortoises, or turtles enough; but now and then one was
as much as I could put to any use: I had timber enough to have
built a fleet of ships; I had grapes enough to have made wine,
or to have cured into raisins, to have loaded that fleet when
they had been built.

I had, as I hinted before, a parcel of money, as well gold as
silver, about thirty-six pounds sterling; alas! there the nasty,
sorry, useless stuff lay; I had no manner of business for it, and I
often thought with myself, that I would have given a handful
of it for a gross of tobacco-pipes, or for a hand-mill to grind my
corn; nay, I would have given it all for six-penny worth of turnip
and carrot seed out of England, or for a handful of pease and
beans, and a bottle of ink.

I had now been here so long, that many things which I
brought on shore for my help, were either quite gone, or very
much wasted, and near spent. My ink, as I observed, had been
gone for some time, all but a very little, which I eked out with
water a little and a little, till it was so pale it scarce left any
appearance of black upon the paper. As long as it lasted, I
made use of it to minute down the days of the month on which
any remarkable thing happened to me, and first, by casting up
times past, I remembered that there was a strange concurrence
of days, in the various providences which befell me, and which,
if I had been superstitiously inclined to observe days as fatal or
fortunate, I might have had reason to have looked upon with
a great deal of curiosity.

First, I had observed, that the same day that I broke away
from my father and my friends, and ran away to Hull in order

to go to sea, the same day afterwards I was taken by the Sallee man-of-war, and made a slave.

The same day of the year that I escaped out of the wreck of that ship in Yarmouth Roads, that same day of the year afterwards I made my escape from Sallee in the boat.

The same day of the year I was born on, namely, the 30th of September, the same day I had my life so miraculously saved 26 years after, when I was cast on shore in this island; so that my wicked life, and solitary life, both began on a day.

The next thing to my ink being wasted, was that of my bread, I mean the biscuit which I brought out of the ship. This I had husbanded to the last degree, allowing myself but one cake of bread a day for above a year, and yet I was quite without bread for near a year before I got any corn of my own; and great reason I had to be thankful that I had any at all, the getting it being, as has been already observed, next to miraculous.

My clothes too began to decay mightily: as to linen, I had had none a good while, except some checkered shirts which I found in the chests of the other seamen, and which I carefully preserved, because many times I could bear no other clothes on but a shirt; and it was a very great help to me, that I had among all the men's clothes of the ship almost three dozen of shirts. There were also several thick watch-coats of the seamen's, which were left indeed, but they were too hot to wear; and though it is true, that the weather was so violent hot that there was no need of clothes, yet I could not go quite naked; no, though I had been inclined to it, which I was not; nor could I abide the thoughts of it, though I was all alone.

One reason why I could not go quite naked, was, I could not bear the heat of the sun so well when quite naked, as with some clothes on; nay, the very heat frequently blistered my skin; whereas, with a shirt on, the air itself made some motion

nd whistling under the shirt, was twofold cooler than without
t. No more could I ever bring myself to go out in the heat of
he sun without a cap or hat; the heat of the sun beating with
uch violence as it does in that place, would give me the head-
che presently, by darting so directly on my head, without a
ap or hat on, so that I could not bear it; whereas if I put on
ny hat, it would presently go away.

Upon these views, I began to consider about putting the few
ags I had, which I called clothes, into some order. I had worn
ut all the waistcoats I had, and my business was now to try
f I could not make jackets out of the great watch-coats which
had by me, and with such other materials as I had; so I set to
vork a-tailoring, or rather indeed a-botching; for I made most
iteous work of it. However, I made shift to make two or three
vaist-coats, which I hoped would serve me a great while; as for
reeches or drawers, I made but a very sorry shift indeed, till
fterwards.

I have mentioned that I saved the skins of all the creatures
hat I killed, I mean four-footed ones; and I had hung them up
tretched out with sticks in the sun, by which means some of
hem were so dry and hard, that they were fit for little; but
thers, it seems, were very useful. The first thing I made of
hese was a great cap for my head, with the hair on the outside
o shoot off the rain, and this I performed so well, that after
his I made a suit of clothes wholly of those skins; that is to say,
waistcoat, and breeches open at the knees, and both loose;
or they were rather wanted to keep me cool than to keep me
varm. I must not omit to acknowledge that they were wretch-
dly made; for if I was a bad carpenter, I was a worse tailor;
owever, they were such as I made very good shift with; and
vhen I was abroad, if it happened to rain, the hair of the waist-
oat and cap being outmost, I was kept very dry.

After this I spent a deal of time and pains to make me an umbrella. I was indeed in great want of one, and had a great mind to make one. I had seen them made in the Brazils, where they are very useful in the great heats which are there; and I felt the heats every jot as great here, and greater too, being nearer the equinox; besides, as I was obliged to be much abroad, it was a most useful thing to me, as well for the rains as the heats. I took a world of pains at it, and was a great while before I could make anything likely to hold; nay, after I thought I had hit the way, I spoiled two or three before I made one to my mind; but at last I made one that answered indifferently well; the main difficulty I found was to make it to let down. I could make it to spread; but if it did not let down too, and draw in, it would not be portable for me any way, but just over my head, which would not do. However, at last, as I said, I made one to answer. I covered it with skins, the hair upwards, so that it cast off the rain like a penthouse, and kept off the sun so effectually, that I could walk out in the hottest of the weather with greater advantage than I could before in the coolest; and when I had no need of it, I could close it, and carry it under my arm.

Thus I lived mighty comfortably, my mind being entirely composed by resigning to the will of God, and throwing myself wholly upon the disposal of his Providence.

I cannot say, that after this, for five years, any extraordinary thing happened to me; but I lived on in the same course, in the same posture and place, just as before; the chief thing was employed in, besides my yearly labor of planting my barley and rice, and curing my raisins, of both which I always kept up just enough to have sufficient stock of the year's provision beforehand; I say, besides this yearly labor, and my daily labor of going out with my gun, I had one labor to make me a canoe which at last I finished: so that by digging a canal to it six feet wide, and four feet deep, I brought it into the creek, almost half a mile.

However, though my little periagua was finished, yet the size of it was not at all answerable to the design which I had in view, when I made the first; I mean of venturing over to the terra firma, where it was above forty miles broad; accordingly, the smallness of my boat assisted to put an end to that design, and now I thought no more of it. But as I had a boat, my next design was to make a tour round the island; for as I had been on the other side, in one place, crossing, as I have already described it, over the land, so the discoveries I made in that journey, made me very eager to see other parts of the coast; and now I had a boat, I thought of nothing but sailing round the island.

For this purpose, and that I might do everything with discretion and consideration, I fitted up a little mast to my boat, and made a sail to it out of some of the pieces of the ship's sails, which lay in store, and of which I had a great store by me.

Having fitted my mast and sail, and tried the boat, I found she would sail very well. Then I made little lockers and boxes at each end of my boat, to put provisions, necessaries, and ammunition, &c., into, to be kept dry, either from rain, or the spray of the sea; and a little long hollow place I cut in the inside of the boat, where I could lay my gun, making a flap to hang down over it to keep it dry.

I fixed my umbrella also in a step at the stern, like a mast, to stand over my head, and keep the heat of the sun off me, like an awning; and thus I every now and then took a little voyage upon the sea, but never went far out, nor far from the little creek. But at last, being eager to view the circumference of my little kingdom, I resolved upon my tour, and accordingly

I victualed my ship for the voyage; putting in two dozen of my loaves (cakes I should rather call them) of barley bread; an earthen pot full of parched rice, a food I ate a great deal of; a little bottle of rum, half a goat, and powder with shot for killing more, and two large watch-coats, of those which, as I mentioned before, I had saved out of the seamen's chests; these I took, one to lie upon, and the other to cover me in the night.

It was the sixth of November, in the sixth year of my reign, or my captivity, which you please, that I set out on this voyage, and I found it much longer than I expected; for though the island itself was not very large, yet when I came to the east side of it, I found a great ledge of rocks lie out about two leagues into the sea, some above water, some under it; and beyond this a shoal of sand, lying dry half a league more; so that I was obliged to go a great way out to sea to double that point.

When I first discovered them, I was going to give over my enterprise, and come back again, not knowing how far it might oblige me to go out to sea, and above all, doubting how I should get back again; so I came to an anchor, for I had made me a kind of an anchor, with a piece of broken grappling, which I got out of the ship.

Having secured my boat, I took my gun, and went on shore, climbing up a hill, which seemed to overlook that point, where I saw the full extent of it, and resolved to venture.

In my viewing the sea from that hill where I stood, I perceived a strong, and indeed, a most furious current, which ran to the east, and even came close to the point; and I took the more notice of it, because I saw there might be some danger, that when I came into it, I might be carried out to sea by the strength of it, and not be able to make the island again. And indeed, had I not gotten first upon this hill, I believe it would have been so; for there was the same current on the other side of the island, only that it set it off at a farther distance; and I saw there was a strong eddy under the shore; so I had nothing to do but to get out of the first current, and I should presently be in an eddy.

I lay here, however, two days; because the wind blowing pretty fresh (E. at S. E. and that being just contrary to the said current) made a great breach of the sea upon the point; so that it was not safe for me to keep too close to the shore for the breach, nor to go too far off because of the stream.

The third day in the morning, the wind having abated overnight, the sea was calm, and I ventured; but I am a warning-piece again to all rash and ignorant pilots; for no sooner was I come to the point, when I was not my boat's length from the shore, but I found myself in a great depth of water, and a cur-

rent like the sluice of a mill. It carried my boat along with it
with such violence, that all I could do could not keep her so
much as on the edge of it; but I found it hurried me farther
and farther out from the eddy, which was on the left hand.
There was no wind stirring to help me, and all that I could do
with my paddles signified nothing. And now I began to give
myself over for lost; for, as the current was on both sides of
the island, I knew in a few leagues' distance they must join
again, and then I was irrecoverably gone; nor did I see any possibility of avoiding it: so that I had no prospect before me but
of perishing; not by the sea, for that was calm enough, but of
starving for hunger. I had indeed found a tortoise on the shore,
as big almost as I could lift, and had tossed it into the boat; and
I had a great jar of fresh water, that is to say, one of my earthen
pots. But what was all this to being driven into the vast ocean,
where, to be sure, there was no shore, no mainland or island,
for a thousand leagues at least!

And now I saw how easy it was for the providence of God
to make the most miserable condition that mankind could be
in worse. Now I looked back upon my desolate, solitary island,
as the most pleasant place in the world, and that all the happiness my heart could wish for, was to be there again. I stretched
out my hands to it with eager wishes. O happy desert, said I, I
shall never see thee more! O miserable creature! said I, whither
am I going? Then I reproached myself with my unthankful
temper, and how I had repined at my solitary condition. And
now what would I give to be on shore there again! Thus we
never see the true state of our condition, till it is illustrated to
us by its contraries; nor know how to value what we enjoy, but
by the want of it. It is scarce possible to imagine the consternation I was now in, being driven from my beloved island (for
so it appeared to me now to be) into the wild ocean, almost

two leagues, and in the utmost despair of ever recovering it again. However, I worked hard, till indeed my strength was almost exhausted, and kept my boat as much to the northward, that is, towards the side of the current which the eddy lay on, as possibly I could; when about noon, as the sun passed the meridian, I thought I felt a little breeze of wind in my face, springing up from the S. S. E. This cheered my heart a little, and especially when in about half an hour more, it blew a pretty small gentle gale. By this time I was gotten at a frightful distance from the island; and, had the least cloud or hazy weather intervened, I had been undone another way too; for I had no compass on board, and should never have known how to have steered towards the island, if I had but once lost sight of it. But the weather continuing clear, I applied myself to get up my mast again, and spread my sail, standing away to the north as much as possible, to get out of the current.

Just as I had set my mast and sail, and the boat began to stretch away, I saw even by the clearness of the water, some alteration of the current was near; for where the current was so strong, the water was foul. But perceiving the water clear, I found the current abate, and presently I found to the east, at about half a mile, a breach of the sea upon some rocks. These rocks, I found, caused the current to part again; and as the main stress of it ran away more southerly, leaving the rocks to the northeast, so the other returned by the repulse of the rock, and made a strong eddy, which ran back again to the northwest with a very sharp stream.

They who know what it is to have a reprieve brought to them upon the ladder, or to be rescued from thieves just going to murder them, or who have been in such like extremities, may guess what my present surprise of joy was, and how gladly I put my boat into the stream of this eddy. And the wind also freshening, how gladly I spread my sail to it, running cheerfully before the wind, and with a strong tide or eddy under foot.

This eddy carried me about a league in my way back again directly towards the island, but about two leagues more towards the northward than the current lay, which carried me away at first; so that when I came near the island, I found myself open to the northern shore of it, that is to say, the other end of the island, opposite to that which I went out from.

When I had made something more than a league of way by the help of this current or eddy, I found it was spent, and served me no further. However, I found, that being between the two great currents, namely, that on the south side which had hurried me away, and that on the north, which lay about two leagues on the other side; I say, between these two, in the west of the island, I found the water at least still, and running no way; and having still a breeze of wind fair for me, I kept on steering directly for the island, though not making such fresh way as I did before.

About four o'clock in the evening, being then within about a league of the island, I stretched across this eddy, slanting northwest, and in about an hour came within about a mile of the shore; it being smooth water, I soon got to land.

When I was on shore, I fell on my knees, and gave God thanks for my deliverance, resolving to lay aside all thoughts of my deliverance by my boat; and refreshing myself with such things as I had, I brought my boat close to the shore, in a little cove that I had espied under some trees, and laid me down to sleep, being quite spent with the labor and fatigue of the voyage.

CHAPTER 13: *The years pass*

I WAS now at a great loss which way to get home with my boat. I had run so much hazard, and knew too much the case, to think of attempting it by the way I went out; and what might be at the other side (I mean the west side) I knew not, nor had I any mind to run any more ventures; so I only resolved in the morning to make my way westward along the shore, and to see if there was no creek where I might lay up my frigate in safety, so as to have her again if I wanted her. In about three miles, or thereabouts, coasting the shore, I came to a very good inlet, or bay, about a mile over, which narrowed till it came to a very little rivulet, or brook, where I found a convenient harbor for my boat, and where she lay as if she had been in a little dock made on purpose for her. Here I put in, and having stowed my boat very safe, I went on shore to look about me and see where I was. I soon found I had but a little passed by the place where I had been before when I travelled on foot to that shore; so taking nothing out of my boat but my gun and my umbrella, for it was exceeding hot, I began my march. The way was comfortable enough after such a voyage as I had been upon, and I reached my old bower in the evening, where I found everything standing as I left it; for I always kept it in good order, being, as I said before, my country-house.

I got over the fence, and laid me down in the shade to rest my limbs, for I was very weary, and fell asleep. But judge you, if you can, that read my story, what a surprise I must be in, when I was awaked out of my sleep by a voice calling me by my name several times, "Robin, Robin, Robin Crusoe, poor Robin Crusoe!" "Where are you, Robin Crusoe?" "Where are you?" "Where have you been?"

I was so dead asleep at first, being fatigued with rowing, or paddling, as it is called, the first part of the day, and walking the latter part, that I did not awake thoroughly; and dozing between sleeping and waking, thought I dreamed that somebody spoke to me; but as the voice continued to repeat "Robin Crusoe, Robin Crusoe," at last I began to awake more perfectly, and was at first dreadfully frighted, and started up in the utmost consternation. But no sooner were my eyes open, but I saw my Poll sitting on the top of the hedge, and immediately knew that this was he that spoke to me; for just in such bemoaning language I had used to talk to him, and teach him. And he had learned it so perfectly, that he would sit upon my finger, and lay his bill close to my face, and cry, "Poor Robin Crusoe, where are you?" "Where have you been?" "How come you here?"—and such things as I had taught him.

However, even though I knew it was the parrot, and that indeed it could be nobody else, it was a good while before I could compose myself. First, I was amazed how the creature got thither, and then how he should just keep about the place, and nowhere else: but as I was well satisfied it could be nobody but honest Poll, I got it over; and holding out my hand, calling him by his name, Poll, the sociable creature came to me, and sat upon my thumb, as he used to do, and continued talking to me, Poor Robin Crusoe, and how did I come here? and where had I been? just as if he had been overjoyed to see me again; and so I carried him home along with me.

I had enough of rambling to sea for some time, and enough to do for many days to sit still, and reflect upon the danger I had been in. I would have been very glad to have had my boat again on my side of the island, but I knew not how it was practicable to get it about. As to the east side of the island, which I had gone round, I knew well enough there was no venturing that way; my very heart would shrink, and my very blood run chill, but to think of it; and as to the other side of the island, I did not know how it might be there; but supposing the current ran with the same force against the shore at the east, as it passed by it on the other, I might run the same risk of being driven down the stream, and carried by the island, as I had been before of being carried away from it; so with these thoughts I contented myself to be without any boat, though it had been the product of many months' labor to make it, and of so many more to get it into the sea.

In this government of my temper I remained near a year, lived a very sedate, retired life, as you may well suppose; and my thoughts being very much composed as to my condition, and fully comforted in resigning myself to the dispensations of Providence, I thought I lived really very happily in all things except that of society.

I improved myself, in this time, in all the mechanic exercises which my necessities put me upon applying myself to; and I believe could, upon occasion, have made a very good carpenter, especially considering how few tools I had.

Besides this, I arrived at an unexpected perfection in my earthen ware, and contrived well enough to make them with a wheel, which I found infinitely easier and better, because I made things round and shapeable, which before were filthy things indeed to look on. But I think I never was more vain of my own performance, or more joyful for anything I found out, than for my being able to make a tobacco-pipe; and though it was a very ugly, clumsy thing when it was done, and only burnt red like other earthen ware, yet as it was very hard and firm, and would draw the smoke, I was exceedingly comforted with it; for I had always been used to smoke, and there were pipes in the ship, but I forgot them at first, not knowing there was tobacco in the island; and afterwards when I searched the ship again I could not come at any pipes at all.

In my wicker ware I also improved much, and made abundance of necessary baskets as well as my invention showed me, though not very handsome, yet convenient for my laying things up in, or fetching things home in. For example, if I killed a goat abroad, I could hang it up in a tree, flay it, and dress it, and cut it in pieces, and bring it home in a basket; and the like by a turtle; I could cut it up, take out the eggs, and a piece or two of the flesh, which was enough for me, and bring them home in a basket, and leave the rest behind me: also large deep baskets were my receivers for my corn, which I always rubbed out as soon as it was dry and cured; and kept it in great baskets instead of a granary.

I began now to perceive my powder abated considerably; and this was a want which it was impossible for me to supply; then I began seriously to consider what I must do when I should have no more powder; that is to say, how should I do to kill any goats. I had, as I observed, in the third year of my being here, kept a young kid and bred her tame. I was in hopes of getting a he-kid, but I could not by any means bring it to pass, till my kid grew an old goat; and I could never find in my heart to kill her, till she died at last of mere age.

But being now in the eleventh year of my residence, and, as I have said, my ammunition growing low, I set myself to study some art to trap and snare the goats, to see whether I could not catch some of them alive; and particularly I wanted a she-goat great with young. To this purpose I made snares to hamper them; and believe they were more than once taken in them; but my tackle was not good, for I had no wire, and always found them broken, and my bait devoured. At length I resolved to try a pit-fall; so I dug several large pits in the earth, in

I arrived at an unexpected perfection

places where I had observed the goats used to feed, and over these pits I placed hurdles of my own making too, with a great weight upon them; and several times I put ears of barley, and dry rice, without setting the trap; and I could easily perceive that the goats had gone in, and eaten up the corn, for I could see the marks of their feet; at length, I set three traps in one night, and going the next morning, I found them all standing, and yet the bait eaten and gone. This was very discouraging; however, I altered my trap; and, not to trouble you with particulars, going one morning to see my traps, I found in one of them a large old he-goat; and, in one of the others, three kids, a male and two females.

As to the old one, I knew not what to do with him; he was so fierce I durst not go into the pit to him; that is to say, to bring him away alive, which was what I wanted; I could have killed him, but that was not my business, nor would it answer my end; so I e'en let him out, and he ran away as if he had been frightened out of his wits; but I did not then know what I afterwards learned, that hunger would tame a lion: if I had let him stay there three or four days without food, and then have carried him some water to drink, and then a little corn, he would have been as tame as one of the kids; for they are mighty sagacious, tractable creatures, where they are well used.

However, for the present I let him go, knowing no better at that time; then I went to the three kids, and taking them one by one, I tied them with strings together; and with some difficulty brought them all home.

It was a good while before they would feed; but throwing them some sweet corn, it tempted them, and they began to be tame; and now I found that if I expected to supply myself with goat's flesh, when I had no powder or shot left, breeding some up tame was my only way, when perhaps I might have

them about my house like a flock of sheep. But then it presently occurred to me that I must keep the tame from the wild,
or else they would always run wild when they grew up; and
the only way for this was to have some inclosed piece of
ground, well fenced either with hedge or pale, to keep them
in so effectually that those within might not break out, or
these without break in.

This was a great undertaking for one pair of hands; yet as
I saw there was an absolute necessity of doing it, my first piece
of work was to find out a proper piece of ground; namely, where
there was likely to be herbage for them to eat, water for them
to drink, and cover to keep them from the sun.

Those who understand such inclosures, will think I had very
little contrivance, when I pitched upon a place very proper for
all these, being a plain open piece of meadow-land, or savanna
(as our people call it in the western colonies), which had two
or three little rills of fresh water in it, and at one end was very
woody; I say they will smile at my forecast, when I shall tell
them I began my inclosing of this piece of ground in such a
manner, that my hedge, or pale, must have been at least two
miles about; nor was the madness of it so great as to the compass; for if it was ten miles about, I was like to have time enough
to do it in; but I did not consider that my goats would be as
wild in so much compass, as if they had had the whole island;
and I should have so much room to chase them in that I should
never catch them.

My hedge was began and carried on, I believe, about fifty
yards, when this thought occurred to me; so I presently stopped
short, and for the first beginning I resolved to inclose a piece of
about 150 yards in length, and 100 yards in breadth, which, as
it would maintain as many as I should have in any reasonable
time, so, as my flock increased, I could add more ground to
my inclosure.

This was acting with some prudence, and I went to work with courage. I was about three months hedging in the first piece; and till I had done it, I tethered the three kids in the best part of it, and used them to feed as near me as possible, to make them familiar; and very often I would go and carry them some ears of barley, or a handful of rice, and feed them out of my hand; so that after my inclosure was finished, and I let them loose, they would follow me up and down, bleating after me for a handful of corn. This answered my end, and in about a year and a half I had a flock of about twelve goats, kids and all; and in two years more I had three-and-forty, besides several I took and killed for my food; and after that I inclosed five several pieces of ground to feed them in, with little pens to drive them into, to take them as I wanted them; and gates out of one piece of ground into another.

But this was not all; for now I not only had goat's flesh to feed on when I pleased, but milk, too, a thing which indeed in my beginning I did not so much as think of, and which, when it came into my thoughts, was really an agreeable surprise; for now I sat up my dairy, and had sometimes a gallon or two of milk in a day. And as Nature, who gives supplies of food to every creature, dictates even naturally how to make use of it, so I, that had never milked a cow, much less a goat, or seen butter or cheese made, very readily and handily, though after a great many essays and miscarriages, made me both butter and cheese at last, and never wanted it afterwards.

How mercifully can our great Creator treat his creatures, even in those conditions in which they seemed to be overwhelmed in destruction! How can he sweeten the bitterest providences, and give us cause to praise him for dungeons and prisons! What a table was here spread for me in a wilderness, where I saw nothing at first but to perish for hunger!

It would have made a stoic smile, to have seen me and my little family sit down to dinner: there was my majesty, the prince and lord of the whole island! I had the lives of all my subjects at absolute command; I could hang, draw, give liberty, and take it away, and no rebels among all my subjects!

Then to see how like a king I dined, too, all alone, attended by my servants! Poll, as if he had been my favorite, was the only person permitted to talk to me; my dog, which was now grown old and crazy, and found no species to multiply his kind upon, sat always at my right hand; and two cats, one on one side the table, and one on the other, expecting now and then a bit from my hand as a mark of special favor.

But these were not the two cats which I brought on shore at first, for they were both of them dead, and had been interred near my habitation by my own hands; but one of them having multiplied by I know not what kind of creature, these were two which I preserved tame, whereas the rest ran wild into the woods, and became indeed troublesome to me at last; for they would often come into my house, and plunder me too, till at last I was obliged to shoot them, and did kill a great many. At length they left me with this attendance, and in this plentiful manner I lived; neither could I be said to want anything but society, and of that, in some time after this, I was like to have too much.

I was something impatient, as I have observed, to have the use of my boat, though very loth to run any more hazard: and therefore sometimes I sat contriving ways to get her about the island, and at other times I sat myself down contented enough without her. But I had a strange uneasiness in my mind to go down to the point of the island, where, as I have said, in my last ramble, I went up the hill to see how the shore lay and how the current set, that I might see what I had to do: this inclina-

tion increased upon me every day; and at length I resolved to travel thither by land, and following the edge of the shore, I did so: but had any one in England been to meet such a man as I was, it must either have frighted them or raised a great deal of laughter; and, as I frequently stood still to look at myself, I could not but smile at the notion of my travelling through Yorkshire with such an equipage, and in such a dress. I had a great high shapeless cap, made of goat's-skin, with a flap hanging down behind, as well to keep the sun from me, as to shoot the rain off from running into my neck; nothing being so hurtful in these climates as the rain upon the flesh under the clothes. I had a short jacket of goat's-skin, the skirts coming down to about the middle of my thighs, and a pair of open-kneed breeches of the same; the breeches were made of the skin of an old he-goat, whose hair hung down such a length on either side, that, like pantaloons, it reached to the middle of my legs. Stockings and shoes I had none, but I made me a pair of something, I scarce know what to call them, like buskins, to flap over my legs, and lace on either side like spatterdashes; but of a most barbarous shape, as indeed were all the rest of my clothes.

I had on a broad belt of goat's-skin dried, which I drew together with two thongs of the same, instead of buckles; and in a kind of frog on either side of this, instead of a sword and dagger, hung a little saw and hatchet; one on one side, one on the other: I had another belt not so broad, and fastened in the same manner, which hung over my shoulder; and at the end of it, under my left arm, hung two pouches, both made of goat's-skin too; in one of which hung my powder, in the other my shot: at my back I carried my basket, on my shoulder my gun, and over my head a great clumsy ugly goat's-skin umbrella, but which, after all, was the most necessary thing I had about me, next to my gun: as for my face, the color of it was really not so Mulatto-like as one might expect from a man not at all careful of it, and living within nine or ten degrees of the equinox. My beard I had once suffered to grow till it was about a quarter of a yard long; but as I had both scissors and razors sufficient, I had cut it pretty short, except what grew on my upper lip, which I had trimmed into a large pair of Mahometan whiskers, such as I had seen worn by some Turks whom I saw at Sallee: for the Moors did not wear such though the Turks did. Of these mustachios, or whiskers, I will not say they were long enough to hang my hat upon them; but they were of length and shape monstrous enough, and such as in England would have passed for frightful.

But all this is by-the-by; for, as to my figure, I had so few to observe me that it was no manner of consequence, so I say no more to that part: in this kind of figure I went my new journey, and was out five or six days. I travelled first along the sea-shore, directly to the place where I first brought my boat to an anchor to get up upon the rocks, and having no boat now to take care of it, I went over the land a nearer way to the same height that I was upon before; when looking forward to the point of the rock I was obliged to double with my boat, as I said above, I was surprised to see the sea all smooth and quiet; no rippling, no motion, no current, any more there than in other places.

I was at a strange loss to understand this, and resolved to spend some time in the observing of it, to see if nothing from the sets of the tide had occasioned it; but I was presently convinced how it was; namely, that the tide of ebb setting from the west, and joining with the current of waters from some great river on the shore, must be the occasion of this current; and that, accordingly as the wind blew more forcibly from the west, or from the north, this current came nearer or went farther from the shore; for, waiting thereabouts till evening, I went up to the rock again, and then the tide of ebb being made, I plainly saw the current again as before, only that it ran farther off, being near half a league from the shore: whereas in my case it set close upon the shore, and hurried me and my canoe along with it, which at another time it would not have done.

This observation convinced me that I had nothing to do but to observe the ebbing and the flowing of the tide, and I might very easily bring my boat about the island again. But when I began to think about putting it in practice I had such terror upon my spirits at the remembrance of the danger I had been in, that I could not think of it again with any patience; but, on the contrary, I took up another resolution, which was more safe, though more laborious; and this was, that I would build, or rather make me another periagua, or canoe and so have one for one side of the island, and one for the other.

You are to understand that now I had, as I may call it, two plantations in the island; one, my little fortification or tent, with the wall about it under the rock, with the cave behind me, which by this time I had enlarged into several apartments or caves, one within another. One of these, which was the driest and largest, and had a door yet beyond my wall or fortification, that is to say, beyond where my wall joined to the rock, was all filled up with large earthen pots, of which I have given an account, and with fourteen or fifteen great baskets, which would hold five or six bushels each, where I laid up my stores of provision, especially my corn, some in the ear cut off short from the straw, and the other rubbed out with my hands.

As for my wall, made as before, with long stakes or piles, those piles grew all like trees, and were by this time grown so big, and spread so very much, that there was not the least appearance, to any one's view, of any habitation behind them.

Near this dwelling of mine, but a little farther within the land, and upon lower ground, lay my two pieces of corn-ground, which I kept duly cultivated and sowed, and which duly yielded me their harvest in its season; and whenever I had occasion for more corn, I had more land adjoining as fit as that.

Besides this, I had my country-seat, and I had now a tolerable plantation there also; for, first, I had my little bower, as I called it, which I kept in repair; that is to say, I kept the hedge which circled it in constantly fitted up to its usual height, the ladder standing always in the inside: I kept the trees, which at first were no more than my stakes, but were now grown very firm and tall,—I kept them always so cut, that they might spread and grow thick and wild, and make the more agreeable shade, which they did effectually to my mind. In the middle of this I had my tent always standing, being a piece of sail spread over poles set up for that purpose, and which never wanted any repair or renewing; and under this I had made me a squab or couch, with the skins of the creatures I had killed, and with other soft things, and a blanket laid on them, such as belonged to our sea-bedding, which I had saved, and a great watch-coat to cover me; and here, whenever I had occasion to be absent from my chief seat, I took up my country habitation.

Adjoining to this I had my inclosures for my cattle, that is to say, my goats; and as I had taken an inconceivable deal of pains to fence and inclose this ground, I was so uneasy to see it kept entire, lest the goats should break through, that I never left off, till with infinite labor I had stuck the outside of the hedge so full of small stakes, and so near to one another, that it was rather a pale than a hedge, and there was scarce room to put a hand through between them, which afterwards, when those stakes grew, as they all did in the next rainy season, made the inclosure strong like a wall, indeed stronger than any wall.

This will testify for me that I was not idle, and that I spared no pains to bring to pass whatever appeared necessary for my comfortable support; for I considered the keeping up a breed of tame creatures thus at my hand would be a living magazine of flesh, milk, butter, and cheese for me, as long as I lived in the place, if it were to be forty years; and that keeping them in my reach depended entirely upon my perfecting my inclosures to such a degree that I might be sure of keeping them together; which, by this method, indeed, I so effectually secured that, when these little stakes began to grow, I had planted them so very thick I was forced to pull some of them up again.

In this place also I had my grapes growing, which I principally depended on for my winter store of raisins, and which I never failed to preserve very carefully as the best and most agreeable dainty of my whole diet; and indeed they were not only agreeable, but physical, wholesome, nourishing, and refreshing to the last degree.

As this was also about half way between my other habitation and the place where I had laid up my boat, I generally stayed and lay here in my way thither; for I used frequently to visit my boat, and I kept all things about or belonging to her in very good order. Sometimes I went out in her to divert myself, but no more hazardous voyages would I go, nor scarce ever above a stone's cast or two from the shore, I was so apprehensive of being hurried out of my knowledge again by the currents, or winds, or any other accident. But now I come to a new scene of my life.

CHAPTER 14: *The strange footprint*

IT HAPPENED one day about noon, going towards my boat, I was exceedingly surprised with the print of a man's naked foot on the shore, which was very plain to be seen in the sand. I stood like one thunderstruck, or as if I had seen an apparition. I lis-

tened, I looked round me; I could hear nothing, nor see any-thing; I went up to a rising ground to look farther. I went up the shore, and down the shore, but it was all one, I could see no other impression but that one. I went to it again, to see if there were any more, and to observe if it might not be my fancy, but there was no room for that, for there was exactly the very print of a foot, toes, heel, and every part of a foot: how it came thither I knew not, nor could in the least imagine. But after innumerable fluttering thoughts, like a man perfectly con-fused, and out of myself, I came home to my fortification, not feeling, as we say, the ground I went on, but terrified to the last degree, looking behind me at every two or three steps, mis-taking every bush and tree, and fancying every stump at a dis-tance to be a man. Nor is it possible to describe how many various shapes an affrighted imagination represented things to me in; how many wild ideas were formed every moment in my fancy, and what strange unaccountable whimsies came into my thoughts by the way.

When I came to my castle, for so I think I called it ever after this, I fled into it like one pursued; whether I went over by the ladder, as first contrived, or went in at the hole in the rock, which I called a door, I cannot remember; no, nor could I remember the next morning; for never frighted hare fled to cover, or fox to earth, with more terror of mind than I to this retreat.

I had no sleep that night; the farther I was from the occasion of my fright the greater my apprehensions were; which is some-thing contrary to the nature of such things, and especially to the usual practice of all creatures in fear. But I was so em-barrassed with my own frightful ideas of the thing, that I formed nothing but dismal imaginations to myself, even though I was now a great way off it.

At last I concluded that it must be some more dangerous creature; namely, that it must be some of the savages of the main-land over against me, who had wandered out to sea in their canoes, and, either driven by the currents or by contrary winds, had made the island, and had been on shore, but were going away again to sea, being as loath, perhaps to have stayed in this desolate island as I would have been to have had them.

While these reflections were rolling upon my mind, I was very thankful in my thought that I was so happy as not to be thereabouts at that time, or that they did not see my boat, by which they would have concluded that some inhabitants had been in the place, and perhaps have searched farther for me. Then terrible thoughts racked my imaginations about their having found my boat, and that there were people here; and that, if so, I should certainly have them come again in great numbers, and devour me; that if it should happen so that they should not find me, yet they would find my inclosure, destroy all my corn, carry away all my flock of tame goats, and I should perish at last for mere want.

Thus my fear banished all my religious hope; all that former confidence in God which was founded upon such wonderful experience as I had had of his goodness, now vanished; as if he that had fed me by miracle hitherto, could not preserve by his power the provision which he had made for me by his goodness. I reproached myself with my easiness, that would not sow any more corn one year than would just serve me till the next season, as if no accident could intervene to prevent my enjoying the crop that was upon the ground. And this I thought so just a reproof, that I resolved for the future to have two or three years' corn beforehand, so that whatever might come, I might not perish for want of bread.

These thoughts took me up many hours, days, nay, I may

say, weeks and months; and one particular effect of my cogitations on this occasion I cannot omit; namely, one morning
early, lying in bed and filled with thoughts about my danger
from the appearance of savages, I found it discomposed me
very much; upon which those words of the Scripture came into
my thoughts, "Call upon me in the day of trouble, and I will
deliver thee, and thou shalt glorify me."

In the middle of these cogitations, apprehensions, and reflections, it came into my thoughts one day, that all this might be
a mere chimera of my own, and that this foot might be the
print of my own foot when I came on shore from my boat.
This cheered me up a little too, and I began to persuade myself
it was all a delusion; that it was nothing else but my own foot;
and why might not I come that way from the boat as well as
I was going that way to the boat? Again, I considered also that
I could by no means tell for certain where I had trod, and
where I had not; and that, if at last this was only the print of
my own foot, I had played the part of those fools who strive to
make stories of spectres and apparitions, and then are themselves frighted at them more than anybody else.

Now I began to take courage, and to peep abroad again; for
I had not stirred out of my castle for three days and nights, so
that I began to starve for provision; for I had little of nothing
within doors but some barley cakes and water. Then I knew
that my goats wanted to be milked too, which usually was my
evening diversion; and the poor creatures were in great pain and
inconvenience for want of it; and indeed it almost spoiled some
of them, and almost dried up their milk.

Heartening myself, therefore, with the belief that this was
nothing but the print of one of my own feet (and so I might be
truly said to start at my own shadow), I began to go abroad
again, and went to my country-house to milk my flock; but to

see with what fear I went forward, how often I looked behind me, how I was ready, every now and then, to lay down my basket, and run for my life; it would have made any one have thought I was haunted with an evil conscience, or that I had been lately most terribly frighted; and so indeed I had.

However, as I went down thus two or three days, and having seen nothing, I began to be a little bolder, and to think there was really nothing in it but my imagination; but I could not persuade myself fully of this till I should go down to the shore again, and see this print of a foot, and measure it by my own, and see if there was any similitude of fitness, that I might be assured it was my own foot. But when I came to the place first, it appeared evidently to me, that when I laid up my boat, I could not possibly be on shore anywhere thereabouts. Secondly, when I came to measure the mark with my own foot, I found my foot not so large by a great deal. Both these things filled my head with new imaginations, and gave me the vapors again to the highest degree, so that I shook with cold like one in an ague, and I went home again, filled with the belief that some man or men had been on shore there; or, in short, that the island was inhabited, and I might be surprised before I was aware; and what course to take for my security I knew not.

This confusion of my thoughts kept me waking all night, but in the morning I fell asleep, and having by the amusement of my mind been, as it were, tired, and my spirits exhausted, I slept very soundly, and awaked much better composed than I had ever been before. And now I began to think sedately; and, upon the utmost debate with myself, I concluded that this island, which was so exceeding pleasant, fruitful, and no farther from the main-land than as I had seen, was not so entirely abandoned as I might imagine. That although there were no stated inhabitants who lived on the spot, yet that there might sometimes come boats off from the shore, who either with design, or perhaps never but when they were driven by cross winds, might come to this place.

That I had lived here fifteen years now and had not met with the least shadow or figure of any people before; and that, if at any time they should be driven here, it was probable they went away again as soon as ever they could, seeing they had never though fit to fix there upon any occasion to this time.

That the most I could suggest any danger from was from any such casual accidental landing of straggling people from the main, who, as it was likely, if they were driven hither, were here against their wills; so they made no stay here, but went off again with all possible speed, seldom staying one night on shore lest they should not have the help of the tides and daylight back again. And that, therefore, I had nothing to do but to consider of some safe retreat, in case I should see any savages land upon the spot.

Now I began sorely to repent that I had dug my cave so large as to bring a door through again, which door, as I said, came out beyond where my fortification joined to the rock. Upon maturely considering this, therefore, I resolved to draw me a second fortification, in the manner of a semicircle, at a distance from my wall, just where I planted a double row of trees about twelve years before, of which I made mention; these trees having been planted so thick before there wanted but a few piles to be driven between them, that they should be thicker and stronger, and my wall would be finished.

So that I had now a double wall, and my outer wall was thickened with pieces of timber, old cables, and everything I could think of to make it strong; having in it seven holes about as big as I might put my arm out at. In the inside of this I thickened my wall to about ten feet thick, continually bringing earth out of my cave, and laying it at the foot of the wall, and walking upon it; and through the seven holes I contrived to plant muskets, of which I took notice that I got seven on shore out of the ship; these, I say, I planted like my cannon, and fitted them into frames that held them like a carriage, that so I could fire all the seven guns in two minutes' time: this wall I was many a weary month in finishing, and yet never thought myself safe till it was done.

When this was done, I stuck all the ground without my wall, for a great way every way, as full with stakes or sticks of the osier-like wood, which I found so apt to grow, as they could well stand; insomuch that I believe I might set in near twenty thousand of them, leaving a pretty large space between them and my wall, that I might have room to see an enemy, and they might have no shelter from the young trees, if they attempted to approach my outer wall.

Thus in two years' time I had a thick grove, and in five or six years' time I had a wood before my dwelling, grown so monstrous thick and strong that it was indeed perfectly impassable; and no man of what kind soever would ever imagine that there was anything beyond it, much less a habitation. As for the way I proposed myself to go in and out (for I left no avenue), it was by setting two ladders, one to a part of the rock which was low, and then broke in, and left room to place another ladder upon that; so, when the two ladders were taken down, no man living could come down to me without mischiefing himself; and if they had come down, they were still on the outside of my outer wall.

Thus I took all the measures human prudence could suggest for my own preservation; and it will be seen at length, that they were not altogether without just reason, though I foresaw nothing at that time more than my mere fear suggested.

CHAPTER 15: *In which I come upon the remains of a cannibal orgy, and am beset by new problems*

WHILE THIS was doing I was not altogether careless of my other affairs; for I had a great concern upon me for my little herd of goats: they were not only a present supply to me upon every occasion, and began to be sufficient for me without the expense of powder and shot, but also abated the fatigue of my hunting after the wild ones; and I was loath to lose the advantage of them, and to have them all to nurse up over again.

To this purpose, after long consideration, I could think but of two ways to preserve them; one was to find another convenient place to dig a cave under ground, and to drive them into it every night; and the other was to inclose two or three little bits of land, remote from one another, and as much concealed as I could, where I might keep about half a dozen young goats in each place; so that if any disaster happened to the flock in general, I might be able to raise them again with little trouble and time; and this, though it would require a great deal of time and labor, I thought was the most rational design.

Accordingly I spent some time to find out the most retired parts of the island, and I pitched upon one, which was as private, indeed, as my heart could wish; for it was a little damp piece of ground in the middle of the hollow and thick woods where, as is observed, I almost lost myself once before, endeavoring to come back that way from the eastern part of the island. Here I found a clear piece of land, near three acres, so surrounded with woods that it was almost an inclosure by nature at least it did not want near so much labor to make it so as the other pieces of ground I had worked so hard at.

I immediately went to work with this piece of ground, and
178

less than a month's time I had so fenced it round that my
ck or herd, call it which you please, which were not so wild
w as at first they might be supposed to be, were well enough
:ured in it. So, without any farther delay, I removed ten she-
ats and two he-goats to this piece; and when there, I con-
1ued to perfect the fence till I made it as secure as the other,
1ich, however, I did at more leisure, and it took me up more
ne by a great deal.

All this labor I was at the expense of purely from my appre-
:nsions on the account of the print of a man's foot which I
1d seen; for as yet I never saw any human creature come near
.e island, and I had now lived two years under these uneasi-
:sses, which indeed made my life much less comfortable than
was before, as may well be imagined by any who know what
is to live in the constant snare of the fear of man.

But to go on; after I had thus secured one part of my little
ving stock, I went about the whole island searching for an-
.her private place to make such another deposit; when wan-
:ring more to the west point of the island than I had ever done
:t, and looking out to sea, I thought I saw a boat upon the sea
. a great distance. I had found a perspective glass or two in one
f the seamen's chests, which I saved out of our ship; but I had
not about me; and this was so remote that I could not tell
:hat to make of it, though I looked at it till my eyes were not
ble to look any longer. Whether it was a boat or not I do not
now; but as I descended from the hill I could see no more of
, so I gave it over, only I resolved to go no more without a per-
>ective glass in my pocket.

When I was come down the hill, to the end of the island,
:here indeed I had never been before, I was presently convinced
hat the seeing the print of a man's foot was not such a strange
hing in the island as I imagined; and, but that it was a special

Providence that I was cast upon the side of the island whe
the savages never came, I should easily have known that not
ing was more frequent than for the canoes from the main, who
they happened to be a little too far out at sea, to shoot over
that side of the island for harbor; likewise, as they often m
and fought in their canoes, the victors, having taken any pri
oners, would bring them over to this shore, where, according
their dreadful customs, being all cannibals, they would kill an
eat them; of which hereafter.

When I was come down the hill to the shore, as I said abov
being the S. W. point of the island, I was perfectly confounde
and amazed; nor is it possible for me to express the horror o
my mind at seeing the shore spread with skulls, hands, feet, an
other bones of human bodies; and particularly I observed
place where there had been a fire made, and a circle dug in th
earth, like a cock-pit, where it is supposed the savage wretche
had sat down to their inhuman feastings upon the bodies o
their fellow-creatures.

I was so astonished with the sight of these things that I en
tertained no notions of any danger to myself from it for a lon
while; all my apprehensions were buried in the thoughts of such
a pitch of inhuman, hellish brutality, and the horror of th
degeneracy of human nature; which, though I had heard o
often, yet I never had so near a view of before; in short,
turned away my face from the horrid spectacle, my stomach
grew sick, and I was just at the point of fainting, when natur
discharged the disorder from my stomach, and, having vomited
with an uncommon violence, I was a little relieved, but could
not bear to stay in the place a moment; so I got me up the hill
again with all the speed I could, and walked on towards my own
habitation.

When I came a little out of that part of the island I stood still

awhile as amazed; and then, recovering myself, I looked up wi
the utmost affection of my soul, and, with a flood of tears in 1
eyes, gave God thanks that had cast my first lot in a p
of the world where I was distinguished from such dreadful cr
tures as these; and though I had esteemed my present con
tion very miserable, had yet given me so many comforts in
that I had still more to give thanks for than to complain of; a
this above all, that I had, even in this miserable condition, be
comforted with the knowledge of himself, and the hope of 1
blessing, which was a felicity more than sufficiently equivale
to all the misery which I had suffered or could suffer.

In this frame of thankfulness I went home to my castle a
began to be much easier now, as to the safety of my circur
stances, than ever I was before; for I observed that the
wretches never came to this island in search of what they cou
get; perhaps not seeking, nor wanting, or not expecting ar
thing here; and having often, no doubt, been up in the cover
woody part of it without finding anything to their purpose.
knew I had been here now almost eighteen years, and never sa
the least footsteps of a human creature there before; and mig
be here eighteen years more as entirely concealed as I was no
if I did not discover myself to them, which I had no manner
occasion to do, it being my only business to keep myself entire
concealed where I was, unless I found a better sort of creatur
than cannibals to make myself known to.

Yet I entertained such an abhorrence of the savage wretch
that I have been speaking of, and of the wretched inhuman cu
tom of their devouring and eating one another up, that I co
tinued pensive and sad, and kept close within my own circle f
almost two years after this: when I say my own circle, I me
by it my three plantations, namely, my castle, my country-sea
which I called my bower, and my inclosure in the woods; n

lid I look after this for any other use than as an inclosure for
my goats; for the aversion which nature gave me to these hellish
wretches was such, that I was as fearful of seeing them as of
seeing the devil himself; nor did I so much as go to look after my
boat in all this time, but began rather to think of never making
any more attempts to bring the other boat round the island
to me, lest I should meet wth some of these creatures at sea, in
which, if I had happened to have fallen into their hands, I knew
what would have been my lot.

Time, however, and the satisfaction I had that I was in no
danger of being discovered by these people, began to wear off
my uneasiness about them; and I began to live just in the same
composed manner as before, only with this difference, that I
used more caution, and kept my eyes more about me than I did
before, lest I should happen to be seen by any of them; and
particularly, I was more cautious of firing my gun, lest any of
them being on the island should happen to hear it; and it was
therefore a very good providence to me, that I had furnished
myself with a tame breed of goats, that I had no need to hunt
any more about the woods, or shoot at them, and if I did catch
any more of them after this, it was with traps and snares, as I
had done before; so that for two years after this, I believe I
never fired my gun once off, though I never went out without it;
and, which was more, as I had saved three pistols out of the
ship, I always carried them out with me, or at least two of them,
sticking them in my goat-skin belt. I likewise furbished up one
of the great cutlasses that I had out of the ship, and made me a
belt to put it in also; so that I was now a most formidable fellow
to look at when I went abroad, if you add to the former description of myself the particular of two pistols, and a great broad-
sword hanging at my side in a belt, but without a scabbard.

Things going on thus, as I have said, for some time, I seemed, excepting these cautions, to be reduced to my former calm sedate way of living; all these things tended to show me more and more how far my condition was from being miserable, compared to some others; nay, to many other particulars of life which it might have pleased God to have made my lot. It put me upon reflecting, how little repining there would be among mankind, at any condition of life, if people would rather compare their condition with those that are worse, in order to be thankful, than be always comparing them with those which are better, to assist their murmurings and complainings.

As in my present condition there were not really many things which I wanted, so indeed I thought the frights I had been in about these savage wretches, and the concern I had been in for my own preservation, had taken off the edge of my invention for my own conveniences; and I had dropt a good design, which I had once bent my thoughts upon; and that was, to try if I could not make some of my barley into malt, and then try to brew myself some beer: this was really a whimsical thought, and I reproved myself often for the simplicity of it; for I presently saw there would be the want of several things necessary to the making my beer, that it would be impossible for me to supply; as, first, casks to preserve it in, which was a thing that, as I have observed already, I could never compass; no, though I spent not many days, but weeks, nay months, in attempting it, but to no purpose. In the next place I had no hops to make it keep, no yeast to make it work, no copper or kettle to make it boil; and yet, had not all these things intervened, I mean the frights and terrors I was in about the savages, I had undertaken it, and perhaps brought it to pass too; for I seldom gave anything over without accomplishing it, when I once had it in my head enough to begin it.

But my invention now ran quite another way; for night and

day I could think of nothing but how I might destroy some of these monsters in their cruel bloody entertainment, and, if possible, save the victim they should bring hither to destroy. It would take up a larger volume than this whole work is intended to be to set down all the contrivances I hatched, or rather brooded upon in my thoughts, for the destroying these creatures, or at least frightening them, so as to prevent their coming hither any more; but all was abortive; nothing could be possible to take effect unless I was to be there to do it myself; and what could one man do among them, when perhaps there might be twenty or thirty of them together, with their darts, or their bows and arrows, with which they could shoot as true to a mark as I could with my gun?

Sometimes I contrived to dig a hole under the place where they made their fire, and put in five or six pounds of gunpowder, which, when they kindled their fire, would consequently take fire, and blow up all that was near it; but, as in the first place I should be very loath to waste so much powder upon them, my store being now within the quantity of a barrel, so neither could I be sure of its going off at any certain time when it might surprise them; and, at best, that it would do but little more than just blow the fire about their ears and fright them, but not sufficient to make them forsake the place; so I laid it aside, and then proposed that I would place myself in ambush, in some convenient place, with my three guns all double-loaded, and in the middle of their bloody ceremony let fly at them, when I should be sure to kill or wound perhaps two or three at every shot: and then falling in upon them with my three pistols and my sword, I made no doubt but that, if there were twenty, I should kill them all: this fancy pleased my thoughts for some weeks, and I was so full of it that I often dreamt of it, and sometimes, that I was just going to let fly at them in my sleep.

I went so far with it in my indignation, that I employed myself several days to find out proper places to put myself in ambuscade, as I said, to watch for them; and I went frequently to the place itself, which was now grown more familiar to me and especially while my mind was thus filled with thoughts of revenge, and of a bloody putting twenty or thirty of them to the sword, as I may call it; but the horror I had at the place, and at the signals of the barbarous wretches devouring one another abated my malice.

Well, at length I found a place in the side of the hill, where I was satisfied I might securely wait till I saw any of the boats coming, and might then, even before they would be ready to come on shore, convey myself unseen into thickets of trees, in one of which there was a hollow large enough to conceal me entirely, and where I might sit and observe all their bloody doings, and take my full aim at their heads, when they were close together so that it would be next to impossible that I should miss my shoot, or that I could fail wounding three or four of them at the first shoot.

In this place, then, I resolved to fix my design, and accordingly I prepared two muskets and my ordinary fowling-piece. The two muskets I loaded with a brace of slugs each, and four or five smaller bullets, about the size of pistol-bullets, and the fowling-piece I loaded with near a handful of swan-shot of the largest size; I also loaded my pistols with about four bullets each; and in this posture, well provided with ammunition for a second and third charge, I prepared myself for my expedition.

After I had thus laid the scheme for my design, and in my imagination put it in practice, I continually made my tour every morning up to the top of the hill, which was from my castle, as I called it, about three miles or more, to see if I could observe any boats upon the sea coming near the island, or standing over towards it: but I began to tire of this hard duty, after I had for two or three months constantly kept my watch; but came always back without any discovery, there having not in all that time been the least appearance, not only on or near the shore, but not on the whole ocean, so far as my eyes or glasses could reach every way.

As long as I kept up my daily tour to the hill to look out, so long also I kept up the vigor of my design, and my spirits seemed to be all the while in a suitable frame for so outrageous an execution as the killing twenty or thirty naked savages, for an offense which I had not at all entered into a discussion of in my thoughts, any further than my passions were at first fired by the horror I conceived at the unnatural custom of the people of that country, who, it seems, had been suffered by Providence, in his wise disposition of the world, to have no other guide than that of their own abominable and vitiated passions; and, consequently, were left, and perhaps had been for some ages, to act such horrid things, and receive such dreadful customs as nothing but nature entirely abandoned of Heaven, and actuated by some hellish degeneracy, could have run them into; but now, when, as I have said, I began to be weary of the fruitless excursion which I had made so long, and so far, every morning in vain; so my opinion of the action itself began to alter, and I began, with cooler and calmer thoughts, to consider what it was I was going to engage in; what authority or call I had to pretend to be judge and executioner upon these men as criminals, whom Heaven had thought fit for so many ages to suffer, unpunished, to go on, and to be, as it were, the executioners of his judgments upon one another; also, how far these people were offenders against me, and what right I had to engage in the quarrel of that blood which they shed promiscuously one upon another. I debated this very often with myself thus: How do I know what

God himself judges in this particular case? It is certain these people do not commit this as a crime; it is not against their own consciences reproving, or their light reproaching them. They do not know it to be an offense, and then commit it in defiance of divine justice, as we do in almost all the sins we commit. They think it no more a crime to kill a captive taken in war, than we do to kill an ox; nor to eat human flesh, than we do to eat mutton.

When I had considered this a little, it followed necessarily that I was certainly in the wrong in it; that these people were not murderers in the sense that I had before condemned them in my thoughts, any more than those Christians were murderers, who often put to death the prisoners taken in battle, or more frequently, upon many occasions, put whole troops of men to the sword, without giving quarter, though they threw down their arms and submitted.

In the next place, it occurred to me, that albeit the usage they gave one another was thus brutish and inhuman, yet it was really nothing to me: these people had done me no injury: that if they attempted me, or if I saw it necessary for my immediate preservation to fall upon them, something might be said for it; but that I was yet out of their power, and they had really no knowledge of me, and consequently no design upon me; and therefore it could not be just for me to fall upon them: that this would justify the conduct of the Spaniards, in all their barbarities practiced in America, where they destroyed millions of these people, who, however they were idolaters and barbarians, and had several bloody and barbarous rites in their customs, such as sacrificing human bodies to their idols, were yet, as to the Spaniards, very innocent people; and that the rooting them out of the country is spoken of with the utmost abhorrence and detestation, even by the Spaniards themselves, at this time, and by all other Christian nations of Europe, as a mere butchery, a bloody and unnatural piece of cruelty, unjustifiable either to God or man; and such, as for which the very name of a Spaniard is reckoned to be frightful and terrible to all people of humanity, or of Christian compassion; as if the kingdom of Spain were particularly eminent for the product of a race of men who were without principles of tenderness, or the common bowels of pity to the miserable, which is reckoned to be a mark of a generous temper in the mind.

These considerations really put me to a pause, and to a kind of full stop; and I began by little and little to be off my design, and to conclude I had taken a wrong measure in my resolutions to attack the savages; that it was not my business to meddle with them, unless they first attacked me, and this it was my business, if possible, to prevent; but that, if I were discovered and attacked, then I knew my duty.

On the other hand, I argued with myself, that this really was the way, not to deliver myself, but entirely to ruin and destroy myself; for unless I was sure to kill every one that not only should be on shore at that time, but that should ever come on shore afterwards, if but one of them escaped to tell their country-people what had happened, they would come over again by thousands to revenge the death of their fellows; and I should only bring upon myself a certain destruction, which at present I had no manner of occasion for. Upon the whole, I concluded, that neither in principles nor in policy, I ought one way or other to concern myself in this affair: that my business was by all possible means to conceal myself from them, and not to leave the least signal to them to guess by, that there were any living creatures upon the island, I mean of human shape.

Religion joined in with this prudential resolution, and I was convinced now many ways that I was perfectly out of my duty,

when I was laying all my bloody schemes for the destruction o
innocent creatures, I mean innocent as to me, as to the crime
they were guilty of towards one another, I had nothing to do
with them; they were national, and I ought to leave them to th
justice of God, who is the governor of nations, and knows how
by national punishments to make a just retribution for nationa
offenses; and to bring public judgments upon those who offen
in a public manner, by such ways as best please him.

In this disposition, I continued for near a year after this: an
so far was I from desiring an occasion for falling upon thes
wretches, that in all that time I never once went up the hill t
see whether there were any of them in sight, or to know whethe
any of them had been on shore there or not; that I might not b
tempted to renew any of my contrivances against them, or b
provoked, by any advantage which might present itself, to fal
upon them; only this I did, I went and removed my boat, which
I had on the other side the island, and carried it down to the eas
end of the whole island, where I ran it into a little cove which
found under some high rocks, and where I knew, by reason o
the currents, the savages durst not, at least would not, come wit
their boats, upon any account whatsoever.

With my boat I carried away everything that I had left ther
belonging to her, though not necessary for the bare goin
thither; namely, a mast and sail, which I had made for her, an
a thing like an anchor, but indeed, which could not be calle
either anchor or grappling: however, it was the best I coul
make of its kind. All these I removed, that there might not b
the least shadow of any discovery, or any appearance of an
boat, or of any habitation upon the island.

Besides this, I kept myself, as I said, more retired than ever
and seldom went from my cell other than upon my constan
employment, namely, to milk my she-goats, and manager m

ttle flock in the wood, which, as it was quite on the other part
f the island, was quite out of danger: for certain it is that these
ivage people, who sometimes haunted this island, never came
'ith any thoughts of finding anything here, and consequently
ever wandered off from the coast, and I doubt not but they
light have been several times on shore after my apprehensions
f them had made me cautious, as well as before; and indeed I
ooked back with some horror upon the thoughts of what my
ondition would have been if I had chopped upon them, and
een discovered when naked and unarmed, except with my gun,
nd that loaded often only with small shot. I walked everywhere
eeping and peeping about the island, to see what I could get.
Vhat a surprise should I have been in, if, when I discovered the
rint of a man's foot, I had instead of that seen fifteen or twenty
ivages, and found them pursuing me, and by the swiftness of
heir running, no possibility of my escaping them!

The thoughts of this sometimes sunk my very soul within me,
nd distressed my mind so much, that I could not soon recover
. I confess that these anxieties, these constant dangers I lived
1, and the concern that was now upon me, put an end to all in-
ention, and to all the contrivances that I had laid for my future
ccommodations and conveniences. I had the care of my
ifety more now upon my hands than that of my food. I cared
ot to drive a nail, or chop a stick of wood now, for fear the
oise I should make should be heard; much less would I fire a
in, for the same reason; and above all, I was intolerably un-
isy at making any fire, lest the smoke, which is visible at a
reat distance in the day, should betray me: and for this reason
removed that part of my business which required fire, such as
irning of pots and pipes, &c., into my new apartment in the
roods; where, after I had been some time, I found, to my un-
peakable consolation, a mere natural cave in the earth, which

went in a vast way, and where, I dare say, no savage, had he
been at the mouth of it, would be so hardy as to venture in, nor
indeed would any man else, but one who, like me, wanted noth
ing so much as a safe retreat.

The mouth of this hollow was at the bottom of a great rock
where, by mere accident (I could say, if I did not see an abund
ant reason to ascribe all such things now to Providence), I was
cutting down some thick branches of trees to make charcoal
and before I go on, I must observe the reason of my making this
charcoal, which was thus:—

I was afraid of making a smoke about my habitation, as I said
before; and yet I could not live there without baking my bread
cooking my meat, &c., so I contrived to burn some wood here
as I had seen done in England, under turf, till it became chark
or dry coal; and then putting the fire out, I preserved the coal to
carry home, and perform the other services which fire was want
ing for at home, without danger of smoke.

But this is by-the-by. While I was cutting down some wood
here, I perceived that behind a very thick branch of low brush
wood, or underwood, there was a kind of hollow place. I was
curious to look into it, and getting with difficulty into the mouth
of it, I found it was pretty large, that is to say, sufficient for me
to stand upright in it, and perhaps another with me; but I must
confess to you, I made more haste out than I did in; when look
ing farther into the place, which was perfectly dark, I saw two
broad shining eyes of some creature, whether devil or man I
knew not, which twinkled like two stars, the dim light from
the cave's mouth shining directly in, and making the reflection

However, after some pause, I recovered myself, and began to
call myself a thousand fools, and tell myself that he that was
afraid to see the devil, was not fit to live twenty years in an island
all alone, and that I durst to believe there was nothing in this

cave that was more frightful than myself; upon this, plucking up
my courage, I took up a great firebrand, and in I rushed again,
with the stick flaming in my hand. I had not gone three steps in,
but I was almost as much frighted as I was before; for I heard a
very loud sigh, like that of a man in some pain; and it was followed by a broken noise, as if of words half-expressed, and then
a deep sigh again. I stepped back, and was indeed struck with
such a surprise, that it put me into a cold sweat; and if I had had
a hat on my head, I will not answer for it that my hair might
not have lifted it off. But still, plucking up my spirits as well as
I could, and encouraging myself a little, with considering that
the power and presence of God was everywhere, and was able
to protect me; upon this I stepped forward again, and by the
light of the firebrand, holding it up a little over my head, I saw
lying on the ground a most monstrous frightful old he-goat,
just making his will, as we say, and gasping for life, and dying
indeed of mere old age.

I stirred him a little to see if I could get him out, and he es-
sayed to get up, but was not able to raise himself: and I thought
with myself, he might even lie there; for he had frighted me
so, he would certainly fright any of the savages, if any of them
should be so hardy as to come in there, while he had any life in
him.

I was now recovered from my surprise, and began to look
round me, when I found the cave was but very small; that is to
say, it might be about twelve foot over, but in no manner of
shape, either round or square, no hands ever having been employed in making it, but those of mere nature. I observed also,
that there was a place at the farther side of it that went in
farther, but was so low, that it required me to creep upon my
hands and knees to go into it, and whither I went I know not;
so having no candle, I gave it over for some time, but resolved

to come again the next day, provided with candles and a tinder-box, which I had made of the lock of one of the muskets, with some wild-fire in the pan.

Accordingly, the next day, I came provided with six large candles of my own making (for I made very good candles now of goat's tallow); and going into this low place, I was obliged to creep upon all fours, as I have said, almost ten yards; which, by the way, I thought was a venture bold enough, considering that I knew not how far it might go, nor what was beyond it. When I was got through the streight, I found the roof rose higher up, I believe near twenty foot; but never was such a glorious sight seen in the island, I dare say, as it was, to look round the side and roof of this vault or cave. The walls reflected an hundred thousand lights to me from my two candles: what it was in the rock, whether diamonds, or any other precious stones, or gold, which I rather suppose it to be, I knew not.

The place I was in was a most delightful cavity, or grotto, of its kind, as could be expected, though perfectly dark; the floor was dry and level, and had a sort of small loose gravel upon it; so that there was no nauseous or venomous creature to be seen, neither was there any damp or wet on the sides or roof; the only difficulty in it was the entrance, which, however, as it was a place of security, and such a retreat as I wanted, I thought that was a convenience; so that I was really rejoiced at the discovery, and resolved, without any delay, to bring some of those things which I was most anxious about to this place; particularly, I resolved to bring hither my magazine of powder, and all my spare arms, namely, two fowling-pieces (for I had three in all) and three muskets (for of them I had eight in all); so I kept at my castle only five, which stood ready mounted, like pieces of cannon, on my outmost fence, and were ready also to take out upon any expedition.

Upon this occasion of removing my ammunition, I took occasion to open the barrel of powder which I took up out of the sea, and which had been wet; and I found that the water had penetrated about three or four inches into the powder on every side, which, caking and growing hard, had preserved the inside like a kernel in a shell; so that I had near sixty pound of very good powder in the centre of the cask; and this was an agreeable discovery to me at that time; so I carried all away thither, never keeping above two or three pound of powder with me in my castle, for fear of a surprise of any kind. I also carried thither all the lead I had left for bullets.

I fancied myself now like one of the ancient giants, which are said to live in caves and holes in the rocks, where none could come at them; for I persuaded myself while I was here, if five hundred savages were to hunt me, they could never find me out; or if they did, they would not venture to attack me here.

The old goat, whom I found expiring, died in the mouth of the cave the next day after I made this discovery; and I found it much easier to dig a great hole there, and throw him in, and cover him with earth, than to drag him out; so I interred him there, to prevent offense to my nose.

I was now in my twenty-third year of residence in this island, and was so naturalized to the place, and to the manner of living, that could I have but enjoyed the certainty that no savages would come to the place to disturb me, I could have been content to have capitulated for spending the rest of my time there, even to the last moment, till I had laid me down and died, like the old goat in the cave. I had also arrived to some little diversions and amusements, which made the time pass more pleasantly with me a great deal than it did before; as, first, I had taught my Poll, as I noted before, to speak; and he did it so familiarly, and talked so articulately and plain, that it was very pleasant to me; and he lived with me no less than six-and-twenty years: how long he might live afterwards I know not; though I know they have a notion in the Brazils that they live a hundred years; perhaps poor Poll may be alive there still, calling after poor Robin Crusoe to this day; I wish no Englishman the ill luck to come there and hear him; but if he did, he would certainly believe it was the devil. My dog was a very pleasant and loving companion to me for no less than sixteen years of my time, and then died of mere old age; as for my cats, they multiplied, as I have observed, to that degree, that I was obliged to shoot several of them at first to keep them from devouring me and all I had; but at length, when the two old ones I brought with me were gone, and after some time continually driving them from me, and letting them have no provision with me, they all ran wild into the woods, except two or three favorites, which I kept tame, and whose young, when they had any, I always drowned, and these were part of my family. Besides these, I always kept two or three household kids about me, which I taught to feed out of my hand; and I had also more parrots which talked pretty well, and would all call Robin Crusoe, but none like my first; nor indeed did I take the pains with any of them that I had done with him. I had also several tame sea-fowls, whose names I know not, which I caught upon the shore, and cut their wings; and the little stakes, which I had planted before my castle wall, being now grown up to a good thick grove, these fowls all lived among these low trees, and bred there, which was very agreeable to me, so that, as I said above, I began to be very well contented with the life I led, if it might but have been secured from the dread of the savages.

But it was otherwise directed; and it may not be amiss for all people who shall meet with my story to make this just observation from it, namely, How frequently, in the course of our lives, the evil which in itself we seek most to shun, and which, when we are fallen into, is the most dreadful to us, is oftentimes the very means or door of our deliverance, by which alone we can be raised again from the affliction we are fallen into. I could give many examples of this in the course of my unaccountable life; but in nothing was it more particularly remarkable than in the circumstances of my last two years of solitary residence in this island.

CHAPTER 16: *A visit from the savages; a wrecked ship*

IT WAS now the month of December, as I said before, in my twenty-third year; and this being the southern solstice, for winter I cannot call it, was the particular time of my harvest, and required my being pretty much abroad in the fields; when going out pretty early in the morning, even before it was thorough daylight, I was surprised with seeing a light of some fire upon the shore, at a distance from me of about two miles, towards the end of the island, where I had observed some savages had been before; but not on the other side; but to my great affliction, it was on my side of the island.

I was indeed terribly surprised at the sight, and stepped short within my grove, not daring to go out, lest I might be surprised; and yet I had no more peace within, from the apprehensions I had, that if these savages, in rambling over the island, should find my corn standing, or cut, or any of my works and improvements, they would immediately conclude that there were people in the place, and would then never give over till they had found me out. In this extremity I went back directly to my castle, pulled up the ladder after me, having made all things without look as wild and natural as I could.

Then I prepared myself within, putting myself in a posture

of defense. I loaded all my cannon, as I called them, that is to
say, my muskets, which were mounted upon my new fortification, and all my pistols, and resolved to defend myself to the last
gasp; not forgetting seriously to commend myself to the divine
protection and earnestly to pray to God to deliver me out of
the hands of the barbarians; and in this posture I continued
about two hours, but began to be mighty impatient for intelli-
gence abroad, for I had no spies to send out.

After sitting a while longer, and musing what I should do in
this case, I was not able to bear sitting in ignorance longer; so
setting up my ladder to the side of the hill where there was a
flat place, as I observed before, and then pulling the ladder up
after me, I set it up again, and mounted to the top of the hill;
and pulling out my perspective glass, which I had taken on purpose, I laid me down flat on my belly on the ground, and began
to look for the place. I presently found there was no less than
nine naked savages sitting round a small fire they had made; not
to warm them, for they had no need of that, the weather being
extreme hot; but, as I supposed, to dress some of their barbarous
diet of human flesh, which they had brought with them,
whether alive or dead I could not know.

They had two canoes with them, which they had hauled up
upon the shore; and as it was then tide of ebb, they seemed to
me to wait for the return of the flood to go away again. It is not
easy to imagine what confusion this sight put me into, especially seeing them come on my side the island, and so near me
too; but when I observed their coming must be always with the
current of the ebb, I began afterwards to be more sedate in my
mind, being satisfied that I might go abroad with safety all the
time of the tide of flood, if they were not on shore before; and
having made this observation, I went abroad about my harvest
work with the more composure.

As I expected, so it proved; for as soon as the tide made to the westward, I saw them all take boat, and row (or paddle as we call it) all away. I should have observed, that for an hour and more before they went off, they went to dancing, and I could easily discern their postures and gestures by my glasses: I could not perceive, by my nicest observation, but that they were stark naked, and had not the least covering upon them; but whether they were men or women, that I could not distinguish.

As soon as I saw them shipped and gone, I took two guns upon my shoulders, and two pistols at my girdle, and my great sword by my side, without a scabbard; and with all the speed I was able to make, I went away to the hill, where I had discovered the first appearance of all. And as soon as I got thither, which was not less than two hours (for I could not go apace, being so loaded with arms as I was), I perceived there had been three canoes more of savages on that place; and looking out farther, I saw they were all at sea together, making over for the main.

This was a dreadful sight to me, especially when going down to the shore, I could see the marks of horror which the dismal work they had been about had left behind it, namely, the blood, the bones, and part of the flesh of human bodies, eaten and devoured by those wretches with merriment and sport. I was so

filled with indignation at the sight, that I began now to pre-
meditate the destruction of the next that I saw there, let them
be who or how many soever.

It seemed evident to me that the visits which they thus made
to this island were not very frequent; for it was above fifteen
months before any more of them came on shore there again,
that is to say, I never saw them, or any footsteps or signals of
them in all that time; and I found they did not come in the
rainy season; yet all this while I lived uncomfortably, by reason
of the constant apprehensions I was in of their coming upon
me by surprise.

However, I wore out a year and three months more, before I
saw any of the savages; but in the month of May, as near as I
could calculate, and in my four-and-twentieth year, I had a very
strange encounter with them, of which in its place.

The perturbation of my mind, during this fifteen or sixteen
months' interval was very great. In the day great troubles overwhelmed my mind; in the night I dreamed often of killing savages, and the reasons why I might justify the doing of it. But, to
waive all this for a while, it was the middle of May, on the six-
teenth day, I think, that it blew a very great storm of wind all
day, with a great deal of lightning and thunder, and a very foul
night it was. I know not what was the particular occasion of it,
but as I was reading the Bible, and taken up with serious
thoughts about my present condition, I was surprised with the
noise of a gun, as I thought, fired at sea.

This was, to be sure, a surprise of quite a different nature
from any I had met with before, for the notions that this put
into my thoughts were quite of another kind. I started up in the
greatest haste imaginable, and, in a trice, clapped up my ladder
in the middle place of the rock, and pulled it after me, and
mounting it the second time, got to the top of the hill; that

moment a flash of fire bade me listen for a second gun, which, accordingly, in about half a minute I heard, and by the sound, knew that it was from that part of the sea where I was driven out with the current in my boat.

I immediately considered that this must be some ship in distress, and that they had some comrade, or some other ship in company, and fired these guns for signals of distress, and to obtain help. I had this presence of mind at that minute, as to think, that though I could not help them, it may be they might help me; so I brought together all the dry wood I could get at hand, and making a good sized pile, I set it on fire upon the hill; the wood was dry, and blazed freely, and though the wind blew very hard, yet it burnt fairly out, so that I was certain, if there was any such thing as a ship, they must needs see it, and no doubt they did, for as soon as my fire blazed up, I heard another gun, and after that several others, all from the same quarter. I plied my fire all night long, till day broke, and when it was broad day, and the air cleared up, I saw something at a great distance at sea, full east of the island, whether a sail, or a hull, I could not distinguish, no, not with my glasses, the distance was so great, and the weather still being hazy also: at least it was so out at sea.

I looked frequently at it all that day, and soon perceived that it did not move; so I presently concluded that it was a ship at anchor, and being eager, you may be sure, to be satisfied, I took my gun in my hand and ran towards the southeast side of the island, to the rocks, where I had been formerly carried away with the current, and getting up there, the weather by this time being perfectly clear, I could plainly see, to my great sorrow, the wreck of a ship cast away in the night upon these concealed rocks, which I found when I was out in my boat, and which rocks, as they checked the violence of the stream, and made a kind of counter stream, or eddy, were the occasion of my recovering then from the most desperate, hopeless condition, that ever I had been in.

Thus, what is one man's safety is another man's destruction; for it seems these men, whoever they were, being out of their knowledge, and the rocks being wholly under water, had been driven upon them in the night; the wind blowing very hard at E. and E. N. E. Had they seen the island, as I must necessarily suppose they did not, they must, as I thought, have endeavored to have saved themselves on shore by the help of their boat; but the firing of their guns for help, especially when they saw, as I imagined, my fire, filled me with many thoughts.

In the condition I was in, I could do no more than look upon the misery of the poor men, and pity them, which had still this good effect on my side, that it gave me more and more cause to give thanks to God, who had so happily and comfortably provided for me in my desolate condition; and that of two ships' companies, who were now cast away upon this part of the world, not one life should be spared but mine. I learnt here again to observe, that it is very rare the providence of God casts us into any condition of life so low, or any misery so great, but we may see something to be thankful for, and may see others worse than ourselves.

Such certainly was the case of these men, of whom I could not so much as see room to suppose any of them were saved; nothing could make it rational, so much as to wish or expect that they did not all perish there, except the possibility only of their being taken up by another ship in company; and this was but mere possibility indeed; for I saw not the least signal or appearance of any such thing. I cannot explain by words, what a strange longing or hankering of desires I felt in my soul upon this sight, breaking out sometimes thus: "O that there had been but one or two, nay, but one soul saved out of the ship, to have escaped to me, that I might have had one companion, one fellow-creature, to have spoken to me, and to have conversed with!" In all the time of my solitary life, I never felt so earnest, so strong a desire, after the society of my fellow-creatures, or so deep a regret at the want of it.

But it was not to be; either their fate, or mine, or both, forbade it; for, till the last year of my being in this island, I never knew whether any were saved out of the ship or not; and had only the affliction, some days after, to see the corpse of a drowned boy washed on shore, at the end of the island which was next the shipwreck. He had on a seaman's waistcoat, a pair of open-kneed linen drawers, and a blue linen shirt; but nothing to direct me to guess what nation he was of. He had nothing in his pocket but two pieces of eight, and a tobacco-pipe. The last was of more value to me than the first.

It was now calm, and I had a great mind to venture out in my boat to this wreck, not doubting but I might find something on board that might be useful to me; and possibly there might be yet some living creature on board, whose life I might not only save, but might, by saving that life, comfort my own to the last degree; and this thought clung so to my heart, that I could not be quiet night or day, but I must venture out in my boat on board this wreck; and committing the rest to God's providence, I thought the impression was so strong upon my mind, that it could not be resisted, that it must come from some invisible direction, and that I should be wanting to myself if I did not go.

Under the power of this impression, I hastened back to my castle, prepared everything for my voyage, took a quantity of bread, a great pot of fresh water, a compass to steer by, a bottle of rum (for I had still a great deal of that left), a basket full of raisins, and thus loading myself with everything necessary, I went down to my boat, got the water out of her, and got her afloat, loaded all my cargo in her, and then went home again for more. My second cargo was a great bag full of rice, the umbrella to set up over my head for a shade, another pot full of fresh water, and about two dozen of my small loaves, or barley cakes, more than before, and a bottle of goat's milk, and a cheese; all which, with great labor and sweat, I brought to my boat, and praying to God to direct my voyage, I put out; and rowing, or paddling the canoe along the shore, I came at last to the utmost point of the island on that side, namely, N. E. And now I was to launch out into the ocean, and either to venture, or not venture. I looked on the rapid currents which ran constantly on both sides of the island at a distance, and which were very terrible to me, from the remembrance of the hazard I had been in before, and my heart began to fail me; for I foresaw, that if I was driven into either of these currents, I should be carried a vast way out to sea, and perhaps out of reach or sight, of the island again; and that, as my boat was but small, if any little gale of wind should rise, I should be inevitably lost.

These thoughts so oppressed my mind, that I began to give over my enterprise, and having hauled my boat into a little creek on the shore, I stepped out, and sat me down upon a little spot of rising ground, very pensive and anxious, between fear and desire, about my voyage; when, as I was musing, I could perceive that the tide was turned, and the flood came on, upon which my going was for so many hours impracticable. Upon this it presently occurred to me, that I should go up to the highest piece of ground I could find, and observe, if I could how the sets of the tides or currents lay when the flood came in, that I might judge whether, if I was driven one way out, I might not expect to be driven another way home, with the same rapidness of the currents. This thought was no sooner in my head, but I cast my eye upon a little hill, which sufficiently overlooked the sea both ways, and from whence I had a clear view of the currents, or sets of the tide, and which way I was to guide myself in my return. Here I found that as the current of the ebb set out close by the south point of the island, so the current of the flood set in close by the shore of the north side; and that I had nothing to do but to keep to the north of the island in my return, and I should do well enough.

Encouraged with this observation, I resolved the next morning to set out with the first of the tide; and reposing myself for that night in the canoe, under the great watchcoat I mentioned, I launched out in the morning. I made first a little out to sea, full north, till I began to feel the benefit of the current, which set eastward, and which carried me at a great rate, and yet did not so hurry me as the southern side current had done before, and so as to take from me all government of the boat; but, having a strong steerage with my paddle, I went directly for the wreck, and in less than two hours I came up to it.

It was a dismal sight to look at: the ship, which by the building was Spanish, stuck fast jammed in between two rocks; all the stern and quarter of her was beaten to pieces with the sea; and as her forecastle, which stuck in the rocks, had run on with great violence, her mainmast and foremast were brought by the board, that is to say, broken short off; but her bowsprit was sound, and the head and bow appeared firm. When I came close to her, a dog appeared upon her, who, seeing me coming, yelped and cried; and as soon as I called him, jumped into the sea to come to me; and I took him into the boat, and found him almost dead for hunger and thirst. I gave him a cake of my bread, and he eat it like a ravenous wolf that had been starving for a fortnight in the snow. I then gave the poor creature some fresh water, with which, if I would have let him, he would have burst himself.

After this I went on board. The first sight I met with was two men drowned in the cook-room, or forecastle of the ship, with their arms fast about one another. I concluded, as is indeed probable, that when the ship struck, it being in a storm, the sea broke so high, and so continually over her, that the men were not able to bear it, and were strangled with the constant rushing in of the water, as much as if they had been under water. Besides the dog, there was nothing left in the ship that had life, or any goods that I could see, but what were spoiled by the water. There were some casks of liquor, whether wine or brandy I knew not, which lay lower in the hold, and which, the water being ebbed out, I could see, but they were too big to meddle with. I saw several chests, which I believed belonged to some of the seamen, and I got two of them into the boat, without examining what was in them.

Had the stern of the ship been fixed, and the fore part broken off, I am persuaded I might have made a good voyage; for, by what I found in these two chests, I had room to suppose the ship had a great deal of wealth on board; and if I may guess by the course she steered, she must have been bound from Buenos Ayres, or the Rio de la Plata, in the south part of America, beyond the Brazils, to the Havannah, in the Gulf of Mexico, and so perhaps to Spain.

I found, besides these chests a little cask full of liquor, of about twenty gallons, which I got into my boat with much difficulty. There were several muskets in the cabin, and a great powder-horn, with about four pounds of powder in it: as for the muskets, I had no occasion for them, so I left them, but took the powder-horn. I took a fire-shovel and tongs, which I wanted extremely; as also two little brass kettles, a copper pot to make chocolate, and a gridiron; and with this cargo and the dog I came away, the tide beginning to make home again; and the same evening, about an hour within night, I reached the island again, wearied and fatigued to the last degree.

I reposed that night in the boat, and in the morning I resolved to harbor what I had gotten in my new cave, not to carry it home to my castle. After refreshing myself, I got all my cargo on shore, and began to examine it. The cask of liquor I found to be a kind of rum, but not such as we had at the Brazils, and, in a word, not at all good. But when I came to open the chests, I found several things I wanted; for example, I found in one a fine case of bottles, of an extraordinary kind, and filled with cordial waters, fine, and very good: the bottles held about three pints each, and were tipped with silver. I found two pots of very good succades, or sweetmeats, so fastened on top, that the salt water had not hurt them; and two more of the same, which the water had spoiled. I found some very good shirts, which were very welcome to me, and about a dozen and a half of white linen handkerchiefs, and colored neckcloths; the former were also very welcome, being exceedingly refreshing to wipe my face on in a hot dry day. Besides this, when I came to the till in the chest, I found there three great bags of pieces of eight, which held about eleven hundred pieces in all; and in one of them, wrapt up in a paper, six doubloons of gold, and some small bars of gold; I suppose they might all weigh near a pound.

The other chest I found had some clothes in it, but of little value; but by the circumstances it must have belonged to the gunner's mate, though there was no powder in it, but about two pounds of glazed powder in three small flasks, kept, I suppose, for charging their fowling-pieces on occasion. Upon the whole, I got very little by this voyage that was of much use to me, for, as to the money, I had no manner of occasion for it, it was to me as the dirt under my feet, and I would have given it all for three or four pair of English shoes and stockings, which were things I greatly wanted, for I had not had a pair on my feet for many years. I had, indeed, gotten two pair of shoes now, which I took off the feet of the two men whom I found drowned in the wreck; and I found two pair more in one of the chests, which were very welcome to me; but they were not like our English shoes, either for ease or service, being rather what we call pumps than shoes. I found in this seaman's chest about fifty pieces of eight in royals, but no gold; I suppose this belonged to a poorer man than the other, which seemed to belong to some officer.

Having now brought all my things on shore, and secured them, I went back to my boat, and rowed or paddled her along the shore to her old harbor, where I laid her up, and made the best of my way to my old habitation, where I found everything safe and quiet; so I began to repose myself, live after my old fashion, and take care of my family affairs, and for a while I lived easy enough, only that I was more vigilant than I used to be, looked out oftener, and did not go abroad so much: and if any time I did stir with any freedom, it was always to the east part of the island, where I was pretty well satisfied the savages never came, and where I could go without so many precautions, and such a load of arms and ammunition as I always carried with me if I went the other way.

One night in the rainy season, in March, the four-and-twentieth year of my first setting foot in this land of solitariness, I had the following dream, namely, that as I was going out in the morning, as usual, from my castle, I saw upon the shore two canoes, and eleven savages coming to land, and that they brought with them another savage, whom they were going to kill, in order to eat him, when on a sudden the savage that they were going to kill, made his escape, and ran for his life; and then I thought in my sleep, that he came running into my little grove, before my fortification, to hide himself; and that I, seeing him, and not perceiving that the others sought him that way, showed myself to him, and encouraged him; that he kneeled down to me, seeming to pray to me to assist him; upon which I showed him my ladder, made him go up, and carried him into my cave, and he became my servant; and that as soon as I had got this man, I said to myself, "Now I may venture to the main-land, for this fellow will serve me as a pilot, and tell me what to do, and whither to go for provisions, and whither not to go for fear of being devoured; what places to venture into, and what to escape." I awoke with this thought, and was under such inexpressible impressions of joy at the prospect of my escape in my dream, that the disappointment I felt upon coming to myself, and finding it was no more than a dream, was really extravagant the other way, and threw me into a very great dejection of spirits.

Upon this, however, I made this conclusion, that my only way to go about an attempt for an escape, was to try to get a savage in my possession; and, if possible, it should be one of their prisoners, whom they had condemned to be eaten, and should bring hither to kill.

CHAPTER 17: *My man Friday*

WITH THESE resolutions in my thoughts, I set myself upon the scout, as often as possible, and indeed so often, till I was heartily tired of it. I was not at first more careful to shun the sight of these savages, and avoid being seen by them, than I was now eager to be upon them.

Besides, I fancied myself able to manage one, nay, two or

three savages, if I had them, so as to make them entirely slaves to me, to do what I should direct them, and to prevent their being able at any time to do me any hurt. It was a great while that I pleased myself with this affair; but nothing still presented; all my fancies and schemes came to nothing, for no savages came near me for a great while.

About a year and a half after I had entertained these notions, and by long musing had, as it were, resolved to put them into execution, I was surprised one morning early with seeing no less than five canoes all on shore together, on my side of the island, and the people who belonged to them all landed. The number of them broke all my measures, for seeing so many, and knowing that they always came four, or sometimes more in a boat, I could not tell what to think of it, or how to take my measures to attack twenty or thirty men, single-handed, so I lay still in my castle, perplexed and discomforted. However, I put myself into all the same postures for an attack that I had formerly provided, and was just ready for action, if anything had presented. Having waited a good while, listening to hear if they made any noise, at length, being very impatient, I set my guns at the foot of my ladder, and clambered up to the top of the hill by my two stages, as usual, standing so, however, that my head did not appear above the hill; so that they could not perceive me by any means. I here observed, by the help of my perspective glass, that they were no less than thirty in number, that they had a fire kindled, and that they had meat dressed; how they cooked it, that I knew not, or what it was; but they were all dancing, in I know not how many barbarous gestures and figures, round the fire.

While I was thus looking on them, I perceived, by my perspective glass, two miserable wretches dragged from the boats, where, it seems, they were laid by, and were now brought out for the slaughter. I perceived one of them immediately fall, being knocked down, I suppose, with a club, or wooden sword, for that was their way; and two or three others were at work, cutting him open for their cookery, while the other victim was left standing by himself till they should be ready for him. In that very moment, the poor wretch, seeing himself a little at liberty, nature inspired him with hopes of life, and he started away from them, and ran with incredible swiftness along the sands, directly towards me, I mean towards that part of the coast where my habitation was.

I was dreadfully frightened (that I must acknowledge) when I perceived him to run my way, and especially when, as I thought, I saw him pursued by the whole body; and I expected that part of my dream was coming to pass, and that he would take shelter in my grove; but I could not depend, by any means, upon my dream for the rest of it, namely, that the savages would not pursue him thither, and find him there. However, I kept my station and my spirits began to recover when I found that there were not above three men that followed him; and still more was I encouraged, when I found that he outstripped them exceedingly in running, and gained ground of them, so that if he could but hold out for half an hour, I saw he would fairly get away from them all.

There was between them and my castle, the creek, which I mentioned often at the first part of my story, when I landed my cargoes out of the ship; and this I knew he must necessarily swim over, or the poor wretch would be taken there; but when the savage who was escaping came thither, he made nothing of it, though the tide was then up, but plunging in, he swam through it in about thirty strokes, or thereabouts, landed, and ran on with exceeding strength and swiftness. When the three pursuers came to the creek, I found that two of them could swim, but the third could not, and that he, standing on the other side, looked at the others, but went no farther, and soon after went softly back again, which, as it happened, was very well for him.

I observed that the two who swam were yet twice as long swimming over the creek as the fellow was that fled from them. It came now very warmly upon my thoughts, and indeed, irresistibly, that now was my time to get me a servant, and perhaps, a companion or assistant, and that I was called plainly by Providence to save this poor creature's life. I immediately got down the ladders, fetched my two guns, for they were both at the foot of the ladders, and getting up again with the same haste to the top of the hill, I crossed towards the sea; and, having a very short cut, and all down hill, clapped myself in the way between the pursuers and the pursued, hallooing aloud to him that fled, who, looking back, was at first as much frightened at me as at them; but I beckoned with my hand to him to come back, and, in the meantime, I slowly advanced towards the two that followed; then rushing at once upon the foremost, I knocked him down with the stock of my piece; I was loath to fire, because I would not have the rest to hear, thought at that distance it would not have been easily heard, and being out of sight of the smoke, too, they would not have known what to make of it. Having knocked this fellow down, the other who followed him, stopped, as if he had been frightened, and I advanced apace towards him; but as I came nearer, I perceived presently he had a bow and arrow, and was fitting it to shoot at me, so I was then necessitated to shoot at him first, which I did, and killed him at the first shot. The poor savage who fled, but had stopped, though he saw both his enemies fallen, and killed (as he thought), yet was so frightened with the noise and fire of my piece, that he stood stock-still, and neither came forward nor

went backward, though he seemed rather inclined to fly still, than to come on. I hallooed again to him, and made signs to him to come forward, which he easily understood, and came a little way, then stopped again, and then a little farther, and stopped again; and then he stood trembling, as if he had been taken prisoner, and had just been to be killed, as his two enemies were. I beckoned to him again to come to me, and gave him all the signs of encouragement that I could think of; and he came nearer and nearer, kneeling down every ten or twelve steps, in token of acknowledgment for saving his life. I smiled at him, and looked pleasantly, and beckoned to him to come still nearer. At length he came close to me, and then he kneeled down again, kissed the ground, and, taking my foot, set it upon his head; this, it seems, was in token of swearing to be my slave forever. I took him up, and made much of him, and encouraged him all I could. But I perceived the savage whom I knocked down was not killed, but stunned with the blow, and began to come to himself. So I pointed to him, showing him the savage, that he was not dead; upon this he spoke some words to me, and though I could not understand them, yet I thought they were pleasant to hear, for they were the first sound of a man's voice that I had heard, my own excepted, for above five-and-twenty years. But there was no time for such reflections now. The savage who was knocked down recovered himself so far as to sit upon the ground, and I perceived that my savage began to be afraid; but when I saw that, I presented my other piece at the man, as if I would shoot him; upon this my savage, for so I call him now, made a motion to me to lend him my sword, which hung naked in a belt by my side; so I did. He no sooner had it than he ran to his enemy, and, at one blow, cut off his head so cleverly, no executioner in Germany could have done it sooner or better; which I thought very strange for one who, I had reason to believe, never saw a sword in his life before, except their own wooden swords. However, it seems, as I learned afterwards, they make their wooden swords so sharp, so heavy, and the wood is so hard, that they will cut off heads and arms with them, and at one blow, too. When he had done this, he came laughing to me in sign of triumph, and brought me the sword again, and laid it down, with the head of the savage he had killed, just before me.

He was astonished how I had killed the other Indian so far off and going to him, he stood like one amazed, looking at him, turning him, first on one side, then on the other; looked at the wound the bullet had made, which was in the breast, where it had made a hole, and no great quantity of blood had flowed, but he had bled inwardly, for he was quite dead. Then he took up his bows and arrows, and came back, and I beckoned for us to go away, making signs that more might come after them. Upon this, he signed to me, that he should bury them with sand, that they might not be seen by the rest, if they followed; so I made signs for him to do so; he fell to work, and had them both buried in the sand in about a quarter of an hour. I then called him away, and took him not to my castle, but my cave, on the farther part of the island; so I did not let my dream come to pass in that respect, namely, that he came into my grove for shelter. Here I gave him bread, and a bunch of raisins to eat, and a draught of water, which he was in great distress for, by his running; and having refreshed him, I made signs for him to go to sleep, pointing to a place where I had laid a great parcel of rice straw, and a blanket upon it, which I used to sleep upon myself sometimes; so the poor creature lay down, and went to sleep.

He was a comely handsome fellow, perfectly well made, tall, and well-shaped, and, as I reckon, about twenty-six years of age.

He had a very good countenance, not a fierce and surly aspect, but seemed to have something very manly in his face, and yet he had all the sweetness and softness of an European in his countenance too, especially when he smiled. His hair was long and black, not curled like wool, his forehead very high and large, and a great vivacity and sparkling sharpness in his eyes. The color of his skin was not quite black, but very tawny, and yet not of an ugly, yellow, nauseous tawny, as the Brazilians, and Virginians, and other natives of America are, but of a bright kind of dun olive color that had in it something very agreeable, though not very easy to describe. His face was round and plump, his nose small, not flat like the Negroes, a very good mouth, thin lips, and his teeth fine, well set, and white as ivory. After he had slumbered about half an hour, he waked, and came out of the cave to me, for I had been milking the goats in the inclosure just by. When he espied me, he came running, and laid himself on the ground again, with all the possible signs of an humble, thankful disposition, making many antic gestures to show it. At last he lays his head flat upon the ground, close to my foot, and sets my other foot upon his head, as he had done before, and after this, made all the signs to me of subjection, servitude, and submission imaginable, to let me know how much he would serve me as long as he lived. I understood him in many things, and let him know I was well pleased with him. In a little time I began to speak to him, and teach him to speak to me; and first, made him know his name should be Friday, which was the day I saved his life. I likewise taught him to say, "Master," and then let him know that was to be my name. I also taught him to say, "Yes," and "No," and to know the meaning of them. I gave him some milk in an earthen pot, and some bread, and let him see me drink some before him, and sop my bread in it, which he quickly imitated, and made signs that it was very good for him.

I kept there with him all that night; but as soon as it was day, I took him away with me. As we went by the place where he had buried the two men, he pointed exactly to the spot, and showed me the marks he had made to find them again, making signs to me that we should dig them up and eat them; at this I appeared very angry, expressed my abhorrence of it, made as if I would vomit at the thoughts of it, and beckoned with my hand to him to come away, which he immediately did, with great submission. I then led him to the top of the hill, to see if his enemies were gone, and pulling out my glass, I looked, and saw plainly the place where they had been, but no appearance of them or their canoes; so they were quite gone.

I then took my man Friday with me, giving him the sword in his hand, with the bow and arrows, at his back, which I found he could use very dexterously, making him carry one gun for me, and I two for myself, and away we marched to the place where these creatures had been. When I came there, my very blood ran chill in my veins, and my heart sank within me at the horror of the spectacle. Indeed, it was a dreadful sight; the place was covered with human bones, the ground dyed with the blood, great pieces of flesh left here and there, half eaten, mangled, and scorched, and in short, all the tokens of the triumphant feast they had been making there, after a victory over their enemies. I saw three skulls, five hands, and the bones of three or four legs and feet, and abundance of other parts of the bodies; and Friday, by his signs, made me understand that they brought over four prisoners to feast upon, that three of them were eaten, and that he, pointing to himself, was the fourth; that there had been a great battle between them and their next king, whose subjects it seems he had been one of, and that they had taken a great number of prisoners, all of which were carried to several places by those that had taken them in the fight, in order to feast upon them, as was done here by these wretches.

I caused Friday to gather all the bones and flesh that re-mained, and lay them together in a heap, and burn them to ashes. I found that he had still a hankering stomach after the flesh, and was still a cannibal in his nature, but I displayed such abhorrence at the very thoughts of it, that he durst not discover it; for I let him know that I would kill him if he offered it.

When we had done this, we came back to our castle, where I gave Friday first of all a pair of linen drawers, which I had out of the poor gunner's chest I found in the wreck, and which, with a little alteration, fitted him very well; then I made him a jerkin of goat's skin, as well as I was able; and I gave him a cap, which I had made of a hare's skin; and thus he was dressed, for the present, tolerably well; and mighty well was he pleased to see himself almost as well clothed as his master. He went awk-wardly in these things at first; wearing the drawers was very awkward to him, and the sleeve of the jerkin galled his shoul-ders and the inside of his arms; but he soon got used to them.

The next day after I came home to my hut with him, I began to consider where I should lodge him; so I made a little tent for him in the vacant place between the two fortifications, in the inside of the last, and in the outside of the first; and as there was an entrance there into my cave, I made a formal framed door-case, and a door to it of boards, and set it up in the passage, a little within the entrance, and causing the door to open in the inside, I barred it up in the night, taking in my ladders, too; so that Friday could no way come at me in the inside of my inner-most wall, without making so much noise in getting over, that it must needs awaken me, for my first wall had now a complete roof over it of long poles, covering all my tent, and leaning up to the side of the hill, which was again laid across with small sticks instead of laths, and then thatched over a great thickness with the rice straw, which was strong like reeds; and at the hole or place which was left to go in or out by the ladder, I had placed a kind of trap-door, which, if it had been attempted on the outside, would not have opened at all, but would have fallen down and made a great noise. I took care to take all the weapons into my side every night.

But I needed none of these precautions, for never was a more faithful, loving, sincere servant than Friday was to me; without passions, sullenness, or designs; his very affections were tied to me, like those of a child to its father, and, I dare say, he would have sacrificed his life for the saving of my own, upon any occasion whatever.

I was greatly delighted with him, and made it my business to teach him everything that was proper and useful, and especially to make him speak, and understand me when I spoke; and he was a very apt scholar, and he was so merry, so diligent, and so pleased when he could understand me, or make me understand him, that it was very pleasant for me to talk to him. And now my life began to be very easy and happy.

After I had been two or three days returned to my castle, I thought, that in order to bring Friday off from his horrid way of feeding, and from the relish of a cannibal's stomach, I ought to let him taste other flesh. So I took him out with me one morning to the woods, and I saw a she-goat lying down in the shade, and two young kids close by her. I catched hold of Friday; "Hold," said I; "stand still;" and made signs to him not to stir; immediately I presented my piece, shot, and killed one of the kids. The poor creature who had, at a distance indeed, seen me kill the savage, his enemy, but did not know, nor could imagine how it was done, was sensibly surprised, trembled, and shook, and looked so amazed, that I thought he would have sunk down. He did not see the kid I had shot at, nor perceived I had killed it, but ripped up his waistcoat to feel if he was not wounded; and, as I found, thought I was resolved to kill him; for he came and kneeled down to me, and embracing my knees, said a great many things I did not understand, but I could see that his meaning was to pray to me not to kill him.

I soon found a way to convince him that I would do him no harm; and, taking him up by the hand, laughed at him, and, pointing to the kid I had killed, beckoned to him to run and fetch it, which he did; and while he was looking to see how the creature was killed, I loaded my gun again, and by and by I saw a great fowl, like a hawk, sit upon a tree within shot; so, to let Friday understand a little what I would do, I called him to me again, pointing at the fowl, which was a parrot, though I thought it had been a hawk; I say, pointing to the parrot and to my gun, and to the ground under the parrot, to let him see I would make him fall, I made him understand that I would shoot and kill that bird; accordingly I fired, and bade him look, and immediately he saw the parrot fall. He stood like one frightened again, notwithstanding all I had said to him; and I found he was the more amazed, because he did not see me put anything into the gun; but thought there must be some wonderful fund of death and destruction in that thing, able to kill man, beast, bird, or any other thing, near or far off; and I believe, if I would have let him, he would have worshipped me and my gun; as for the gun itself, he would not so much as touch it for several days after, but would speak to it, and talk to it, as if it had answered him, which as I afterwards learned of him, was to desire it not to kill him.

Well, after his astonishment was a little over at this, I pointed to him to run and fetch the bird I had shot, which he did, but stayed some time, for the parrot, not being quite dead, was fluttered a good way off from the place where she fell. However, he found her, took her up, and brought her to me; and, as I had perceived his ignorance about the gun before, I took this advantage to charge the gun again, and not let him see me do it, that I might be ready for any other mark, but nothing offered at that time. So I brought home the kid, and the same evening took the skin off, and cut it up as well as I could; and having a pot for that purpose, I boiled or stewed some of the flesh, and made some very good broth. After I had begun to eat some, I gave some to my man, who seemed very glad of it, and liked it very well; but that which was strangest to him, was to see me eat salt with it. He made a sign to me that the salt was not good to eat, and putting a little into his own mouth, he seemed to nauseate it, and would spit and sputter at it, washing his mouth with fresh water after it. On the other hand, I took some meat in my mouth without salt, and I pretended to spit and sputter for want of salt, as fast as he had done at it, but it would not do.

Having thus fed him with boiled meat and broth, I was resolved to feast him the next day with roasting a piece of the kid; this I did by hanging it before the fire in a string, as I had seen many people do in England, setting two poles up, one on each side of the fire, and one across the top, and tying the string to the cross stick, letting the meat turn continually. This Friday admired much; but when he came to taste the flesh, he took so many ways to tell me how well he liked it, that I could not but understand him; and at last he told me he would never eat man's flesh any more, which I was very glad to hear.

The next day I set him to work to beating some corn out, and sifting it in the manner I used to do; and he soon understood how to do it as well as I, especially after he had seen what the meaning of it was, and that it was to make bread of; for after that I let him see me make my bread, and bake it, too; and in a little time Friday was able to do all the work for me as well as I could do it myself.

I began now to consider that having two mouths to feed instead of one, I must provide more ground for my harvest, and plant a larger quantity of corn than I used to do, so I marked out a larger piece of land, and began the fence in the same manner as before, in which Friday not only worked very hard, but very cheerfully; and I told him that it was for corn to make more bread, because he was now with me, and that I might have enough for him and myself, too. He appeared very sensible of that part, and let me know that he would work the harder for me, if I would tell him what to do.

This was the pleasantest year of all the life I led in this place. Friday began to talk pretty well, and understand the names of almost everything I had occasion to call for, and of every place I had occasion to send him to, and talk a great deal to me; so that, in short, I began to have some use for my tongue again. Besides the pleasure of talking to him, I had a singular satisfaction in the fellow himself; his simple, unfeigned honesty appeared to be more and more every day, and I began really to love the creature; and I believe he loved me as much as possible.

I had a mind once to try if he had any lingering inclination to his own country; and having learned him English so well that he could answer me almost any questions, I asked him whether the nation that he belonged to never conquered in battle. At which he smiled, and said, "Yes, yes; we always fight the better;" that is, he meant, always get the better in fight, and so we began the following discourse: "You always fight the better!" said I; "how came you to be taken prisoner, then, Friday?"

Friday. My nation beat much for all that.

Master. How beat? If your nation beat them, how came you to be taken?

Friday. They more than my nation in the place where me was; they take one, two, three, and me. My nation over-beat them in yonder place, where me no was; there my nation take one, two, great thousand.

Master. But why did not your side recover you from the hands of your enemies, then?

Friday. They run one, two, three and me, and make go in the canoe; my nation have no canoe that time.

Master. Well, Friday, and what does your nation do with the men they take? Do they carry them away, and eat them, as these did?

Friday. Yes, my nation eat mans too, eat all up.

Master. Where do they carry them?

Friday. Go to other place, where they think.

Master. Do they come hither?

Friday. Yes, yes, they come hither; come other else place.

Master. Have you been here with them?

Friday. Yes, I been here. (Points to the N. W. side of the island, which it seems was their side.)

By this I understood that my man Friday had formerly been among the savages, who had used to come on shore on the farther parts of the island, on the said man-eating occasions that he had been now brought for; and some time after, when I took courage to carry him to that side, he presently knew the place, and told me he was there once when they eat up twenty men, two women, and one child.

After I had had this discourse with him, I asked him how far it was from our island to the shore; whether the canoes were not often lost? He told me that there was no danger, no canoes ever lost; but that, after a little way out to sea, there was a current, and a wind always one way in the morning, the other in the afternoon.

This I thought to be no more than the sets of the tide, as going out or coming in; but I afterwards understood it was occasioned by the great draught and reflux of the mighty river Oroonoque; in the mouth of which river, as I thought afterwards, our island lay; and that this land, which I perceived to the W. and N. W. was the great island Trinidad, on the north point of the mouth of the river. I asked Friday a thousand questions about the country, the inhabitants, the sea, the coast, and what nations were near; he told me all he knew, with the greatest openness imaginable. I asked him the names of the several nations of his sort of people, but could get no other names than Caribs; from whence I easily understood that these were the Caribbees, which our maps place on that part of America which reaches from the mouth of the river Oroonoque to Guiana, and onwards to St. Martha. He told me that up a great way beyond the moon, which must be west from their country, there dwelt white, bearded men like me, and pointed to my great whiskers, which I mentioned before, and that they had killed "much mans," that was his word. By all which I understood he meant the Spaniards, whose cruelties in America had been spread over whole countries, and were remembered by all the nations from father to son.

I inquired if he could tell me how I might come from this island, and get among those white men? He told me yes, yes, I might go in "two canoe." I could not understand what he meant by "two canoe," till at last, with difficulty, I found he meant that it must be a large boat, as big as two canoes.

This part of Friday's discourse began to relish with me very well; and from this time I entertained some hopes that, one time or other, I might find an opportunity to make my escape from this place, and that this poor savage might be a means to help me to do it.

CHAPTER 18: *Preparations for departure*

I WAS now wanting to lay a foundation of religious knowledge in Friday's mind; particularly I asked him one time who made him. The poor creature did not understand me, but thought I had asked him who was his father. But I took it another way, and asked him who made the sea, the ground he walked on, and the hills and woods. He told me it was one old Benamuckee, that lived beyond all. He could describe nothing of this great person, but that he was very old; much older, he said, than the sea or the land, than the moon or the stars. I asked him then, if this person had made all things, why did not all things worship him? He looked very grave, and with a perfect look of innocence said, "All things said O to him." I asked him if the people who die in his country went away anywhere. He said, yes, they all went to Benamuckee. Then I asked him whether those they eat up went thither, too. He said, "Yes."

From these things I began to instruct him in the knowledge of the true God. I told him that the great Maker of all things lived up there, pointing up towards the heaven; that he governs the world by the same power and providence by which he had made it; that he was omnipotent, could do everything for us, give everything to us, take everything from us, and thus, by degrees, I opened his eyes. He listened with great attention, and received with pleasure the notion of Jesus Christ being sent to redeem us, and of the manner of making our prayers to God, and his being able to hear us, even into heaven. He told me one day, that if our God could hear us up beyond the sun, he must needs be a greater God than their Benamuckee, who lived but a little way off, and yet could not hear till they went up to the great mountains where he dwelt, to speak to him. I asked him if ever he went thither to speak to him. He said, no; they never went that were young men; none went thither but the old men, whom he called their Oowokakee, that is, as I made him explain it to me, their religious, or clergy; and that they went to say O (so he called saying prayers), and then came back, and told them what Benamuckee said. By this I observed that there is priestcraft even amongst the most blinded ignorant pagans in the world.

Sending him for something a great way off, I seriously prayed to God that he would enable me to instruct this poor savage, assisting by his Spirit the heart of the poor ignorant creature to receive the light of the knowledge of God in Christ, reconciling him to himself, and would guide me to speak so to him from the word of God, as his conscience might be convinced, his eyes opened, and his soul saved. When he came again to me, I entered into a long discourse with him upon the subject of the redemption of man, by the Saviour of the world, and of the doctrine of the gospel preached from heaven, namely, of repentance towards God, and faith in our blessed Lord Jesus. I then explained to him, as well as I could, why our blessed Redeemer took not on him the nature of angels, but the seed of Abraham, and how, for that reason, the fallen angels had no share in the redemption; that he came only to the lost sheep of the house of Israel, and the like.

I had, God knows, more sincerity than knowledge, in all the methods I took for this poor creature's instruction, and must acknowledge what I believe all that act upon the same principle will find, that, in laying things open to him, I really informed and instructed myself in many things that I either did not know or had not fully considered before, but which occurred naturally to my mind, upon my searching into them for the information of this poor savage; and I had more affection in my inquiry after things upon this occasion than ever I felt before; so that whether this poor wild wretch was the better for me or no, I had great reason to be thankful that ever he came to me; my grief sat lighter upon me, my habitation grew comfortable to me beyond measure, and when I reflected, that, in this solitary life which I had been confined to, I had not only been moved myself to look up to heaven, and to seek to the hand that brought me thither, but was now to be made an instrument, under Providence, to save the life, and, for aught I knew, the soul, of a poor savage, and bring him to the true knowledge of religion, and of the Christian doctrine, that he might know Christ Jesus, "to know whom is life eternal."

In this thankful frame I continued all the remainder of my time, and the conversation which employed the hours between Friday and me was such as made the three years, which we lived there together, perfectly and completely happy, if any such thing as complete happiness can be found in a sublunary state. The savage was now a good Christian, a much better one than I, though I have reason to hope, and bless God for it, that we were equally penitent, and comforted restored penitents. We had here the word of God to read, and no farther off from his Spirit to instruct, than if we had been in England. I always applied myself to reading the Scriptures, and to let him know, as well as I could, the meaning of what I read.

After Friday and I became more intimately acquainted, and that he could understand almost all I said to him, and speak fluently, though in broken English to me, I acquainted him with my history. I let him into the mystery of gunpowder and bullets, and taught him how to shoot. I gave him a knife, which he was wonderfully delighted with, and I made him a belt with a frog hanging to it, such as in England we wear hangers in, and in the frog, instead of a hanger, I gave him a hatchet.

I described to him the countries of Europe, and particularly England, which I came from; how we lived; how we worshipped God, how we behaved to one another, and how we traded in ships to all parts of the world. I gave him an account of the wreck which I had been on board of, and showed him, as near as I could, the place where she lay; but she had all been gone long ago. I showed him the ruins of our boat, which we lost when I escaped, and which was now fallen almost to pieces. Upon seeing this boat, Friday stood musing some time, and said nothing. I asked him what he studied upon; at last, says he, "Me see such boat like come to place at my nation."

I did not understand him a good while; but at last, when I had examined farther into it, I understood by him, that a boat, such as that had been, came on shore upon the country where he lived, that is, as he explained it, was driven thither by stress of weather. I presently imagined that some European ship must have been cast away upon their coast, and the boat might get loose, and drive ashore; but was so dull that I never once thought of men making their escape from a wreck thither, much less whence they might come, so I only inquired after a description of the boat.

Friday described the boat to me well enough; but brought me better to understand him when he added, with some warmth, "We save the white mans from drown." Then I presently asked him if there were any white mans, as he called them, in the boat. "Yes," he said, "the boat full of white mans." I asked him, "How many?" He told me upon his fingers, seventeen. I asked him, "What became of them?" He told me, "They live, they dwell at my nation."

This put new thoughts into my head again, for I presently imagined that these might be the men belonging to the ship that was cast away in sight of my island, and who, after the ship was struck on the rock, and they saw her inevitably lost, had saved themselves in their boat, and were landed upon that wild shore among savages.

Upon this I inquired of him more critically, what was become of them; he assured me they still lived there, that they had been there about four years, that the savages let them alone, and gave them victuals to live. I asked him how it came to pass that they did not kill them, and eat them. He said, "No, they make brother with them," that is, as I understood him, a truce; and then he added, "They no eat mans, but when make the war, fight;" that is to say, they never eat any men, but such as come to fight with them, and are taken in battle.

It was after this, some considerable time, that being on the top of the hill, at the east side of the island, from whence I had, in a clear day, discovered the main, or continent of America, Friday, the weather being very serene, looks very earnestly towards the main-land, and in a kind of surprise, falls a jumping and dancing, and calls out to me; I asked him what was the matter. "O joy!" says he, "O glad! There see my country! there my nation!"

I observed an extraordinary sense of pleasure appear in his face, his eyes sparkled, and his countenance discovered a strange eagerness, as if he had a mind to be in his own country again; and this observation of mine put a great many thoughts into me, which made me at first not so easy about my new man Friday as I was before; and I made no doubt, but that if Friday could get back to his own nation again, he would not only forget all his religion, but all his obligations to me.

But I wronged the poor honest creature very much, for which I was very sorry afterwards; however, as my jealousy increased, and held me some weeks, I was a little more circumspect, and not so familiar and kind to him as before, in which I was certainly in the wrong.

Whilst my jealousy of him lasted, I was every day pumping him, to see if he would discover any of the new thoughts, which I suspected were in him; but I found everything he said was honest, and so innocent, that I could find nothing to nourish my suspicion, and, in spite of all my uneasiness, he made me at last entirely his own again; nor did he in the least perceive that I was uneasy, and therefore I could not suspect him of deceit.

One day walking up the same hill, but the weather being hazy at sea, so that we could not see the continent, I called to him and said, "Friday, do not you wish yourself in your own country, your own nation?" "Yes," he said; "I be much glad to be at my own nation." "What would you do there?" said I; "would you turn wild again, eat man's flesh again, and be savage as you were before?" He looked full of concern and shaking his head, said, "No, no; Friday tell them to live good; tell them to pray God; tell them to eat corn-bread, cattle-flesh, milk; no eat man again." "Why, then," said I to him, "they will kill you." He looked grave at that, and then said, "No, they no kill me; they willing love learn." He meant by this they would be willing to learn; he added they learned much of the bearded mans that came in the boat. Then I asked if he would go back to them. He smiled at that, and told me he could not swim so far. I told him I would make a canoe for him. He told me he would go, if I would go with him. "I go," said I, "why they will eat me if I come there." "No, no," said he, "me make them no eat you; me make they much love you." He meant he would tell them how I had killed his enemies, and saved his life, and so he would make them much love me.

From this time, I confess, I had a mind to venture over, and see if I could possibly join with these bearded men, who, I made no doubt, were Spaniards or Portuguese; not doubting but, if I could, we might find some method to escape from thence, being upon the continent, and a good company together, better than I could from an island, forty miles off the shore, and alone without help. So, after some days, I took Friday to work again, by way of discourse, and told him I would give him a boat to go back to his own nation; and accordingly carried him to my frigate, which lay on the other side of the island, and having cleared it of the water, I brought it out, showed it him, and we both went into it.

I found he was very dexterous at managing it, and would make it go almost as swift again as I could; so I said to him, "Well, now, Friday, shall we go to your nation?" He looked very dull at my saying so, which, it seems, was because he thought the boat was too small to go so far. I told him then I had a bigger one; so the very next day I went to the place where the first boat lay, which I had made, but which I could not get into the water. He said that was big enough; but as I had taken no care of it, and it had lain two or three-and-twenty years there, the sun had split and dried it, that it was in a manner rotten. Friday told me that such a boat would do very well, and would carry "much enough vittle, drink, bread;" that was his way of talking.

Upon the whole, I was by this time so fixed upon my design of going over with him to the continent, that I told him we would go and make one as big as that, and he should go home in it. He answered not one word, but looked very grave and sad. I asked him what was the matter with him. He asked me again thus: "Why you angry mad with Friday? What me done?" I asked him what he meant; I told him I was not angry with him at all. "No angry! no angry!" says he, repeating the words several times, "why send Friday home away to my nation?" "Why," said I, "Friday, did you not say you wished you were there?" "Yes, yes," says he, "wish we both there; no wish Friday there, no master there." In a word, he would not think of going there without me. "You shall go without me; leave me here to live by myself as I did before." He looked confused at this, and running to one of the hatchets which he used to wear, he takes it up hastily, and gives it me. "What must I do with this?" said I to him. "You take kill Friday," says he. "What must I kill you for?" said I again. He returns very quick. "What you send Friday away for? Take kill Friday; no send Friday away." As he spoke, tears stood in his eyes, and I was so affected, that I said I would never send him away, if he was willing to stay with me.

I found that all the foundation of his desire to go to his own country was laid in his ardent affection to the people, and his hopes of my doing them good: a thing, which as I had no notion of myself, so I had not the least thought, or intention, or desire of undertaking it. But still I found a strong inclination to attempting an escape, as above, founded on the supposition gathered from the former discourse, namely, that there were seventeen bearded men there; and therefore, without any more delay, I went to work with Friday, to find out a great tree proper

to fell, and make a large periagua, or canoe, for the voyage.
After searching some time, Friday at last pitched upon a tree,
for I found he knew much better than I what kind of wood was
fittest for it; nor can I tell, to this day, what wood to call the tree
we cut down, except that it was very like the tree we call fustic,
or between that and the Nicaragua wood, for it was much of the
same color and smell. Friday was for burning the hollow or
cavity of this tree out, to make it into a boat; but I showed him
how rather to cut it out with tools, which after I showed him
how to use he did it very handily, and in about a month's hard
labor we finished it, and made it very handsome, especially
when with our axes, which I showed him how to handle, we cut
and hewed the outside into the true shape of a boat. After this,
however, it cost us near a fortnight's time to get her along, as it
were, inch by inch, upon great rollers, into the water; but when
she was in, she would have carried twenty men with ease.

It amazed me to see with what dexterity, and how swift my
man Friday would manage her, turn her, and paddle her along.
So I asked him if he would, and if we might venture over in her.
"Yes," he said, "me venture over in her very well, though great
blow wind." However, I had a farther design that he knew
nothing of, and that was to make a mast and a sail, and to fit her
with an anchor and cable. As to the mast, that was easy enough
to get, so I pitched upon a straight young cedar-tree, which I
found near the place, and which there was plenty of in the
island; and I set Friday to work to cut it down, and gave him
directions how to shape and order it; but as to the sail, that was
my particular care. I knew I had pieces of old sails, but as I had
had them now twenty-six years by me, and not being very careful to preserve them, they were nearly all rotten. However, I
found two pieces which appeared pretty good, and with a great
deal of pains and awkward, tedious stitching, for want of

needles, I at length made a three-cornered ugly thing, like what we call in England a shoulder-of-mutton sail, to go with a boom at the bottom, and a little short sprit at the top, such as usually our ships' long boats sail with, and such as I best knew how to manage, because it was such a one as I used in the boat in which I made my escape from Barbary.

I was near two months in rigging and fitting out my mast and sails, for I fitted them very complete, making a small stay, and a sail, or foresail to it, to assist, if we should turn to windward; and, which was more than all, I fixed a rudder to the stern of her to steer with, and though I was but a bungling shipwright, yet, as I knew the usefulness and even necessity of such a thing, I applied myself with so much pains to do it, that at last I brought it to pass.

After all this was done, I had my man Friday to teach as to what belonged to the navigation of my boat; for though he knew very well how to paddle the canoe, he knew nothing what belonged to a sail and a rudder, and how the sail gibbed, and filled this way or that way, as the course we sailed changed; I say, when he saw this, he stood like one astonished and amazed. However, with a little use, I made all these things familiar to him, and he became an expert sailor, except that as to the compass I could make him understand very little of that; but there was not much occasion for the compass in these parts.

I was now entered on the seven-and-twentieth year of my captivity in this place; though the three last years that I had this creature with me ought rather to be left out of the account, my habitation being quite of another kind than in all the rest of the time. I kept the anniversary of my landing here with the same thankfulness to God for his mercies as at first; and if I had such cause of acknowledgment at first, I had much more so now, having such additional testimonies of the care of Providence over me, and the great hopes I had of being effectually and speedily delivered; for I had an invincible impression upon my thoughts, that my deliverance was at hand, and that I should not be another year in this place. However, I went on with all my work as usual.

CHAPTER 19: *In which we fight the savages, and rescue two prisoners*

THE RAINY season was in the mean time upon me, when I kept more within doors than at other times; so I had stowed our new vessel as secure as we could, bringing her up into the creek, where, as I said in the beginning, I landed my rafts from the ship; and thus we waited for the months of November and December, in which I designed to make my adventure.

When the settled season began to come in, the first thing I did was to lay by a certain quantity of provisions, being the store for our voyage; and I intended in a week or a fortnight's time to open the dock and launch out our boat. I was busy one morning upon something of this kind, when I called to Friday and bade him go to the sea-shore, and see if he could find a turtle or tortoise—a thing which we generally got once a week for the sake of the eggs, as well as the flesh. Friday had not been long gone, when he came running back, and flew over my outward wall, or fence, like one that felt not the ground, and before I had time to speak to him, he cried out to me, "O master! O master! O sorrow! O bad!" "What's the matter, Friday?" said I. "O yonder there," says he, "one, two, three canoe! one, two, three!" By this way of speaking, I concluded there were six; but, on inquiry, I found there were but three. "Well, Friday," said I, "do not be frightened;" so I heartened him up as well as I could. However, I saw the poor fellow was most terribly scared, for nothing ran in his head but that they were come to look for him, and would cut him in pieces and eat him; and the poor fellow trembled so, that I scarce knew what to do with him. I comforted him as well as I could, and told him I was in as much danger as he, and that they would eat me as well as him. "But," said I, "Friday, we must resolve to fight them. Can you fight, Friday?" "Me shoot," says he; "but there come many great number." "No matter for that," said I again, "our guns will fright them that we do not kill." So I asked him whether, if I resolved to defend him, he would defend me, and stand by me, and do just as I bade him. He said, "Me die when you bid die, master." So I gave him a good dram of rum; and when he had drunk it, I made him take the two fowling-pieces, and load them with swan-shot, as big as small pistol-bullets; then I took four muskets, and loaded them with two slugs and five small bullets each; and my two pistols I loaded with a brace of bullets each. I hung my great sword, as usual, naked by my side, and gave Friday his hatchet.

When I had thus prepared myself I took my perspective glass, and went up to the side of the hill to see what I could discover, and I found quickly by my glass that there were twenty-one savages, three prisoners, and three canoes; and that their whole business seemed to be the triumphant banquet upon these three human bodies; but nothing more than as I had observed as usual with them.

They were landed, not where they had done when Friday made his escape, but nearer to my creek, where the shore was low, and where a thick wood came close almost down to the sea. This, with the abhorrence of the inhuman errand these wretches came about, so filled me with indignation, that I came down to Friday, and told him I was resolved to go down to them and kill them all, and asked him if he would stand by me. He had now gotten over his fright, and his spirits being a little raised with the dram I had given him, he was very cheerful, and told me as before, "He would die when I bid die."

In this fit of fury, I took first and divided the arms which I had charged, as before, between us. I gave Friday one pistol to stick in his girdle, and three guns upon his shoulder; and I took one pistol and the other three myself, and in this posture we marched out. I took a small bottle of rum in my pocket, and gave Friday a large bag with more powder and bullets; and as to orders, I charged him to keep close behind me, and not to stir, or shoot, or do anything till I bade him; and, in the mean time, not to speak a word. In this posture I fetched a compass to my right hand of near a mile, as well to get over the creek as to get into the wood, so that I might come within a shot of them before I should be discovered, which I had seen by my glass it was easy to do.

I entered the wood with all possible wariness and silence (Friday following close at my heels) and marched till I came to the skirt of the wood, on the side which was next to them, only that one corner of the wood lay between me and them. Here I called softly to Friday, and showing him a great tree, which was just at the corner of the wood, I bade him go to the tree, and bring me word if he could see there plainly what they were doing. He did so, and came immediately back to me, and told me they might be plainly viewed there; that they were all about the fire, eating the flesh of one of their prisoners, and that another lay bound upon the sand, a little from them, whom, he said, they would kill next, and which fired the very soul within me. He told me it was not one of their own nation, but one of the bearded men whom he had told me of, that came to their country in the boat. I was filled with horror at the very naming the white, bearded man, and going to the tree, I saw plainly by my

glass a white man, who lay upon the beach of the sea, with his
hands and feet tied with flags, or things like rushes, and that he
was an European, and had clothes on.

There was another tree, and a little thicket beyond it, about
fifty yards nearer to them than the place where I was, which, by
going a little way about, I saw I might come at undiscovered,
and that then I should be within half a shot of them. So I with-
held my passion, and, going back about twenty paces, I got behind some bushes, which held all the way till I came to the
other tree, and then I came to a little rising ground, which gave
me a full view of them, at the distance of about eighty yards.

I had now not a moment to lose, for nineteen of the dreadful
wretches sat upon the ground, all close huddled together, and
had just sent the other two to butcher the poor Christian, and
bring him, perhaps limb by limb, to their fire, and they were
stooped down to untie the bands at his feet. I turned to Friday:
"Now, Friday," said I, "do as I bid thee." Friday said he would.
"Then, Friday," said I, "do exactly as you see me do; fail in
nothing." So I set down one of the muskets and the fowling-
piece upon the ground, and Friday did the like by his; and with
the other musket I took my aim at the savages, bidding him do
the like: then asking him if he was ready, he said, "Yes." "Then
fire at them," said I, and the same moment I fired also.

Friday took his aim so much the better than I, that on the
side he shot he killed two of them and wounded three more;
and, on my side, I killed one and wounded two. They were in
a dreadful consternation; and all of them who were not hurt
jumped up upon their feet immediately, but did not know
which way to run or which way to look, for they knew not from
whence their destruction came. Friday kept his eyes close upon
me, that, as I bid him, he might observe what I did; so, as soon
as the first shot was made, I threw down the piece and took up
the fowling-piece, and Friday did the like; he sees me cock and

present; he did the same again. "Are you ready, Friday?" said I. "Yes," said he. "Let fly, then," said I; and with that I fired again among the amazed wretches, and so did Friday, and as our pieces were now loaded with what I call swan-shot, or small pistol bullets, we found only two drop; but so many were wounded, that they ran about yelling and screaming like mad creatures, all bloody and wounded most of them, and three more fell quickly after, but not quite dead.

"Now, Friday," said I, laying down the discharged pieces and taking up the musket, which was yet loaded, "follow me," which he did with a deal of courage; upon which I rushed out of the wood and showed myself, and Friday close at my foot. As soon as I perceived they saw me, I shouted as loud as I could, and bade Friday do so too; and running as fast as I could, which, by the way, was not very fast, I made directly towards the poor victim, who was, as I said, lying upon the beach or shore, between the place where they sat and the sea. The two butchers, who were just going to work with him, had left him at the surprise of our first fire and fled, in a terrible fright, to the sea-side, and had jumped into a canoe, and three more of the rest made the same way. I turned to Friday, and bade him step forwards and fire at them. He understood me immediately, and, running about forty yards to be nearer them, he shot at them, and I thought he had killed them all, for I saw them all fall on a heap in the boat, though I saw two of them up again quickly. However, he killed two of them, and wounded the third, so that he lay in the bottom of the boat as if he had been dead.

While Friday fired at them, I pulled out my knife and cut the flags that bound the poor victim; and loosing his hands and feet, I lifted him up, and asked him, in the Portuguese tongue, what he was. He answered in Latin, "Christianus;" but was so weak and faint, that he could scarce stand or speak. I took my bottle out of my pocket and gave it him, making signs that he should drink, which he did; and I gave him a piece of bread, which he eat. Then I asked him what countryman he was, and he said "Espagniole;" and, being a little recovered, let me know, by all the signs he could possibly make, how much he was in my debt for his deliverance. I said, in as good Spanish as I could, "We will talk afterwards, but we must fight now; if you have any strength left, take the pistol and sword and lay about you." He took them very thankfully, and no sooner had he the arms in his hands, but, as if they had put new vigor into him, he flew upon his murderers like a fury, and had cut two or three in pieces in an instant, for they were so surprised and frightened, that they could make no resistance, nor attempt to escape.

I kept my piece in my hand still, without firing, being willing to keep my charge ready, because I had given the Spaniard my pistol and sword; so I called to Friday, and bade him run up to the tree from whence we first fired, and fetch the arms which lay there that had been discharged, which he quickly did; and then giving him my musket, I sat down to load all the rest again, and bade them come to me when they wanted. While I was loading these pieces, there happened a fierce engagement between the Spaniard and one of the savages, who made at him with one of their great wooden swords, the same weapon that was to have killed him before, if I had not prevented it. The Spaniard, who was very bold, though weak, had fought this Indian a good while, and had cut him two great wounds on his head; but the savage, being a stout, lusty fellow, closing in with him, had thrown him down, and was wringing my sword out of his hand, when the Spaniard, though undermost, wisely quitted the sword, drew the pistol from his girdle, and shot him dead on the spot.

Friday, being now left at his liberty, pursued the flying

wretches with no weapon in his hand but his hatchet; and with that he dispatched those three who were wounded at first and fallen, and all the rest he could come up with; and the Spaniard coming to me for a gun, I gave him one of the fowling-pieces, with which he pursued two of the savages, and wounded them both; but as he was not able to run, they both got from him into the wood, where Friday pursued them, and killed one of them, but the other was too mimble for him; and though he was wounded, yet had plunged into the sea, and swam with all his might off to those who were left in the canoe; which three in the canoe, with one wounded, we know not whether he died or no, were all that escaped our hands of one-and-twenty.

Those that were in the canoe worked hard to get out of gun-shot; and though Friday made two or three shots at them, I did not find that he hit any of them. Friday would fain have had me take one of their canoes and pursue them, and indeed I was very anxious about their escape, lest, carrying the news home to their people, they should come back, perhaps, with two or three hundred of their canoes, and devour us by mere multitude; so I consented to pursue them by sea; and running to one of their canoes, I jumped in, and bade Friday follow me; but when I was in the canoe, I was surprised to find another poor creature lie there alive, bound hand and foot, as the Spaniard was, for the slaughter, and almost dead with fear, not knowing what the matter was, for he had not been able to look up over the side of the boat; he was tied so hard, neck and heels, and had been tied so long, that he had little life in him.

I immediately cut the twisted flags, or rushes, that bound him, and would have helped him up; but he could not stand or speak, but groaned most piteously, believing, it seems, still, that he was only unbound in order to be killed. When Friday came, I bade him speak to him, and tell him of his deliverance; and pulling out my bottle, made him give the poor wretch a dram, which, with the news of being delivered, revived him, and he sat up in the boat. But when Friday came to hear him speak, and looked in his face, it would have moved any one to tears to have seen how Friday kissed him, embraced him, hugged him, cried, laughed, hallooed, jumped about, danced, sung, and then cried again, wrung his hands, beat his own face and head, and then sung and jumped about again, like a distracted creature. It was a good while before I could make him speak to me, or tell me what was the matter; but when he came a little to himself, he said that it was his father.

It is not easy for me to express how it moved me, to see what ecstasy and filial affection had worked in this poor savage, at the sight of his father, and of his being delivered from death: nor indeed can I describe half the extravagance of his affection after this, for he went into the boat and out of the boat a great many times. When he went in to him, he would sit down by him, open his breast, and hold his father's head close to his bosom half an hour together, to nourish it; then he took his arms and ankles, which were numbed and stiff with the binding, and chafed and rubbed them with his hands; and I perceiving what the case was, gave him some rum out of my bottle to rub them with, which did them a deal of good.

This action put an end to our pursuit of the canoe with the other savages, who were now gotten almost out of sight; and it was happy for us that we did not, for it blew so hard within two hours after, and before they could be gotten a quarter of their way, and continued blowing so hard all night, and that from the northwest, which was against them, that I could not suppose their boat could live, or that they ever reached to their own coast.

But to return to Friday, he was so busy about his father, that

I could not find in my heart to take him off for some time; but
after I thought he could leave him a little, I called him to me,
and he came jumping and laughing, and pleased to the highest
extreme. Then I asked him if he had given his father any bread.
He shook his head, and said, "None; ugly dog eat all up self." So
I gave him a cake of bread, out of a little pouch I carried on purpose; I also gave him a dram for himself, but he would not taste
it, but carried it to his father. I had in my pocket also two or
three bunches of my raisins, so I gave him a handful of them for
his father. He had no sooner given his father these raisins, but I
saw him come out of the boat, and run away, as if he had been
bewitched. He ran at such a rate (for he was the swiftest fellow
of his foot that ever I saw), I say, he ran at such a rate, that he
was out of sight, as it were, in an instant; and though I called
and hallooed to after him, it was all one: away he went, and in a
quarter of an hour I saw him come back again, though not so
fast as he went; and as he came near I found his pace was
slacker, because he had something in his hand.

When he came to me, I found he had been quite home for
an earthen jug, or pot, to bring his father some fresh water, and
that he had got two more cakes or loaves of bread. The bread he
gave me, but the water he carried to his father; however, as I
was very thirsty too, I took a little sup of it. The water revived
his father more than all the rum or spirits I had given him, for
he was just fainting with thirst.

When his father had drunk, I called to him to know if there
was any water left; he said, "Yes," and I bade him give it to the
poor Spaniard, who was as much in want of it as his father, and
I sent one of the cakes that Friday brought to the Spaniard too,
who was indeed very weak, and was reposing himself upon a
green place, under the shade of a tree, and whose limbs were
also very stiff, and very much swelled with the rude bandage he

had been tied with. When I saw that, upon Friday's coming up
to him with the water, he sat up and drank, and took the bread
and began to eat, I went up to him and gave him a handful of
raisins. He looked up in my face with all the tokens of gratitude
and thankfulness that could appear in any countenance; but
was so weak, notwithstanding he had so exerted himself in the
fight, that he could not stand upon his feet. He tried to do it two
or three times, but was really not able, his ankles were so swelled
and so painful to him; so I bade him sit still, and caused Friday
to rub his ankles, and bathe them with rum, as he had done his
father's.

I observed the poor affectionate creature, every two minutes,
or perhaps less, all the while he was there, turned his head about
to see for his father; and at last he missed him, at which he
started up, and without speaking a word, flew with that swiftness to him, that one could scarce perceive his feet to touch the
ground as he went; but when he came, he found he had only
laid himself down to ease his limbs. So Friday came back to me
presently, and I then told him to help the Spaniard to the boat;
so he took him upon his back, and carried him beside his father
in the boat, and stepping out again, launched the boat off, and
paddled it along the shore faster than I could walk, though the
wind blew pretty hard too; so he brought them both safe into
our creek, and leaving them in the boat, runs away to fetch the
other canoe. As he passed me, I spoke to him, and asked him
whither he went. He told me, "Go fetch more boat." So away
he went, like the wind, for sure never man or horse ran like him;
and he had the other canoe in the creek almost as soon as I got
to it by land; so he wafted me over, and then went to help our
new guests out of the boat, which he did; but they were neither
of them able to walk, so that poor Friday knew not what to do.

At last, we made a kind of hand-barrow to lay them on, and

Friday and I carried them up both together upon it between us. But when we got them to the outside of our wall or fortification, we were at a worse loss than before, for it was impossible to get them over; and I was resolved not to break it down. So I set to work again; and Friday and I, in about two hours' time, made a very handsome tent, covered with old sails, and above with boughs of trees, being in the same space without our outward fence, and between that and the grove of young wood which I had planted; and here we made them two beds of such things as I had, namely, of good rice straw, with blankets laid upon it to lie on, and another to cover them on each bed.

My island was now peopled, and I thought myself very rich in subjects; and it was a merry reflection which I frequently made, how like a king I looked. First of all, the whole country was my own mere property, so that I had an undoubted right of dominion. Secondly, my people were perfectly subjected; I was the absolute lord and lawgiver; they all owed their lives to me, and were ready to lay down their lives, if there had been occasion of it, for me. It was remarkable, too, I had but three subjects, and they were of three different religions: my man Friday was a Protestant; his father was a pagan and a cannibal; and the Spaniard was a Papist. However, I allowed liberty of conscience to all my subjects.

As soon as I had secured my two weak, rescued prisoners, and given them shelter, and a place to rest upon, I began to think of making some provision for them; and the first thing I did, I ordered Friday to take a yearling goat, betwixt a kid and a goat, out of my particular flock, to be killed. Then I cut off the hinder quarter, and chopping it into small pieces, I set Friday to work to boiling and stewing, and made them a very good dish of flesh and broth, and we all enjoyed it and eat heartily.

After we had dined, or rather supped, I ordered Friday to

take one of the canoes and go and fetch our muskets and other fire-arms from the place of battle; and the next day I ordered him to go and bury the dead bodies of the savages, which lay open to the sun, and would presently be offensive; and I also ordered him to bury the horrid remains of their barbarous feast: all of which he punctually performed.

I then began to enter into a little conversation with my two new subjects; and first I set Friday to inquire of his father what he thought of the escape of the savages in that canoe, and whether we might expect a return of them with a power too great for us to resist. His first opinion was, that the savages in the boat never could live out the storm which blew that night they went off, but must be drowned, or driven south to those other shores, where they were as sure to be devoured as they were to be drowned, if they were cast away; but as to what they would do, if they came on shore, he said, he knew not; but it was his opinion that they were so dreadfully frightened with the manner of their being attacked, the noise and the fire, that he believed they would tell their people they were all killed by thunder and lightning, and not by the hand of man; and that the two which appeared (namely Friday and I) were two heavenly spirits and furies come down to destroy them, and not with weapons. And this old savage was right; for though they escaped the sea, they gave such dreadful accounts in their own country (as I heard afterwards), that they never ventured from that part to my island again.

But I was under continual apprehensions for some time, and and kept upon my guard, I and all my army; for, as we were now four of us, I would have ventured upon a hundred of them in the open field.

In a little time, however, no more canoes appearing, the fear of them coming wore off, and I began to take my former

thoughts of a voyage to the main into consideration, being likewise assured, by Friday's father, that I might depend upon good
usage from their nation, on his account, if I would go.

But my thoughts were a little suspended, when I had a serious discourse with the Spaniard, and when I understood that
there were sixteen more of his countrymen and Portuguese,
who having been cast away, and made their escape to that side,
lived there at peace indeed with the savages, but were very sore
put to it for necessaries, and indeed for life. I asked him all the
particulars of their voyage, and found they were a Spanish ship,
bound from the Rio de la Plata to the Havannah, being directed
to leave their loading there, which was chiefly hides and silver,
and to bring back what European goods they could meet with
there; that they had five Portuguese seamen on board, whom
they took out of another wreck; that five of their own men were
drowned when first their ship was lost; and that these escaped
through infinite dangers and hazards, and arrived, almost
starved, on the cannibal coast, where they expected to be devoured every moment.

He told me they had some arms with them, but they were
perfectly useless, for they had neither powder nor ball, the washing of the sea having spoiled all their powder, but a little, which
they used at their first landing to provide themselves some food.

I asked him what he thought would become of them there,
and if they had formed no design of making an escape. He said
they had many consultations about it, but having neither vessel,
nor tools to build one, nor provisions of any kind, their counsels
always ended in tears and despair. I asked him how he thought
they would receive a proposal from me, which might tend towards an escape; and, whether, if they were all here, it might
not be done.

He told me they were all under the greatest distress imaginable, and if I would undertake their relief, they would live and die by me.

Upon these assurances, I resolved to venture to relieve them, if possible, and to send the old savage and the Spaniard over to them to treat. But when he had gotten all things in readiness to go, the Spaniard himself started an objection, which had so much prudence in it on the one hand, and so much sincerity on the other hand, that I could not but be well satisfied in it; and, by his advice, put off the deliverance of his comrades for at least half a year. The case was thus:—He had been with us now about a month, during which time I had let him see in what manner I had provided, with the assistance of Providence, for my support; and he saw evidently what stock of corn and rice I had laid up, which, as it was more than sufficient for myself, so it was not sufficient, at least without good husbandry, for my family, now it was increased to the number of four; but much less would it be sufficient, if his countrymen, who were, as he said, fourteen, still alive, should come over; and, least of all, would it be sufficient to victual our vessel, if we should build one, for a voyage to any of the Christian colonies of America. So he told me he thought it would be more advisable to let him and the two others dig and cultivate more land, as much as I could spare seed to sow; and that we should wait another harvest, then we might have a supply of corn for his countrymen, when they should come; for want might be a temptation to them to disagree, or not think themselves delivered, otherwise than out of one difficulty into another.

His caution was so seasonable, and his advice so good, that I could not but be very well pleased with his proposal, as well as I was satisfied with his fidelity. So we fell to digging, all four of us, as well as the wooden tools we were furnished with permitted; and in about a month's time, by the end of which it was seed-time, we had gotten as much land cured, and trimmed up, as we sowed twenty-two bushels of barley on, and sixteen jars of rice, which was, in short, all the seed we had to spare.

Having now society enough, and our number being sufficient to put us out of fear of savages, if they had come, unless their number had been very great, we went freely all over the island, wherever we found occasion; and as we had our escape or deliverance upon our thoughts, it was impossible, at least for me, to have the means of it out of mine. To this purpose, I marked out several trees, which I thought fit for our work, and I set Friday and his father to cutting them down; and then I caused the Spaniard to oversee and direct their work. I showed them with what indefatigable pains I had hewed a large tree into single planks, and I caused them to do the like; till they had made about a dozen large planks of good oak, near two feet broad, thirty-five feet long, and from two inches to four inches thick. What prodigious labor it took up, any one may imagine.

At the same time, I contrived to increase my little flock of tame goats as much as I could; and to this purpose I made Friday and the Spaniard go out one day, and myself with Friday the next day, for we took our turns; and, by this means, we got about twenty young kids to breed up with the rest; for whenever we shot the dam we saved the kids, and added them to our flock. But, above all, the season for curing the grapes coming on, I caused such a prodigious quantity to be hung up in the sun, that I believe, had we been at Alicant, where raisins are cured, we should have filled sixty or eighty barrels; and these with our bread, was a great part of our food.

It was now harvest, and our crop in good order. It was not the most plentiful increase I had seen in the island; but, however, it was enough to answer our end, for, from our twenty-two bushels of barley, we brought in and thrashed out above two hundred and twenty bushels, and the like in proportion of the rice, which was store enough for our food to the next harvest, though all the fourteen Spaniards had been on shore with me; or, if we had been ready for a voyage, it would very plentifully have victualled our ship to have carried us to any part of the world, that is to say, of America. When we had thus housed and secured our magazine of corn, we fell to work to make more wicker work, namely, great baskets in which we kept it; and the Spaniard was very handy and dexterous at this part.

And now, having a full supply of food for all the guests I expected, I gave the Spaniard leave to go over to the main, to see what he could do with those he had left behind him there. I gave him strict charge not to bring any man with him, who would not first swear, in the presence of himself and the old savage, that he would in no way injure, fight with, or attack the person he should find in the island, who was so kind as to send for them, in order to their deliverance; but that they would stand by and defend him against all such attempts, and wherever they went, would be entirely under and subjected to his command: and that this should be put in writing, and signed with their hands.

Under these instructions, the Spaniard and the old savage, went away in one of the canoes which they came in, when they were brought as prisoners to be devoured by the savages. I gave each of them a musket, and about eight charges of powder and ball, charging them to be very careful of both, and not to use either of them, but upon very urgent occasions.

This was a cheerful work, being the first measures used by me, in view of my deliverance, for now twenty-seven years and some days. I gave them provisions of bread and of dried grapes, sufficient for themselves for many days, and sufficient for all their countrymen for about eight days; and wishing them a good voyage, I let them go, agreeing with them about a signal they should hang out at their return, by which I should know them again, when they came back, at a distance before they came on shore. They went away, with a fair gale, on the day that the moon was at the full, by my account, in the month of October, as near as I could tell.

CHAPTER 20: *Which relates of the sighting of a boat, and the singular events which followed*

IT WAS no less than eight days I waited for them, when a strange and unforeseen occurrence intervened, of which the like has not, perhaps, been heard of in history. I was fast asleep in my hut one morning, when my man Friday came running in to me, and called aloud, "Master, master, they are come, they are come!" I jumped up, and, regardless of danger, went out, as soon as I could get my clothes on, through my little grove; I went without my arms, which it was not my custom to do; but I was surprised, when, turning my eyes to the sea, I presently saw a boat, at about a league and a half distance, standing in for the shore, with a shoulder-of-mutton sail, as they call it, and the wind blowing pretty fair to bring them in. Also, I observed, that they did not come from that side which the shore lay on, but from the southern-most end of the island. Upon this I called Friday in, and bade him lie close, for these were not the people we looked for, and that we did not know yet whether they were friends or enemies. In the next place, I went in to fetch my per-spective glass, to see what I could make of them; and, having taken the ladder out, I climbed up to the top of the hill, as I used to do when I was apprehensive of anything, and to take my view plainer, without being discovered. I had scarce set my foot on the hill, when my eye discovered a ship lying at anchor, at

about two leagues and a half distance from me, S. S. E., but not above a league and a half from the shore. It appeared plainly to be an English ship, and the boat an English long-boat.

I cannot express the confusion I was in, though the joy of seeing a ship, and one which I had reason to believe was manned by my own countrymen, and consequently friends, was such as I cannot describe; but yet I had some secret doubts hanging about me, I cannot tell from whence they came, bidding me to be on my guard. I began to consider what business an English ship could have here; since it was not the way to or from any part of the world where the English had any traffic; and I knew there had been no storm to drive them in there, as in distress; and that if they were English really, it was probable they were here upon no good design, and that I had better continue as I was than fall into the hands of thieves and murderers.

When they were on shore, I was fully satisfied they were Englishmen, at least most of them; one or two I thought were Dutch, but it did not prove so. There were in all, eleven men, whereof three I found were unarmed, and (as I thought) bound; and when the first four or five of them were jumped on shore, they took these three out of the boat as prisoners. One of the three I could perceive using the most passionate gestures of entreaty, affliction, and despair; the other two lifted up their hands sometimes, and appeared concerned indeed, but not so much as the first.

I was perfectly confounded at the sight, and knew not what the meaning of it could be. Friday called out to me, in English, as well as he could, "O master, you see English mans eat prisoners as well as savage mans." "Why," said I, "do you think they are going to eat them, then?" "Yes," says Friday, "they will eat them." "No, no," said I, "Friday, I am afraid they will murder them, indeed, but you may be sure they will not eat them."

All this while I had no thoughts of what the matter really was, but expected every moment the three prisoners would be killed; and once I saw one of the villains lift up his arm, with a great cutlass or sword, to strike one of the poor men, and I expected to see him fall every moment. I wished heartily now for my Spaniard, and the savage that was gone with him; or that I had any way to have come undiscovered within shot of them, that I might have rescued the three men, for they had no firearms that I saw.

After I had observed the outrageous usage of the three men by the insolent seamen, I saw that the fellows ran scattering about the land, as if they wanted to see the country. I observed, also, that the three other men had liberty to go where they pleased, but that they sat down all three upon the ground, very pensive, and looked like men in despair.

It was just at the top of high water when these people come on shore, and while partly they stood parleying with the prisoners they brought, and partly while they rambled about to see what kind of place they were in, they had carelessly stayed till the tide was spent, and the water was ebbed considerably away, leaving the boat aground.

It was my design, as I said before, not to have made any attempt until it was dark; but about two o'clock, being the heat of the day, I found that they were all gone straggling into the woods, and, as I thought, were all laid down to sleep. The three poor distressed men, too anxious for their condition to get any sleep, were, however, sat down under the shelter of a great tree, at about a quarter of a mile from me, and, as I thought, out of sight of any of the rest.

Upon this I resolved to discover myself to them, and learn something of their condition. Immediately I marched with my man Friday at a good distance behind me, as formidable for his arms as I, but not making quite so staring a spectre-like figure as I did. I came as near them undiscovered as I could, and then, before any of them saw me, I called aloud to them, in Spanish, "What are ye, gentlemen?"

They started up at the noise, but were ten times more confounded when they saw me, and the uncouth figure I made. They made no answer at all, but I thought I perceived them just going to fly from me, when I spoke to them in English:— "Gentlemen," said I, "do not be surprised at me; perhaps you may have a friend near you when you do not expect it." "He must be sent directly from heaven, then," said one of them very gravely to me, and pulling off his hat at the same time, "for our condition is past the help of man." "All help is from heaven, sir," said I, "but can you put a stranger in the way how to help you, for you seem to be in some great distress? I saw you when you landed; and when you seemed to make application to the brutes that came with you, I saw one lift up his sword to kill you." The poor man, with tears running down his face, and trembling, looking like one astonished, returned, "Am I talking to God or man? Is it a real man, or an angel?" "Be in no fear about that, sir," said I, "if God had sent an angel to relieve you, he would have come better clothed, and armed after another manner, than you see me. Pray lay aside your fears; I am a man, an Englishman, and disposed to assist you, you see. I have one servant only; we have arms and ammunition, tell us freely, can we serve you? What is your case?"

"Our case, sir," said he, "is too long to tell you, while our murderers are so near; but, in short, sir, I was commander of that ship, my men have mutinied against me, they have been hardly prevailed upon not to murder me, and, at last, have set me on shore in this desolate place, with these two men with me, one my mate, the other a passenger, where we expected to perish, believing the place to be uninhabited, and know not yet what to think of it."

"Where are those brutes, your enemies?" said I; "do you know where they are gone?" "There they are, sir," said he, pointing to a thicket of trees; "my heart trembles for fear they have seen us, and heard you speak; if they have, they will murder us all."

"Have they any fire-arms?" said I. He answered, "They had only two pieces, and one which they left in the boat." "Well, then," said I, "leave the rest to me. I see they are asleep. It is an easy thing to kill them all; but shall we rather take them prisoners?" He told me there were two desperate villains among them, that was scarce safe to show any mercy to, but if they were secured, he believed all the rest would return to their duty. I asked him which they were. He told me he could not, at that distance, describe them; but he would obey my orders in anything I would direct. "Well," said I, "let us retreat out of their view or hearing, lest they awake, and we will resolve farther." So they willingly went back with me, till the woods covered us from them. "Look you, sir," said I, "if I venture upon your deliverance, are you willing to make two conditions with me?" He anticipated my proposals, by telling me, that both he and the ship, if recovered, should be wholly directed and commanded by me in everything; and if the ship was not recovered, he would live and die with me, in what part of the world soever I would send him, and the two others said the same.

"Well," said I, "my conditions are but two; first, that while you stay on this island with me, you will not pretend to any authority here; and if I put arms in your hands, you will, upon all occasions, give them up to me, and do no prejudice to me or mine, upon this island; and, in the mean time, be governed by my orders. Secondly, that if the ship is, or may be, recovered, you will carry me and my man to England passage free." He gave me all the assurances that the invention and faith of man could devise, that he would comply with these most reasonable demands, and, besides, would owe his life to me, and acknowledge it, upon all occasions, as long as he lived.

"Well, then," said I, "here are three muskets for you, with powder and ball. Tell me next what you think is proper to be done." He showed all the testimony of his gratitude that he was able; but offered to be wholly guided by me. I told him I thought it was hard venturing anything, but the best method I could think of was to fire upon them at once, as they lay; and if any were not killed at the first volley, and offered to submit, we might save them, and so put it wholly upon God's providence to direct the shot.

He said, very modestly, that he was loath to kill them, if he could help it, but that those two were incorrigible villains, and had been the authors of all the mutiny in the ship, and if they escaped we should be undone still, for they would go on board and bring the whole ship's company and destroy us all. "Well, then," said I, "necessity legitimates my advice; for it is the only way to save our lives." However, seeing him still cautious of shedding blood, I told him they should go themselves, and manage as they found convenient.

In the middle of this discourse we heard some of them awake, and soon after we saw two of them on their feet. I asked him if either of them were the men who, he had said, were the heads of the mutiny. He said, "No." "Well, then," said I, "you may let them escape; and Providence seems to have awakened them on purpose to save themselves. Now," said I, "if the rest escape you, it is your fault."

Animated with this, he took the musket I had given him in his hand, and a pistol in his belt, and his two comrades with him, each man a piece in his hand. There were three more in the company, and one of them was also slightly wounded. By this time I was come; and when they saw their danger, and that it was in vain to resist, they begged for mercy. The captain told them he would spare their lives, if they would give him any assurance of their abhorrence of the treachery they had been guilty of, and would swear to be faithful to him in recovering the ship, and afterwards in carrying her back to Jamaica, from whence they came. They gave him all the protestations of their sincerity that could be desired, and he was willing to believe them, and spare their lives, which I was not against; only I obliged him to keep them bound, hand and foot, while they were upon the island.

While this was doing, I sent Friday, with the captain's mate, to the boat, with orders to secure her, and bring away the oars and sail, which they did; and, by the by, three straggling men, that were parted from the rest, came back again upon hearing the guns fired; and seeing their captain, who was before their prisoner, now their conqueror, they submitted to be bound also.

It now remained that the captain and I should inquire into one another's circumstances. I began first, and told him my whole history, which he heard with an attention even to amazement, and particularly at the wonderful manner of my being furnished with provisions and ammunition; and, indeed, as my story is a whole collection of wonder, it affected him deeply, but when he reflected from thence upon himself, and how I seemed to have been preserved there on purpose to save his life, the tears ran down his face, and he could not speak a word more.

After this communication was at an end, I carried him and his two men into my apartment, leading them in just where I came out, namely, at the top of the house, where I refreshed them with such provisions as I had, and showed them all the contrivances I had made during my long inhabiting this place.

All I showed them, all I said to them, was perfectly amazing; but, above all, the captain admired my fortification, and how perfectly I had concealed my retreat with a grove of trees, which, having been now planted near twenty years, and the trees growing much faster than in England, was become a little wood, and so thick, it was impassable in any part of it but that one side where I had reserved my little winding passage into it. This I told him was my castle and my residence, but that I had a seat in the country, as most princes have, whither I could retreat upon occasion, and I would show him that too another time; but at present our business was to consider how to recover the ship. He agreed with me as to that; but told me he was perfectly at a loss what measures to take, for that there were still six-and-twenty hands on board, who, having entered into a cursed conspiracy, by which they had all forfeited their lives to the law, would be hardened in it now by desperation, and would carry it on, knowing that if they were reduced they should be brought to the gallows as soon as they came to England, or to any of the English colonies, and that therefore there would be no attacking them with so small a number as we were.

Upon this, I told him the first thing we had to do was to stave the boat, which lay upon the beach, so that they might not carry her off: and take everything out of her, leave her so far useless as not to be fit to swim. Accordingly we went on board, took the arms which were left on board out of her, and whatever else we found there, which was a bottle of brandy, and another of rum, a few biscuit cakes, a horn of powder, and a great lump of sugar, in a piece of canvas; the sugar was five or six pounds: all which was very welcome to me, especially the brandy and sugar, of which I had been without many years.

When we had carried all these things on shore, we knocked a

great hole in her bottom, that if they had come strong enough to master us, yet they could not carry off the boat.

Indeed, it was much in my thoughts that we could be capable to recover the ship; but my view was, that if they went away without the boat, I did not much question to make her fit again to carry us away to the Leeward Islands, and call upon our friends the Spaniards in my way.

While we were thus preparing our designs, and had first, by main strength, heaved the boat up on the beach, so high that the tide would not float her off at high-water mark; and, besides, had broken a hole in her bottom too big to be quickly stopped, and were sat down musing what we should do, we heard the ship fire a gun, and saw her make a waft with her ancient, as a signal for the boat to come on board; but no boat stirred, and they fired several times, making other signals for the boat.

At last, when all their signals and firings proved fruitless, and they found the boat did not stir, we saw them (by the help of my glasses) hoist another boat off, and row towards the shore; and we found, as they approached, that there were no less than ten men in her, and that they had fire-arms with them.

As the ship lay almost two leagues from the shore, we had a full view of them as they came. The captain knew the persons and characters of all the men in the boat, of whom he said that there were three very honest fellows, who, he was sure, were led into this conspiracy by the rest, being overpowered and frightened: but that as for the boatswain, who, it seems, was the chief officer among them, and all the rest, they were as outrageous as any of the ship's crew, and were, no doubt, made desperate in their new enterprise.

As soon as they got to the place where their other boat lay, they ran their boat into the beach, and came all on shore, hauling the boat up after them, which I was glad to see; for I was afraid they would rather have left the boat, and anchor some distance from the shore, with some hands in her to guard her, and so we should not be able to seize the boat.

Being on shore, they ran all to the other boat; and it was easy to see they were under a great surprise to find her stripped, and a great hole in the bottom. After this, they set up a great shout; but it was all to no purpose: then they came all close in a ring, and fired a volley of their small arms, which indeed we heard, and the echoes made the woods ring, but it was all one; those in the cave we were sure could not hear, and those in our keeping, though they heard it well enough, yet durst give no answer to them.

They were surprised at this, as they told us afterwards, that they resolved to go all on board again to their ship, and let them know there that the men were all murdered, and the long boat staved; accordingly, they immediately launched their boat again, and got all of them on board.

The captain was terribly amazed, and even confounded at this, believing they would go on board the ship again, and set sail, giving their comrades up for lost, and so he should still lose the ship, which he was in hopes we should have recovered, but he was quickly as much frightened the other way.

They had not been long put off with the boat, but we perceived them all coming on shore again; and they left three men in the boat, and the rest went up into the country to look for their fellows. This was a great disappointment to us, for now we were at a loss what to do; for our seizing those seven men on shore would be of no advantage to us if we let the boat escape, because they would then row away to the ship, and then the rest of them would be sure to weigh, and set sail, and so our hope of recovering the ship would be lost. However, we had no remedy but to wait and see what the issue of things might present. The seven men came on shore, and the three who remained in the boat put her off to a good distance from the shore, and came to an anchor, to wait for them, so that it was impossible for us to come at them in the boat. Those that came on shore kept close together, marching towards the top of the little hill, under which my habitation lay, and we could see them plainly, though they could not perceive us.

The captain made a very just proposal to me upon this consultation of theirs, namely, that perhaps they would all fire a volley again, to endeavor to make their fellows hear, and that we should all sally upon them just at the juncture when their pieces were all discharged, and they would certainly yield, and we should have them without bloodshed. I liked the proposal, provided it was done while we were near enough to come up to them before they could load their pieces again.

But this event did not happen, and we lay still a long time, very irresolute what course to take; at length I told them there would be nothing to be done, in my opinion, till night; and then, if they did not return to the boat, perhaps we might use some stratagem with them in the boat to get them on shore.

We waited a great while, and were very uneasy; when we saw them all start up, and march towards the sea. It seems they had such dreadful apprehensions upon them of the danger of the place, that they resolved to go on board the ship again, give their companions over for lost, and so go on their intended voyage with the ship.

As soon as I perceived them go towards the shore, I imagined they had given over their search, and were for going back again; and the captain was ready to sink when I told him my thoughts, but I presently thought of a stratagem to fetch them back again, and which answered my end to a tittle.

I ordered Friday and the captain's mate to go over the little
creek westward, towards the place where Friday was rescued,
and at about half a mile distance, I bade them halloo as loud as
they could, and as soon as they heard the seamen answer them,
they should return it again, and then, keeping out of sight, take
a round, and then wheel about again to me by such ways as I
directed.

They were just going into the boat, when Friday and the mate
hallooed, and they presently heard them, and answering, run
along the shore westward, towards the voice they heard, when
they were stopped by the creek,—the water being up, they could
not get over,—and called for the boat to come and set them
over, as, indeed, I expected.

When they had set themselves over, I observed that they
took one of the three men out of her, and left only two in the
boat, having fastened her to a stump of a little tree on the shore.

This was what I wished for; and immediately leaving Friday
and the captain's mate to their business, I took the rest with
me, and crossing the creek out of their sight, we surprised the
two men before they were aware, one of them lying on the shore
between sleeping and waking, and, going to start up, the captain, who was foremost, ran in upon him and knocked him
down, and then called to him in the boat to yield or he was a
dead man.

There needed very few arguments to persuade a single man
to yield, when he saw five men upon him, and his comrade
knocked down: besides, this was, it seems, one of the three men
who were not so hearty in the mutiny as the rest of the crew,
and, therefore, was easily persuaded, not only to yield but afterwards to join very sincerely with us.

In the mean time, Friday and the captain's mate so well
managed their business with the rest, that they drew them, by

hallooing and answering, from one wood to another, till they not only heartily tired them, but left them where they were sure they could not reach back before it was dark: and indeed they were heartily tired themselves also by the time they came back to us.

It was several hours after Friday came back to me before they came to their boat, and we could hear foremost of them long before they came quite up, calling to those behind to come along, and could hear them answer, and complain how lame and tired they were, and not able to come any faster, which was very welcome news to us.

At length they came up to the boat, but it is impossible to express their confusion when they found the boat fast aground in the creek, and their two men gone; we could hear them telling one another they were gotten into an enchanted island; that either there were inhabitants in it, and they should all be murdered, or else there were devils or spirits in it, and they should be carried away and devoured.

They hallooed again, and called their two comrades by their names, but got no answer. After some time, we could see them by the little light there was run about like men in despair; and that sometimes they would go and sit down in the boat to rest themselves, then come on shore again, and walk about, and so the same thing over again.

My men would have fallen upon them in the dark, but I was willing to spare them, and kill as few of them as I could, being unwilling to hazard the killing any of our men, knowing the others were well armed. I resolved to wait and make sure of them, and drew my ambuscade nearer, and ordered Friday and the captain to creep upon their hands and knees, and get as near them as they possibly could before they offered to fire.

They had not been long in that posture when the boatswain,

who was the principal ringleader, and had now shown himself the most dispirited of all the rest, walked towards them with two more of their crew. The captain was so eager at having the principal rogue so much in his power, that he could hardly have patience to let him come so near as to be sure of him, for he only heard his tongue before; but when they came nearer, the captain and Friday, starting up on their feet, let fly at them.

The boatswain was killed on the spot, the next was shot through the body, and fell just by him, though he did not die till an hour or two after, and the third ran for it.

At the noise of the fire, I immediately advanced with my whole army, which was now eight men, namely, myself, generalissimo; Friday, my lieutenant-general; the captain and his two men; and the three prisoners of war, whom we had trusted with arms.

We came upon them indeed in the dark, so that they could not see our number; and I made the man they had left in the boat, who was now one of us, to call them by name, to try if he could bring them to parley, which fell out just as we desired. So he calls out as loud as he could to one of them, "Tom Smith! Tom Smith!" Tom Smith answered immediately, "Who's that, Robinson?" for it seems he knew his voice. The other answered, "Ay, ay; for God's sake, Tom Smith, throw down your arms and yield, or you are all dead men this moment!"

"Who must we yield to?—where are they?" says Tom Smith again. "Here they are," says he. "Here is our captain, and fifty men with him, have been hunting you this two hours. The boatswain is killed, Will Frye is wounded, and I am a prisoner; if you do not yield, you are all lost."

"Will they give us quarter, then," says Tom Smith, "and we will yield." "I'll go and ask, if you promise to yield," says Robinson. So he asked the captain, and the captain himself then called out, "You, Smith, you know my voice; if you lay down your arms immediately, and submit you shall all have your lives, all but Will Atkins."

Upon this Will Atkins cried out, "For God's sake, captain, give me quarter! What have I done? They have all been as bad as I!" which was not true, for it seems this Will Atkins was the first man that laid hold of the captain when they first mutinied. However, the captain told him he must lay down his arms at discretion, and trust to the governor's mercy; by which he meant me, for they called me governor.

In a word, they all laid down their arms, and begged their lives; and I sent the man that had parleyed with them, and two more, who bound them all; and then my great army of fifty men, which, particularly with those three, were in all but eight, came up and seized upon them all, and upon their boat, only that I kept myself and one more out of sight, for reasons of state.

Our next work was to repair the boat, and to think of seizing the ship; and as for the captain, now he had leisure to parley with them, he expostulated with them upon the villainy of their practices with him, and how certainly it must bring them to misery and distress in the end, and perhaps to the gallows.

They all appeared very penitent, and begged hard for their lives. As for that, he told them that the governor was an Englishman, and that he might hang them all there if he pleased; but, as he had given them quarter, he supposed he would send them to England, except Atkins, whom he was commanded by the governor to advise to prepare for death, for that he would be hanged in the morning. Though this was all a fiction of his own, yet it had the desired effect; Atkins fell upon his knees to beg the captain to intercede with the governor for his life, and all the rest begged of him, for God's sake, not to be sent to England.

It now occurred to me that the time of our deliverance was come, and that it would be a most easy thing to bring these fellows in to be hearty in getting possession of the ship. So I retired in the dark from them, that they might not see what kind of a governor they had, and called the captain to me. When I called, as at a good distance, one of the men was ordered to speak again, and to say to the captain, "Captain, the commander calls for you;" and presently the captain replied, "Tell his excellency I am just a-coming." So they all believed the commander was just by with his fifty men.

Upon the captain's coming to me, I told him my project for seizing the ship, which pleased him, and resolved to put it in execution the next morning.

But in order to execute it with more art, and to be sure of success, I told him we must divide the prisoners, and that he should go and take Atkins, and two more of the worst of them, and send them bound to the cave where the others lay. So Friday, and the two men who came on shore with the captain, conveyed them to the cave as to a prison. The other I ordered to my bower, where they were pinioned, and left secure enough.

To these, in the morning, I sent the captain, who was to enter into a parley with them; in a word, to try them and tell me whether he thought they might be trusted or no, to go on board and surprise the ship. He talked to them of the injury done him, of the condition they were brought to, and that though the governor had given them quarter for their lives, as to the present action, yet that if they were sent to England, they would all be hanged in chains; but that if they would join in so just an attempt as to recover the ship, he would have the governor's engagement for their pardon.

Any one may guess how readily such a proposal would be accepted by men in their condition; they fell down on their knees to the captain, and promised, with deep imprecations, that they would be faithful to him to the last drop, and that they should owe their lives to him, and would go with him all over the world; that they would own him for a father to them as long as they lived. "Well," says the captain, "I must go and tell the governor what you say, and see what I can do to bring him to consent to it." So he brought me an account of the temper he found them in, and that he verily believed they would be faithful. However, that we might be very secure, I told him he should go back again, and choose out five of them, and tell them that they should see he did not want men, but that he would take out those five to be his assistants, and that the governor would keep the other two, and the three that were sent prisoners to the castle (my cave), as hostages for the fidelity of those five; and if they proved unfaithful in the execution, the five hostages should be hanged in chains alive upon the shore.

This looked severe, and convinced them that the governor was in earnest. However, they had no way left them but to accept it; and it was now the business of the prisoners, as much as of the captain, to persuade the other five to do their duty. Our strength was now thus ordered for the expedition: First, the captain, his mate, and passenger. Second, then the two prisoners of the first gang, to whom, having their characters from the captain, I had given their liberty, and trusted them with arms. Third, the other two, whom I had kept in my bower, pinioned, these were now released. Fourth, these five, released at last; so that there were twelve in all, besides five we kept in the cave, as hostages for the fidelity of the others.

I asked the captain if he was willing to venture with those hands on board the ship; for as for me and my man Friday, I did not think it proper for us to stir, having seven men left behind; and it was employment enough for us to keep them asunder, and supply them with victuals.

As to the five in the cave, I resolved to keep them fast; but Friday went twice a day to them, to supply them with necessaries; and I made the other two carry provisions to a certain distance, where Friday was to take it.

When I showed myself to the two hostages, it was with the captain, who told them I was the person the governor had ordered to look after them, and that it was the governor's pleasure they should not stir anywhere, but by my direction; that if they did, they should be fetched to the castle and be laid in irons; so that we never suffered them to see me as governor, so now I appeared as another person, and spoke of the governor, the garrison, the castle, and the like, upon all occasions.

CHAPTER 21: *In which we capture the boat, and I return to civilization*

THE CAPTAIN now had no difficulty before him but to furnish his two boats, stop the breach of one, and man them. He made his passenger captain of one, with four other men: he himself, with his mate and five more, went in the other. And they contrived their business very well, for they came up to the ship about midnight. As soon as they came within call of the ship, he made Robinson hail them, and tell them he had brought off the men and the boat, but that it was a long time before they had found them, and the like; holding them in chat till they came to the ship's side; when the captain and the mate, entering first with their arms, immediately knocked down the second mate and the carpenter with the butt-end of their muskets, being very faithfully seconded by their men. They secured all the rest that were upon the main and quarter-decks, and began to fasten the hatches to keep them down who were below, when the other boat, and the men entering the forechains secured the forecastle of the ship, and the scuttle which went down into the cook-room, making three men they found there prisoners. When this was done, and all safe upon the deck, the captain ordered the mate with three men to break into the round-house, where the new rebel captain lay; and he, having taken the alarm and gotten up, now stood with two men and a boy, having fire-arms in their hands; and when the mate, with a crow, split open the door, the new captain and his men fired boldly among them, and wounded the mate with a musket-ball, which broke his arm, and wounded two more of the men, but killed nobody.

The mate calling for help, rushed, however, into the round-house, wounded as he was, and, with his pistol, shot the new captain through the head, the bullet entering at his mouth, and came out again behind one of his ears, so that he never spoke a word; upon which the rest yielded, and the ship was taken effec-tually, without any more lives lost. As soon as the ship was thus secured, the captain ordered seven guns to be fired, which was the signal agreed upon with me, to give me notice of his suc-cess, which, you may be sure, I was glad to hear, having sat watching upon the shore for it till two o'clock in the morning.

Having heard the signal plainly, I laid me down, and being very much fatigued, I fell sound asleep, when shortly I was awoke by the noise of a gun; and starting up, I heard a man call me by the name of "Governor," and presently I knew the cap-tain's voice, when climbing up to the top of the hill, there he stood, and pointing to the ship, he embraced me in his arms. "My dear friend and deliverer," says he, "there's your ship; for she is all yours, and so are we, and all that belongs to her." I cast my eyes to the ship, and there she rode, about half a mile off the shore, for they had weighed her anchor as soon as they were masters of her, and the weather being fair, had brought her to an anchor just against the mouth of a little creek, and the tide being up, they had brought the pinnace in near the place where I had first landed my rafts, and so landed just at my door.

I was, at first, ready to sink down with surprise, for I saw my deliverance indeed visibly put into my hands, all things easy, and a large ship just ready to carry me away whither I pleased to go. He perceived my situation, and immediately pulls a bottle out of his pocket, and gave me a dram of cordial, which he had brought on purpose for me. After I drank it, I sat down upon the ground, and it was a good while before I could speak to him.

After some time, I came to myself, and then I embraced him in my turn, as my deliverer, and we rejoiced together. I told him, I looked upon him as a man sent from heaven to deliver me, and that the whole transaction seemed to be a chain of wonders; and such things as these were the testimonies we had of a secret hand of Providence governing the world, and an evidence that the eyes of an infinite power could search into the remotest corner of the world, and send help to the miserable whenever he pleased; nor did I forget to return thanks to God for all his mercies.

When we had talked a while, the captain told me he had brought me some little refreshment, such as the ship afforded, and such as the wretches, who had been so long his masters, had not plundered him of. Upon this he called aloud to his men, and told them to bring the things ashore that were for the governor: and it was a splendid present. First, he had brought me a case of bottles full of cordial waters, six large bottles of Madeira wine, two pounds of excellent tobacco, twelve good pieces of the ship's beef, and six pieces of pork, with a bag of peas, and about a hundred weight of biscuit. He brought me also a box of sugar, a box of flour, a bag full of lemons, and two bottles of lime-juice, and abundance of other things. But, besides these, and what was a thousand times more useful to me, he brought me six clean new shirts, six very good neckcloths, two pairs of gloves, one pair of shoes, a hat, and one pair of stockings, and a very good suit of clothes of his own, which had been worn very little; but the clothes felt very awkward and uneasy upon me at first.

After all these things were brought into my little apartment, we began to consult what was to be done with the prisoners we had, and whether we might venture to take them away with us or no, especially two of them, whom we knew to be incorrigible and refractory to the last degree, and the captain said he knew that they were such rogues, that there was no obliging them; and if he did carry them away, it must be in irons, as malefactors, to be delivered over to justice at the first English colony he could come at. Upon this, I told him I durst undertake to bring the two men he spoke of to make it their own request that he should leave them upon the island, of which the captain said he should be very glad. I accordingly sent for them, and entered seriously into discourse with them upon their circumstances. One of them answered in the name of the rest, that they had nothing to say but this, that when they were taken, the captain promised them their lives, and they humbly implored my mercy. But I told them I knew not what mercy to show them; for, as for myself, I had resolved to quit the island with all my men, and had taken passage with the captain to go to England; and as for the captain, he would not carry them to England, but as prisoners in irons, to be tried for mutiny and running away with the ship; the consequence of which, they must needs know, would be the gallows: so that I could not tell which was best for them, unless they had a mind to take their fate in the island; if they desired that, I did not care, as I had liberty to leave it; I had some inclination to give them their lives, if they could shift on shore. They seemed very thankful for it; and said they would rather venture to stay there, than to be carried to England to be hanged.

I then told them I would let them into the story of my living there, and put them into the way of making it easy to them. Accordingly I gave them the whole history of the place, and of my coming to it; showed them my fortifications, the way I made my bread, planted my corn, cured my grapes, and in a word, all that was necessary to make them easy. I told them the story of the Spaniards that were to be expected, for whom I left a letter, and made them promise to treat them in common with themselves.

I left them five muskets, three-fowling pieces, and three swords. I had about a barrel and a half of powder, which I left them. I gave them a description of the way I managed the goats, and directions to milk and fatten them, to make both butter and cheese. In a word, I gave them every part of my own story; and I told them I would prevail with the captain to leave them two barrels of gunpowder more, and some garden seeds, which I told them I would have been very glad of; also I gave

hem the bag of peas which the captain had brought me, and
ade them to be sure to sow and increase them.

Having done this, I left them the next day, and went on
oard the ship. The next morning two of the five men came
wimming to the ship's side, and making a most lamentable
omplaint of the other three, begged to be taken into the ship,
or God's sake, for they should be murdered.

The captain pretended to have no power without me; but,
fter some difficulty, and after their solemn promises of amend-
ment, they were taken on board, and were shortly after soundly
whipped, after which they proved very honest and quiet fellows.

Some time after this, I went with the boat on shore, the tide
being up, with the things promised to the men, with which the
captain, at my intercession, sent their chests and clothes, which
they took, and were very thankful for, I also encouraged them,
by telling them that if it lay in my way to send any vessel to
take them in, I would not forget them.

When I quitted this island, I carried on board, for relics, the
great goat-skin cap I had made, my umbrella, and one of my
parrots; also I forgot not to take the money I had had laid by
me so long useless.

And thus I left the island, the 19th of December, by the
ship's account, in the year 1686, after I had been upon it twenty-
eight years, two months, and nineteen days; being delivered
from the second captivity the same day of the month that I
made my escape from among the Moors at Sallee. In this vessel,
after a long voyage, I arrived in England, the 11th of June, in
the year 1687, having been thirty-five years absent.

When I came to England, I was as perfect a stranger as if I
had never been known there. My benefactor and faithful steward, whom I left in trust with my money, was alive, but had had
great misfortunes in the world, was become a widow the second

time, and was in very low circumstances. I made her easy as to what she owed me, assuring her I would give her no trouble but, on the contrary, in gratitude to her former care and faithfulness to me, I relieved her as much as my little stock would afford, which at that time would indeed allow me to do but little for her; but I assured her I would never forget her former kindness to me; nor did I forget her when I had sufficient to help her at a future time.

I went down afterwards into Yorkshire; but my father was dead, and my mother, and all the family extinct, except two sisters, and two of the children of one of my brothers; and, as I had been long ago given over for dead, there had been no provision made for me, so that, in a word, I found nothing to relieve or assist me, and the little money I had would not do much for me, as to settling in the world.

I met with one piece of gratitude, indeed, which I did not expect; and this was, that the master of the ship, whom I had so happily delivered, having given a very handsome account to the owners of the manner how I had saved the lives of the men and the ship, they invited me to meet them and some other merchants concerned, and all together made me a very handsome compliment upon the subject, and a present of almost two hundred pounds sterling.

But, after making several reflections upon the circumstances of my life, and how little way this would go towards settling me in the world, I resolved to go to Lisbon, and see if I could get any information of the state of my plantation in the Brazils, and of what was become of my partner, who, I supposed, had for some years now given me over for dead.

With this view, I took shipping for Lisbon, where I arrived in April following; my man Friday accompanying me very honestly in all these ramblings, and proving a most faithful servant upon all occasions. When I came to Lisbon, I found out by inquiry, and to my particular satisfaction, my old friend, the captain of the ship, who first took me up at sea, off the shore of Africa. He was now grown old, and had left off the sea, having put his son into the ship, and who still used the Brazil trade. The old man did not know me, and I scarcely knew him; but he soon recollected me when I told him who I was.

After some passionate expressions of our old acquaintance, I inquired after my plantation and my partner. The old man told me he had not been in the Brazils for about nine years; but that he could assure me, that when he came away, my partner was living, but that the trustees, whom I had joined with them to take cognizance of my part, were both dead; that however, he believed that I should have a very good account of the improvement of the plantation, for that, in the general belief of my being cast away and drowned, my trustees had given in the account of the produce of my plantation to the procurator fiscal, who had appropriated it, in case I never came to claim it, one third to the king, and two thirds to the monastery of St. Augustine, to be expended for the benefit of the poor, and for the conversion of the Indians to the Catholic faith; but that if I appeared, or any one for me, to claim the inheritance, it would be restored; only that the improvement, or annual production, being, as he said, distributed to charitable uses, he thought could not be restored.

I was a little concerned and uneasy at this account, and inquired of the old captain how it came to pass that the trustees should thus dispose of my effects, when they knew that I had made my will, and made him, the Portuguese captain, my universal heir, &c. He told me that was true, but as there was no proof of my being dead, he could not act as executor, until some certain account should come of my death; and that, besides, he

was not willing to intermeddle with a thing so remote; that
was true, he had registered my will, and put in his claim, an
could he have given any account of my being dead or alive, h
would have acted by procuration, and taken possession of m
ingenio (the sugar-house), and given his son, who was now i
the Brazils, orders to do it.

The old man then asked me if he should put me in a metho
to make my claim to the plantation. I told him I thought to g
over to it myself. He said I might do so if I pleased; but that
I did not, there were ways enough to secure my right, and im
mediately to appropriate the profits to my use; and as the
were ships in the river of Lisbon just ready to go to the Brazil
he made me enter my name in a public register, with his af
davit, affirming, upon oath, that I was alive, and that I was th
same person who took up the land for planting the said plant
tion at first. This being regularly attested by a notary, and
procuration affixed, he directed me to send it, with a letter o
his writing, to a merchant of his acquaintance at the place, an
then proposed my staying with him till an account came of th
return.

Never anything was more honorable than the proceeding
upon this procuration; for in less than seven months I receive
a large packet from the survivors of my trustees, the merchant
for whose account I went to sea; and as the Brazil ships come a
in fleets, the same ships which brought my letters brought m
goods, and the effects were safe in the Tagus before the lette
came to my hands. By these, it appeared I was now master, al
on a sudden of above five thousand pounds sterling in money
and had an estate, as I might well call it, in the Brazils, of abov
a thousand pounds a-year, as safe as any landed estate in Eng
land, in a word, I was in a condition which I could scarcel
understand, or how to compose myself for its enjoyment.

The first thing I did was to recompense my original benefactor, my good old captain, who had been first charitable, to
me in my distress, kind to me in the beginning, and honest to
me at the end. I showed him all that was sent me. I told him
that, next to the providence of Heaven, which disposes all
things, it was owing to him; and that it now lay on me to reward
him. So I sent for a notary, and caused him to draw a procuration, empowering him to be my receiver of the annual profits
of my plantation, and appointing my partner to account to him,
and make the returns by the usual fleets to him, in my name,
adding a clause in the end, being a grant of one hundred moidores a year during his life, out of the effects; and fifty moidores
a year to his son after him, for his life: and thus I requited my
old man. I was now to consider which way to steer my course
next, and what to do with the estate that Providence had thus
put into my hands; and, indeed, I had more care upon my head
now than I had in my silent state of life on the island, where I
wanted nothing but what I had, and had nothing but what I
wanted.

As I had rewarded the old captain fully, and to his satisfaction, who had been my former benefactor, so I began to think
of my poor widow, whose husband had been my first benefactor, and she, while it was in her power, my faithful steward
and instructor. So the first thing I did I got a merchant in Lisbon to write to his correspondent in London, not only to pay a
bill, but to go find her out, and carry her in money a hundred
pounds from me, and to talk with her and comfort her in her
poverty, by telling her she should, if I lived, have a farther supply. At the same time, I sent my two sisters in the country, each
of them a hundred pounds, they being, though not in want, yet
not in very good circumstances; one having been married, and
left a widow, and the other having a husband not so kind to her

as he should be. But, among all my relations or acquaintances, I could not yet pitch upon one to whom I durst commit the gross of my stock.

I had once a mind to have gone to the Brazils, and have settled myself there, for I was, as it were, naturalized to the place, but that I really did not know with whom to leave my effects behind me; so I resolved at last to go to England with them, where, if I arrived, I concluded I should make some acquaintance or find some relations that would be faithful to me, and accordingly I prepared to go for England with all my wealth. Having settled my affairs, sold my cargo, and turned all my effects into good bills of exchange, my next difficulty was which way to go to England. I had been accustomed enough to the sea, and yet I had a strange aversion to go to England by sea at that time; and though I could give no reason for it, yet the difficulty increased upon me so much, that though I had once shipped my baggage in order to go, yet I altered my mind, and that not once but two or three times. It is true I had been very unfortunate by sea, and this might be one of my reasons; but let no man strike the strong impulses of his own thoughts in cases of such moment. Two ships, each of which I had engaged to go in, but again withdrew my agreement, miscarried, namely, one was taken by the Algerines, and the other was cast away on the Start, near Torbay, and all the people drowned, except three; so that in either of those vessels I had been made miserable, and in which most, it was hard to say.

Having been thus harassed in my thoughts, my old pilot, to whom I communicated everything, pressed me earnestly not to go by sea; but either to go by land to the Groyne, and cross over the Bay of Biscay to Rochelle, from whence it was but an easy and safe journey by land to Paris, and so to Calais and Dover; or go up to Madrid, and so all the way by land through France.

In a word, I was so prepossessed against my going to sea at all, except from Calais to Dover, that I resolved to travel all the way by land, which, as I was not in haste, and did not value the charge, was by much the pleasanter way; and to make it more so, my old captain brought an English gentleman, the son of a merchant in Lisbon, who was willing to travel with me; after which we picked up two more, who were English, and merchants also, and two young Portuguese gentlemen, the last going to Paris only, so that we were in all six of us and five servants; the two merchants, and the two Portuguese, contenting themselves, with one servant between two, to save the charge; and as for me, I got an English sailor to travel with me as a servant, besides my man Friday, who was too much a stranger to be capable of supplying the place of a servant upon the road.

In this manner we set out from Lisbon; and our company being all very well mounted and armed, we made a little troop, whereof they did me the honor to call me captain, as well because I was the oldest man as because I had two servants, and indeed was the originator of the whole journey.

Four French gentlemen, who had been stopped on the French side of the passes, as we were now on the Spanish, had found out a guide, who had brought them over the mountains by such ways, that they were not much incommoded with the snow; and, where they met with snow in any quantity, they said it was frozen hard enough to bear them and their horses.

We sent for this guide, who told us that he would undertake to carry us the same way, with no hazard from the snow, provided we were armed sufficiently to protect us from wild beasts; for, he said, upon these snow regions it was common for wolves to show themselves at the foot of the mountains, being made ravenous for want of food, while the ground was covered with snow. We told him we were well enough prepared for such crea-

tures as they were, if he would insure us from a kind of two-
legged wolves, from which we were told most danger was to be
apprehended, especially on the French side of the mountains.

He satisfied us there was no danger of that kind in the way
that we were to go. So we readily agreed to follow him, as did
also twelve other gentlemen, with their servants, some French,
some Spanish, who, as I said, had attempted to go, and were
obliged to come back again.

Accordingly, we all set out from Pampeluna, with our guide,
on the 15th of November; and, indeed, I was surprised, when,
instead of going forward, he came directly back with us above
twenty miles; on the same road by which we came from Madrid,
when, having passed two rivers, and come into the plain country, we found ourselves in a warm climate again, where the country was pleasant, and no snow was to be seen; but, on a sudden,
turning to the left, he approached the mountains by another
way; and though, it is true, the hills and the precipices looked
dreadful, yet he made so many tours, and meanders, and led us
by such winding ways, that we insensibly passed the height of
the mountains without being much encumbered with the snow;
and, all on a sudden, he showed us the pleasant fruitful prov-
inces of Languedoc and Gascoigne, all green and flourishing,
though indeed they were at a great distance, and we had some
rough way to pass yet.

We were a little uneasy, however, when we found it snowed
so fast one whole day and night that we could not travel; but he
bade us be easy, we should soon be past it all. We found, indeed,
that we began to descend every day, and to come more north
than before; and so, depending upon our guide, we went on.

It was about two hours before night, when our guide, being
something before us, and not just in sight, out rushed three
monstrous wolves, and after them a bear, out of a hollow way,

adjoining to a thick wood. Two of the wolves flew upon the guide, and had he been half a mile before us, he had been devoured, indeed, before we could have helped him. One of them fastened upon his horse, and the other attacked the man with that violence, that he had not time, or not presence of mind enough to draw his pistol, but hallooed and cried out to us most lustily. My man Friday being next to me, I bade him ride up, and see what was the matter. As soon as Friday came in sight of the man, he hallooed as loud as the other, "O master! O master!" but, like a bold fellow, rode directly up to the man, and, with a pistol, shot the wolf that attacked him through the head.

It was happy for the poor man that it was my man Friday, for he, having been used to that kind of creature in his country, had no fear upon him, but went up close to him, and shot him as above, whereas, any of us would have fired at a farther distance, and might, perhaps, have either missed the wolf, or shot the man.

But it was enough to have terrified a bolder man than I; and indeed it alarmed all our company, when, with the noise of Friday's pistol, we heard on both sides the most dismal howling of wolves, and the noise redoubled by the echo of the mountains.

My man Friday had delivered our guide, and when we came up he was helping him off from his horse, for the man was both hurt and frightened, and indeed the last more than the first.

We had one dangerous place to pass, of which our guide told us, if there were any more wolves in the country, we should find them there; and this was a small plain, surrounded with woods on every side, and a long, narrow defile or lane, which we were to pass, to get through the wood, and then we should come to a village where we were to lodge.

It was within half an hour of sunset when we entered the first wood; and a little after sunset we came into the plain. We met with nothing in the first wood, except that, in a little plain within the wood, which was not above two furlongs over, we saw five great wolves cross the road, full speed, one after another, as if they had been in chase of some prey they had in view. They took no notice of us, and were gone, and out of our sight in a few moments.

This gave us leisure to charge our pieces again, and that we might lose no time, we kept going; but we had little more than loaded our fusils, and put ourselves into readiness, when we heard a terrible noise in the wood on our left.

The night was coming on, and the light began to be dusky, which made it the worse on our side; but the noise increasing, we could not perceive that it was the howling of those ravenous creatures; and, on a sudden, we perceived two or three troops of wolves, one on our left, one behind us, and one in our front, and we knew not what course to take; but the creatures resolved us soon, for they gathered about us, in hopes of prey; and I verily believe there were three hundred of them. It happened very much to our advantage, that, at the entrance into the wood there lay some large timber trees, cut down, and I drew my little troop in among these trees, and placing ourselves in a line, behind one long tree, I advised them all to alight, and keeping that tree before us for a breastwork, to stand in a triangle or three fronts, inclosing our horses in the centre. We did so; and it was well we did, for never was a more furious charge than the creatures made upon us in this place: they came on us with a growling kind of noise, and mounted the piece of timber, as if they were only rushing upon their prey; and this fury of theirs, it seems, was principally occasioned by their seeing our horses behind us, which was the prey they aimed at. I ordered our men to fire as before, every other man, and they took their aim so sure, that they killed several wolves at the first volley; but there was a necessity to keep a continual firing, for they came on like

devils, those behind pushing on those before. When we had
fired the second volley of our fusils, we thought they stopped a
little, and I hoped they would have gone off, but it was but a
moment, for others came forward again, so we fired two volleys
of our pistols, and, I believe, in these four firings, we killed
seventeen or eighteen of them, and lamed twice as many; yet
they came on again. I was loath to spend our last shot too hastily; so I called my servant, not Friday, but my other man, and,
giving him a horn of powder, I bid him lay a train all along the
piece of timber, and let it be a large train. He did so; and had but
just time to get away, when the wolves came up to it, and some
were got upon it, when I, snapping an uncharged pistol close to
the powder, set it on fire. Those that were upon the timber were
scorched with it, and six or seven of them fell, or rather jumped
in among us, with the force and fright of the fire. We dispatched
these in an instant, and the rest were so frightened with the
light, that they drew back a little. Upon which I ordered our last
pistols to be fired off in one volley; and after that we gave a
shout: upon this the wolves turned tail, and we sallied immediately upon near twenty lame ones, whose dreadful crying and
howling scared the rest, so that they all fled, and left us.

I have nothing uncommon to take notice of in my passage
through France, nothing but what other travellers have given
an account of, with much more advantage than I can. I travelled from Thoulouse to Paris, and, without any considerable
stay, came to Calais, and landed safe at Dover, the 14th of January, after having a severe cold season to travel in.

I was now come to the centre of my travels, and had, in a
little time, all my newly discovered estate safe about me, the
bills of exchange which I had brought with me having been
currently paid. My principal guide and privy counsellor was my
good old widow, who, in gratitude for the money I had sent her,

thought no pains too much, or care too great, to employ for me.

I began to think of leaving my effects with this woman, and setting out for Lisbon, and so to the Brazils. But now another scruple came in my way, and that was religion; for, as I had entertained some doubts about the Roman religion, even while I was abroad, especially in my state of solitude, so I knew there was no going to the Brazils for me, much less going to settle there, unless I resolved to embrace the Catholic religion, without any reserve; except, on the other hand, I resolved to be a sacrifice to my principles, be a martyr for religion, and die in the Inquisition; so I resolved to stay at home, and, if I could find means, to dispose of my plantation. To this purpose I wrote to my old friend at Lisbon, who, in return, gave me notice that he could easily dispose of it there; but that, if I thought fit to give him leave to offer it in my name to the two merchants, the survivors of my trustees, who lived in the Brazils, and most fully understood the value of it, who lived just upon the spot, and whom I knew to be very rich, so that he believed they would be fond of buying it, he did not doubt but I should make four or five thousand pieces of eight more for it.

Accordingly I agreed, gave him orders to offer it to them, and he did so; and in about eight months more, the ships being then returned, he sent me an account that they had accepted the offer, and had remitted thirty-three thousand pieces of eight to a correspondent of theirs at Lisbon to pay for it.

In return, I signed the instrument of sale in the form which they sent from Lisbon, and sent it to my old man, who sent me bills of exchange for thirty-two thousand eight hundred pieces of eight for the estate, reserving the payment of one hundred moidores a-year to him, the old man, during his life, and fifty moidores afterwards to his son for his life, which I had promised them, and which the plantation was to make good as a rent-charge. And thus I have given the first part of a life of fortune and adventure, a life of Providence's checker-work, and of a variety which the world will seldom be able to show the like of. Beginning foolishly, but closing much more happily than I had ever any reason even to hope for.

Any one would think that, in this state of complicated good fortune, I was past running any more hazards; but I was inured to a wandering life, had no family, nor many relations, nor, however rich, had I contracted much acquaintance; and though I had sold my estate in the Brazils, yet I could not keep that country out of my head, and had a great mind to be upon the wing again, especially I could not resist the strong inclination I had to see my island. My true friend, the widow, earnestly dissuaded me from it, and so far prevailed with me, that for almost seven years she prevented my running abroad; during which time I took my two nephews, the children of one of my brothers, into my care. The eldest, having something of his own, I bred up as a gentleman, and gave him a settlement of some addition to his estate after my decease; the other I put out to the captain of a ship, and, after five years, finding him a sensible, bold, enterprising young fellow, I put him into a good ship, and sent him to sea. And this young fellow afterwards drew me in, old as I was, to farther adventures myself. In the mean time, I in part settled myself here. For, first of all, I married, and had three children, two sons and one daughter. But my wife dying, and my nephew coming home, with good success, from a voyage to Spain, my inclination to go abroad, and his importunity, prevailed, and I engaged to go in his ship as a private trader to the East Indies. In this voyage I visited my new colony in the island, saw my successors, the Spaniards; had the whole story of their coming to and adventures in the island, after my departure. I may write later of all these things.

Robinson Crusoe

illustrated by Roger Duvoisin, is one of the series of

RAINBOW CLASSICS

Edited under the supervision of May Lamberton Becker

Typesetting by Westcott and Thomson

Printing and binding by H. Wolff

Binding pattern by Leo Manso

Designer: Ernst Reichl

2-1484